The Billionaire Wins the Game

Billionaire Bachelors Book One

Melody Anne

Dream!
Melody Anne

ISBN: 1467980757
ISBN-13: 978-1467980753

DEDICATION

This book is dedicated to my beautiful daughter Phoenix for all the help you gave me with the many hours of editing, and for inspiring me to never let go of my dreams.

Books by Melody Anne

*The Billionaire Wins the Game
*The Billionaire's Dance
*The Billionaire Falls
*The Billionaire's Marriage Proposal
*Blackmailing the Billionaire
*Runaway Heiress
*The Billionaire's Final Stand

+The Tycoon's Revenge
+The Tycoon's Vacation
+The Tycoon's Proposal
+The Tycoon's Secret (Coming December 15, 2012)

-Midnight Fire – Rise of the Dark Angel – Book One
-Midnight Moon – Rise of the Dark Angel – Book Two
-Midnight Storm – Rise of the Dark Angel – Book Three (February 2013)

www.facebook.com/authormelodyanne

www.melodyanne.com

Twitter: @authmelodyanne

The Anderson Family

Joseph Anderson – (M) – Katherine Simerly
/
Lucas Alex Mark

Lucas Anderson (m) Amy Harper
/
Jasmine Katherine (c) Isaiah Allen (c)

Alex Anderson (m) Jessica Sanders
/
Jacob (c) Katie (c)

Mark Anderson (m) Emily Jackson
/
Trevor (a,c) Tassia (c)

George Anderson (M) Amelia Grant(d)
(M) Esther Lion
/
Trenton Max Bree Austin

Trenton Anderson (m) Jennifer Stellar
/
Molly (n,a) Weston (c)

Max Anderson (m) Cassie McKentire
/
Ariel (c)

Bree Anderson (m) Chad Redington
/
Mathew (c)

Austin Anderson (m) Kinsey Shelton
/
Isabelle (c)

(m) = Married (d) = deceased (c) = child (n) = niece (a) = adopted

Prologue

"It's just not right, Katherine!" Joseph slammed his fist down on the table, making the dinnerware shake. "Those kids just don't listen to us – not one of them. Can't they see that we aren't getting any younger? I should've had grandchildren bouncing on my knees years ago."

Katherine smiled as she listened to her husband complain about his disobedient children. She knew what he said was nothing but empty words. He adored their kids as much as she did. She had to agree with Joseph, though, that a few beautiful women rocking babies would be an excellent addition to the house. She'd always dreamed of the day she'd be holding grandchildren while her table was surrounded by those she loved.

"Now, Joseph. You know if you go meddling again, the boys are going to disown you," Katherine warned.

"If they don't do something about this grandchildren situation then I'm going to disown them," he growled, though with zero conviction in his voice.

"Since you retired last year, you've had too much time on your hands, Joseph Anderson. The boys have been tossed a lot of responsibility already. Are you sure you want to add more to their plates?" she finished, knowing the answer already.

"The boys are ready for love and marriage. They just need a helping push."

The decision had already been made. He'd have at least one grandchild in his empty mansion before Christmas.

Katherine suppressed her sigh, knowing there was nothing she could say that would change her willful husband's mind. Where did he think their sons acquired that particular trait? Even with their flaws, she couldn't possibly love any of them, including her husband, more than she already did.

"Lucas will be first," Joseph said in his booming voice, startling Katherine out of her reverie. "I've already found him the perfect bride."

Joseph leaned back in his chair with a very pleased expression on his face. Finally, he had a project to keep himself occupied – with the prize of grandchildren as his reward. Lucas was in for wild adventures come Monday morning.

Katherine watched the self-satisfied expression on Joseph's face and thought about warning her sons about what was coming. She decided against it because even though she didn't agree with Joseph meddling, she really did want those grandbabies…

Chapter One

You can do this. Walk in there with confidence. Who cares if this family is worth more than Bill Gates and Donald Trump combined? You were hired for this position, and you need this job. They obviously see something in you, so keep your head held high.

Amy was giving herself a lecture on her long elevator ride up to the twenty-fifth floor of the Anderson Corporation. Her stomach was in knots as she began her journey into the corporate world.

She brushed a few strands of escaped golden hair from her face, more out of nervousness than necessity. She considered herself to be of average looks and tried to downplay the assets she'd been given. She wanted to be respected – not lusted after, like her mother. She had long hair she couldn't find the will to cut off, although when out, she always placed it in an unflattering bun.

She tended to hide her curves from the world. She was well-endowed, in what an ex-boyfriend had called *all the right places* and she was self-conscious of the fact. She also didn't like the fact that her green eyes gave away every emotion she was feeling, and that no matter how hard she tried, she couldn't manage to fix it.

She still couldn't believe she'd been hired as Executive Secretary for Lucas Anderson. Anyone who lived within a thousand-mile radius of Seattle, Washington, knew who the Andersons were. Their corporation had a variety of divisions, which required a large staff. They dealt with everything from construction and farming to high-end corporate takeovers. Although their headquarters was in the US, they did business all around the world, and she was excited to be a part of it.

Her job was in the corporate headquarters, working for the fairly new president, Lucas Anderson. All she really knew was he'd taken over his father's position about a year ago.

Though she'd graduated with honors, she was still fresh out of college and felt a little bit overwhelmed at the prospect of working for such a powerful man. She hadn't actually met Lucas, yet, just his father.

She'd originally met Joseph at a college fair toward the end of her senior year at the University. He'd given her his card and told her to call after graduation, telling her he was impressed with her college transcript. She'd called the day after her commencement ceremony, and he'd gotten her in for an interview faster than she'd dared to even hope for.

As she continued the long ascent in the elevator, she let her thoughts drift back to the previous week when she'd interviewed for the job.

Amy took a fortifying breath as she stepped from the cab, looking up at the huge fortress of a home in front of her. Before she could blink, the yellow car pulled away, leaving her frozen at the bottom of the large cement staircase. There was no turning back, now.

She slowly climbed the steps and approached the door, which was big enough to fit a large truck through. It seemed Mr. Anderson liked to do things on a much larger scale than the average person.

She rang the doorbell, though he must know she was already there as he'd opened the gates at the bottom of the driveway.

Within seconds, the door was opened by an older gentleman who, thankfully, was smiling.

"Hello, I'm Amy Harper. I have an appointment with Mr. Anderson."

"Good morning, Ms. Harper. It's a pleasure to meet you. Please follow me to the sitting room, where Mr. Anderson will join you shortly," the man offered.

Amy nodded, then followed his quick steps as he led her through the overwhelming home. She couldn't help but to look around as her steps echoed off the walls.

The home screamed luxury, from the gorgeous marble floors to the priceless pieces of artwork adorning the walls. The longer they walked, the more out of place she felt. She couldn't figure out what had ever made her think she could handle such a prestigious job as to work for the head of a multi-billion dollar corporation.

They walked through a set of oversized double doors and Amy looked around the warm room as her shoulders relaxed. A fireplace, so large she could literally walk inside of it, was burning what smelled like cedar, giving the room a comforting quality. Though the room was well lit, it was done in soft bulbs, making the space incredibly inviting.

"Would you like something to drink while you wait?"

Amy shook her head and gave the man a small smile. She didn't want to appear rude.

"Go ahead and make yourself comfortable in the seating area. I'll let Mr. Anderson know you've arrived."

Before Amy could respond, he left, leaving her standing near the entrance. Eventually she was able to make her feet respond to her brain and walked over to the comfortable looking sofa. She sank onto the soft leather and leaned back. She wasn't kept waiting long, when a rumbling voice caused her to sit straight up, startling her. She was thankful she hadn't accepted the drink or she would've spilled it all over herself.

"Good morning, Ms. Harper. I'm sorry to have kept you waiting. Sometimes, it's difficult to get off the phone," Joseph said.

"I haven't been waiting long at all, Mr. Anderson. Thank you for getting me in for an interview so

quickly. I really appreciate it." Amy jumped to her feet and moved forward to shake his hand.

"The pleasure's all mine. Now, let's get the formality out of the way. Call me Joseph, please," he said as he held out his hand.

Amy felt like she was caught before an oncoming train. She didn't know how to react. She couldn't be rude, but she was uncomfortable calling him by his first name. She took his hand as she shifted on her feet.

"Thank you. You can call me Amy," she finally replied, deciding to just not call him by any name.

"Now that we have the formalities out of the way, let's sit down and chat. Have you been offered something to drink?"

"Yes, but I don't need anything." She didn't think she'd be able to swallow past the nervous lump in her throat.

Joseph indicated for her to sit back down on the sofa, which she quickly did, grateful to get off her shaky legs. He took the chair opposite her, then trained his light blue eyes on her face. The man was quite intimidating, standing well over six feet tall, with the broadest shoulders she could ever remember seeing.

He had snow white hair, just starting to thin a bit, and a neatly trimmed white mustache and beard. He was actually quite handsome for a man who must be in his early fifties, at least.

"I was impressed with your resume during the job fair at your school. If I remember correctly, you've held regular jobs since you were fourteen, then full-time work all throughout your schooling, correct?

How did you manage to regulate your time to keep such impressive grades?"

"I've always believed in a strong work ethic. I made sure not to overschedule myself, and I took my classes a little later in the morning so I could work the swing shifts at my jobs. I didn't want to graduate with a lot of debt," Amy replied, happy in knowing she'd done exactly that, and was pretty much debt free.

"Very impressive, Amy. Your resume, here, says you graduated with a degree in Business Finance with a minor in Public Relations. What are your future plans?"

"I haven't had a lot of time to think about where I want to go in ten years, but my goal has always been to get my foot in the door of a great corporation, such as yours, and work my way up. I know it's not an easy task, but I learn very quickly, and I'm not afraid of hard work or long hours. I'll do whatever it takes to learn all I need to in order to be a real asset to your company."

"What about marriage and babies?" he asked, never taking his gaze from her eyes.

Amy felt her cheeks heat at his question. She knew a lot of higher up companies were afraid to hire young women due to the fact they'd sometimes get married, then need time off for having children and such. She didn't want to lie, but she knew her answer could lose her the job.

"I'm not involved with anyone right now, but I'd be lying to you if I said I don't want that to happen. I eventually want children, whether I do so in the traditional way or I adopt. I've always wanted to be a

mother, but I can guarantee you I wouldn't let anything affect my job performance. I know the value of secure employment, and I can't be a great mother without first having a solid home for my child," she answered. She knew he didn't know her, but she could obtain letters of recommendation. She'd never once taken a sick day from work, and her school assignments had always been on time, if not early.

Joseph continued watching her for so long, it made her want to fidget in her seat. With sheer will, she remained still as she waited for his response.

"Do you have family or friends close by who'd be willing to help you?"

Amy was surprised by his questions. She'd never before had an interview with so many personal questions. It was throwing her off balance. She had all the answers to typical interview questions, but not the stuff he was asking her. She didn't want anyone to know the true circumstances of her personal life.

"I have a few friends, but no family here," she finally answered, feeling safe in her choice of wording. The reality was that she didn't have any family, period.

Joseph then switched back to asking a few more work-related questions and she relaxed, secure in her knowledge of the business world. She'd studied hard, and spent the very little free time she had researching large corporations, knowing she wanted a high salary job when she graduated.

Her real goals included her working non-stop for several years while saving every extra dime she could so she'd be able to have a family. She'd been alone since she was a child, and she didn't want to die that way.

What Amy didn't know was that Joseph had already run a full background check on her, knew she was an orphan, and he had much bigger ideas in mind than just an executive assistant position. He was looking for a potential daughter-in-law.

"Amy, it's been a true pleasure talking with you today. As you were my last interview, I can safely tell you that the position is yours if you'd like it."

Amy stared back at Joseph in shock. She hadn't expected to hear anything about the job for at least a week, and found herself speechless as his words sunk in. He smiled as he waited for her to compose herself.

"Um…thank you, Mr. Anderson. I…Of course, I'll take the job," she finally stuttered, completely forgetting about his request to call him by his first name.

"That's wonderful. Welcome to the Anderson family corporation…"

The elevator sounding her arrival snapped Amy back to the present. *Do not blow this job, Amy. If it all works out, you could be completely secure within a couple years.* With her final words of encouragement to herself, she took a deep breath and waited for the doors to open.

As she stepped onto the twenty-fifth floor, she was momentarily paralyzed with fear. It was the most beautiful office she'd ever seen. The doors opened up to a massive lobby, a round cherry wood desk strategically placed for easy guest access. Behind the desk was a stunning blonde who looked more efficient than Amy ever hoped to be. White marble columns flanked the entranceway, leading to where Amy assumed the offices were located. Exquisite paintings hung on the walls, adding a depth of warm color. In the corner a seating area offered soft leather furniture and an antique coffee table with a priceless chandelier acting as a centerpiece overhead. She felt increasingly frumpy and inadequate as she stepped forward in her second hand business suit, and three year old heels.

"Can I help you?" the woman asked.

Amy snapped out of her temporary paralysis and walked forward. "Yes, I'm Amy Harper, the new executive secretary for Mr. Anderson," she said with as much confidence as she could rally.

The woman looked at her blankly for a moment before slowly reaching for her phone. "Mr. Anderson, I have Amy Harper here who says she's your new executive secretary." She paused for a few moments. "Okay…Yes, sir."

She hung up the phone and turned back to Amy, "Mr. Anderson says he already has an executive secretary and has hired no one new. He also said that if you're a reporter trying for another story about his family, all his answers are, *no comment*." The woman looked dismissively at Amy before adding, "Have a nice day, Ms. Harper."

She didn't give Amy another glance as she turned back to her computer. As far as she was concerned Amy was dismissed.

"Um, excuse me," Amy looked at the secretary's name plate, "…Shelly, I was interviewed last week by Mr. Anderson. He told me to be in the office at eight a.m. sharp, so you may want to check again," she said a bit more forcefully. Shelly glanced up, as if shocked that the disturbing woman was still there.

Before Shelly had a chance to reply, the elevator chimed and in walked an older woman with smiling blue eyes. "You must be Amy Harper. I'm sorry I'm late but I got stuck behind a car accident," the woman said while walking forward. "I'm Esther Lyon and I'll be working with you this week – getting you trained for the new position. I was so happy when Joseph called to let me know he'd found my replacement," she said, warmth seeping through her voice.

Relief flooded through Amy, knowing the job was really hers – for better or worse. "It's so good to meet you, Esther. I was a bit nervous when Shelly said there wasn't a job," she said.

Esther looked over at the woman in question. "We haven't yet announced I'm retiring, though it's been in the works for some time. Shelly wasn't made aware of the situation. I'm sorry about any lack of communication."

"Walk with me, and I'll show you your new office as I talk a little about the history of this wonderful company. The original building was created a little over one-hundred years ago, but in this growing city, many updates have been added since then. Joseph's grandfather, Benjamin, started Anderson Corporation with little more than a prayer and a few dollars. As I'm sure you know, his hard work paid off. We're now global, with offices all across the United States and the world. Joseph was the next elected CEO after Benjamin's passing, but his son, Lucas, took over last year, and is certainly following in his relative's footsteps. He's a brilliant man, and I'm sure you'll love working for him."

"I have to be honest; this is all a little overwhelming. I mean, the history of this wealthy family, the amount of business to keep track of, even the building, itself. I don't know how one man keeps track of it all," Amy said with awe.

"Oh, it takes a whole team, sweetie, believe me. Don't let yourself get worked up over nothing. The way to keep sane in this chaotic place is simply to do one task at a time. Look at the smaller picture, and before you know it, the day is done and you've accomplished far more than you ever imagined," Esther reassured her.

They walked down the hallway and through a large oak doorway into a huge office. Was everything in the building done on a much grander scale than your average place? In the middle of the room was a huge three-sided desk. On the surface sat a top-of-the-line computer and an overflowing in and out box. Two chairs were placed in front of the desk, and one large chair behind it.

A bookshelf took up most of one wall, its shelves lined from top to bottom with many titles. Amy hoped she wasn't expected to read them all in a short time period. Hopefully, they were only there for either decoration, or for when she needed a specific answer, though with the internet, it was much faster to search online for whatever a person needed, nowadays.

Natural light flooded the room from the floor to ceiling windows lined up on the back wall, behind the desk. Amy was grateful for the uncovered windows, knowing if she got too stressed, she could take a minute to face the amazing city of Seattle while her stress had a chance to diminish. It really was an ideal office.

"Come in and have a seat. Make yourself comfortable while I show you what you need to get started. Before you know it, you'll be excellent on your own, no longer needing my help at all," Esther said kindly.

"I have my doubts about that, but I'm sure glad you're the one training me. You seem very nice."

"Thank you, Amy. Do you mind if I call you by your first name? I've never been huge on the formality thing. I feel that an office environment should be enjoyable, and *really* knowing who you're working with makes a big difference in making it so. Joseph became a dear friend of mine, and so did his beautiful wife, Katherine. I've watched their children grow into fine young men, and have been treated like a part of their family. It's a good thing, too, because there are weeks you'll see far more of this office than your own place. You need to have a healthy working relationship with your boss."

"I'd love to keep it informal. Joseph said the same thing to me during the interview, and I didn't know how to respond, but I'm beginning to see this place isn't what I thought it would be. I was expecting a rigid staff and endless work," Amy replied. As she realized what she said, she quickly tried to correct herself.

"I wasn't trying to say hard work is bad, or being professional is a negative thing. I was just…"

"You don't need to explain, Amy," Esther interrupted. "I understand exactly what you're saying.

Before I was fortunate enough to get a job with Joseph, I worked for a large developer on the other side of the city. He was rude, to me and his clients, never smiled at anyone, and didn't care about those who worked for him. He only cared about the bottom line. There are a lot of corporations like that, but this isn't one of them. They expect a great deal from you, but they're also willing to compensate you for your work. They treat their staff, from the lowest positions to the highest, with respect. The benefits are almost mind-boggling, but you'll soon learn why they can do this. They save a lot of money by having an incredibly low turnover rate, and they never hurt for more business, because they have repeat business in all their divisions. Even in bad economic times, they not only survive, but thrive."

Amy relaxed as she listened to Esther. The woman should be a recruiter for the corporation, not that it looked like they needed to recruit. Before that moment, Amy hadn't realized quite how lucky she was to have gotten her job. It didn't matter, though. She'd work hard no matter what – she didn't know any other way.

Amy felt slightly overwhelmed as the two women worked together the rest of the morning. By the afternoon, she was starting to pick up on some of the tasks, though, and she really enjoyed Esther's company. They worked well together, and Amy wished she had more than one week of training with her. Amy didn't have a mother and tended to enjoy the company of older women, especially when they were open and caring.

Esther put Amy on a project as she cleaned out her email. Amy was glad to find she was able to do the assigned task without asking for help. They sat in a comfortable silence as they worked for a few hours before they were interrupted.

"Esther, can you cancel my appointments for the rest of the day. I need to go to my father's. Before I leave, I also need the Niles reports if you've finished them."

Amy looked up as the most stunning man she'd ever glimpsed walked through a connecting door on the south wall. He was looking at a piece of paper in his hand, which gave her a few moments to secretly observe him.

The first thing she noticed was his build. He had to be at least six-foot-four, with wide shoulders, a full chest, and a flat stomach. As his arm moved, stretching the obviously tailored dark business suit, she could easily guess he was solid muscle, not an ounce of fat daring to attach to his body. The white shirt clearly accentuated his golden tan. The outfit was complete with a loosened tie, making him look like he'd just stepped off the closest movie shoot rather than his office.

He reached up and ran his fingers through his dark brown hair, causing the short strands to stick out in a few places, making him even sexier, in her opinion. In the next moment he looked up, and his deep azure eyes met her startled green ones.

"I'm sorry, Esther. I didn't realize you had a client in here."

Amy was shocked by his words. Why was he calling her a client?

"Lucas Anderson," he said as he held his hand out to her. *I'm in trouble, big, big trouble,* was her only thought as she looked at his hand like it was a snake. Skin to skin contact would feel far too intimate, even though it was simply shaking hands, but when had she ever touched a man of this stunning caliber? She also knew full well she couldn't refuse to shake her boss's hand.

As she hesitated an awkward amount of time, she saw him raise his eyebrows at her questioningly. Her face turned a nice shade of red as she finally broke eye contact.

She snapped out of her trance, realizing he was waiting for her to introduce herself. Finally, she stood and gave him her hand, "Hello, I'm Amy Harper."

Amy was rooted to the spot as his fingers closed around hers, her breath instantly held prisoner inside her lungs.

Chapter Two

As their hands touched, Lucas felt a surge of adrenaline rush through his body, and straight to his groin, shocking him. He tightened his grip around her fingers, tugging a little, enough that she noticed. He didn't like the instant attraction – not one bit.

Amy was beautiful, sure, but so were thousands of other women he was in contact with. It seemed, though, that none of them had the power to electrify him with only a simple touch. The electric moment with Amy was a first for him.

As a myriad of emotions crossed Amy's face, Lucas found himself fascinated by her expressions. She didn't seem capable of hiding a thing from him, though he was sure she'd like to. Their gazes were locked together, her cheeks flushed and eyes wide as he watched a mixture of desire and fear play from deep within their depths. He found himself wanting to lean closer, shock her into gasping, opening those luscious pink lips, but somehow he managed to pull himself back.

He had work to do – important work. He certainly didn't have time to play with the obviously innocent woman.

Slowly, Lucas turned toward Esther, releasing Amy's hand at the same time. "When your guest leaves, step into my office and grab the paper on my desk. I have several letters that need to go out today and a few other tasks I want done before five."

"I think you and your father need to talk right away, Lucas," Esther said, stopping him.

"Talk about what?" He saw the hesitation on Esther's face and got a bad feeling.

"I sent you my notice last month and told you that your father would be hiring a new assistant."

"I told you then that I needed you to stay longer. I assumed the matter was settled," he answered a bit too harshly.

"Lucas, don't you dare use that tone of voice with me. Don't forget, I've seen you running around in nothing but a diaper. You knew when your father retired that I'd be leaving as soon as you got settled in. I stayed on to make sure you had a smooth transition, but now it's my turn for retirement. I love this company but, like your father, I believe sometimes it's best to get on with things and bring in a new generation."

"I'm sorry about the misunderstanding. Can you work one more month so I can find an appropriate replacement to take your position? I'll double your salary, knowing it's an inconvenience," he asked, trying to forget Amy was in the room.

"Your father already conducted the interviews, and Amy's your new assistant. I've been training her all morning, and she's doing a remarkable job," Esther finished and patted Amy on the hand.

His gaze turned immediately to the woman in question, the one who'd seared him with nothing more than the touch of her fingers. There was no possible way she could work for him – not even a chance.

◊◊◊◊◊◊

Suddenly, Amy found herself the object of Lucas's intense gaze. The minute he turned those cold blue eyes back on her, she felt her stomach drop. He had enough heat raging in his eyes to be considered a fire hazard. The intensity flowing between the two of them was enough to leave her shaking, though she really hoped her fear wasn't showing through.

She tried to firm her shoulders and meet his look with an expression of indifference, but she was sure she wasn't pulling it off.

"I'll speak to my father about this, but I should've been informed of the interviews. Don't get too comfortable in your new position, Ms. Harper," he spoke with the utmost authority before storming through the doorway, shutting it a bit harder than necessary.

"I thought he knew I'd been hired. He didn't even know you were leaving," Amy said with apprehension in her voice. She could be losing her dream job before it even started.

"Now, don't you worry about anything, Amy. It will all be just fine."

"I know you've worked here for a lot of years, Esther, but the look on his face wasn't that of a happy man. I wouldn't get too set on retirement if I were you," Amy said, attempting to make a joke, though it fell flat.

"You'll find Lucas is far more bark than bite. He's riled up right now, but he'll settle down soon. Let's finish our work for the afternoon. By tomorrow this will be straightened out and you'll forget all about it," Esther promised.

Amy had her doubts, but there was no use in worrying about it. She figured she'd do the best job she could, and then *maybe* her position would be safe.

They got absorbed in their work, and the incident was placed on the back burner – still there, but put away for the moment.

◊◊◊◊◊◊

"Dad, how do you expect me to run this company when you're stepping in and doing things without letting me know?" Lucas was pacing in front of his father, back and forth across the parlor.

"Now, son, I told you when I left that Esther would be retiring once you got settled in. I also said I'd take care of her replacement. It's not my fault you forgot. And it's not Esther's fault you didn't take her resignation seriously."

"I take everything seriously. At the least, you could have let me know interviews were going on so I could be a part of it. I would've been just fine handling them on my own."

"I know you're more than capable of doing your job. However, when you took over, I promised to tie up any loose ends left from my leaving. This was the final item I had to take care of," Joseph said, leaving Lucas with little argument.

"Dad, I know you're up to something. I just can't figure out what it is this time, but I'm capable of hiring my own staff. It doesn't look good for me when I don't know what's going on in my own offices."

"I interviewed about thirty people, and Ms. Harper was, by far, the most qualified candidate. Believe me, you won't have any problems with her. I checked her out extensively before sending her to you."

It was a good thing Lucas didn't know that Joseph was far more interested in her abilities as a possible wife, than an executive assistant. Luckily, she really had done well in school and was more than capable of doing her job, and doing it well, for that matter. Lucas would've seen right through a woman who was only there looking for a husband.

Joseph felt Amy was a perfect candidate for Lucas. She was smart, strong, and had been through a lot in her short lifetime. She needed a family, and Joseph needed a daughter-in-law. It was a perfect match. Lucas would soon see that.

"You've left me with little choice. I don't think there's any way I can convince Esther to stay on at this point, now that she's made up her mind. I'll see how Ms. Harper works out, but if she doesn't work soundly with me, then I'll fire her and the next person will be someone I find – not you."

"I think that's a reasonable request," Joseph quickly agreed, wanting to change the subject. "Now, on to other business." Joseph knew he couldn't give Lucas too much time to think about the matter. He was a smart boy, and Joseph didn't want him figuring out what he was up to. If Lucas had any idea how much Joseph wanted his sons married, Lucas would go running for the hills before he had a chance to fall in love with Amy. That just wouldn't do for Joseph. He wanted those grandchildren – the earlier, the better.

The two of them spent the rest of the afternoon going over the new benefits package Joseph had modified. Joseph may be retired, but he liked to stay involved. He'd go a little stir-crazy if he left the corporation completely. He'd promised his Katherine he wouldn't work seventy-hour weeks anymore, but he'd never agreed to forget about the corporation his grandfather had started. She understood that, and was supportive of him remaining active with the human resources department. After all, she had a huge heart, herself. It was why he loved her so much, even after thirty-five years of marriage.

◊◊◊◊◊◊

By the time Lucas left his father's house, his frustration had greatly lessened. When he returned to the building, everyone was gone for the day.

As he made his way into his office, he could smell a lingering scent of vanilla in the air, just a hint, but enough to remind him of his new employee. He had a feeling Amy was going to be nothing but trouble for him if he let her stay. The best thing for both of them would be for him to simply fire her. He knew his dad would be upset, but he'd support him.

As he stood in the connecting doorway to their two offices, he struggled with himself while remembering her innocent expression, so open and readable.

With a firm resolve, he stood straighter and turned his back to the room, silently shutting the door behind him. He was in control of his emotions, and there was no way he was going to let a stranger get under his skin. Women came and went from his life, serving an essential purpose, and then quietly exiting. His new employee wasn't going to get the upper hand and control any part of him – certainly not his emotions.

Lucas walked to his desk and picked up a file. He had a lot of work to finish that night, so he relaxed on his couch and started reading. It didn't take him long to feel his eyes start to grow heavy, then he was falling asleep before he knew what hit him.

Lucas often spent his nights in the office after burning the midnight oil. He'd always driven himself hard, putting work ahead of pleasure at all times. He'd known from a young age that he was going to take over the family corporation. It was in his blood.

Lucas's last thought, before succumbing to sleep, was of vivid green eyes filled with hunger.

Chapter Three

"I think you're ready for a few days on your own. I'm just a phone call away if you need me, but I think I'll help you from the beaches in Southern California," Esther said as she gathered her purse and jacket.

It was Amy's second week and she was doing much better, but panic consumed her at the thought of Esther leaving her on her own. Well, it wasn't exactly on her own – Lucas was only a thin piece of wood away.

She couldn't say he'd been rude, but he wasn't friendly, either. His glacier blue eyes would hold her captive as she and Esther sat before him at his desk, his tone commanding, yet always professional. She'd yet to see him smile.

"I'll be fine, Esther, but I'll miss you," Amy finally assured her.

"I'll miss you too, dear, but don't worry about a thing. I'll be back on Monday to start on your final training schedule. You're picking up on all of this much faster than I did way back when, and it wasn't nearly as technical when I was starting out. I think you're a great addition to the team."

"You're too nice to me. Make sure you bottle up some sand so I can at least pretend I occasionally get to visit warm beaches," Amy said with a laugh.

"It won't take long before you're flying all over the world. Part of your job is traveling to different divisions of the corporation with Lucas. Some of the places are incredible. It's very difficult to work from a hotel suite when you can see the sun shining down on a beautiful white beach. Joseph was always good about making sure I had time to get some playing in, though. I'm sure Lucas will be the same way," Esther assured her.

Amy had serious doubts about that. Lucas didn't seem like he was familiar with anything that had to do with fun. The idea of seeing him in nothing but a pair of low-riding swim trunks immediately sent butterflies to her stomach, though.

"Yes, you're probably right," Amy finally answered, realizing Esther was giving her an odd look. It didn't help that her reply came out a bit breathlessly.

Stop daydreaming about your boss. The man hates you, as it is. You, in no way, need to make the situation worse by lusting after him, Amy berated herself.

"All right, then. I'm off. Have a great day," Esther said before breezing out of the office.

Amy sat at the desk, a little bit lost. She had her assignments, but it was her first day all by herself. After a couple minutes she dove in. It wasn't like she could mess up too badly.

A couple hours later she was startled when her intercom buzzed.

"Amy, I need you in my office."

Lucas was short and to the point, never adding more words than he needed to. It was a bit disconcerting. She gathered her notebook and quickly walked to their connecting door. Before turning the knob, she took a fortifying breath, then stepped through.

"Good afternoon, Mr. Anderson."

"I need you to take a few memos for me, then type up the letters. I need them back within the hour. I've been called away for an emergency and I don't know how long I'll be away. Normally, you'd be coming with me, but since you're still in training, that's out the window," he said, his tone curt.

She shifted on her feet, feeling like she was getting a scolding for being new. She knew better than to say anything back, but she felt like apologizing, though she didn't know what for.

"Yes, sir," she replied as she sat before him.

◊◊◊◊◊◊

Lucas had to stare at his computer while he cursed his reaction to Amy as her scent washed over him. If he didn't gain some control over his body's reaction to her, he'd never make it through the next few weeks, let alone a long-term employment. He decided right then, that if a new assistant was hired for him, it was going to either be male, or a much older woman.

He knew he'd been working a lot of hours, but obviously, it was time for him to call one of his female friends. He needed to find relief before he ended up doing something stupid like throwing his new assistant over his desk.

It wasn't like he was a hormone riddled teenage boy. He couldn't understand why the heck he was reacting so strongly to her. Yes, she was attractive, but he'd seen better looking women, who were far more polished, and even more, who knew the score.

He had zero doubts his assistant wasn't the one-night-stand type of girl – and that's the only kind of women he dated. He had no time and no desire for committed relationships.

Lucas pulled himself together, then dictated the notes he wanted typed up. Yes, this was what he did well – business. Most people let their jobs rule them, cause stress, but not Lucas. He thrived in the fast paced world of high finance.

He finally looked up, his throat closing for a moment as he watched her furiously write to keep up with him. The same piece of stubborn hair that was always escaping her unflattering bun was caressing her cheekbone, the end tickling the corner of her mouth, almost framing her luscious pink lips. His groin tightened as he thought about those lips gliding across his skin, her tongue darting out and cooling his overheated body.

When she looked up, her eyes widened, emotions flashing through her expressive face. The fact that she couldn't hide a thing from him didn't help. He knew his employee was just as attracted to him as he was to her.

His groin throbbed as their gazes locked together, neither of them seeming able to pull away. His brothers would have a heyday if they saw what his tiny little assistant was doing to him. They always liked to tease him about being made of steel, always the one in control, even from the time they were teenagers.

They'd get a real kick over his lack of control due to one small woman.

"That will be all," he finally said, knowing his voice was harsh, but not able to stop it. He watched as she jumped in her chair, then as her cheeks flushed a tempting shade of red, he found himself wanting to say 'to hell with it' and just pulling her onto his lap.

"Uh…okay. I'll…um…have this done on time," she stuttered before shakily climbing to her feet.

He watched as she slowly made her way from his office, a bit unsteady. The gentle sway of her hips didn't help his situation – not at all.

Finally, he jumped to his feet, needing to get out of the office. He grabbed his gym bag and exited through his private entrance. He was relieved to be leaving for a while. By the time he got back, he knew he'd have his hormones under control.

Amy stepped off the elevator with an extra bounce in her step. *What a difference a month makes*, she thought with a genuine smile. Though tension was still over the top with Lucas, she really didn't spend too much time with him, making her days bearable. She loved her job and felt confident in performing her tasks, even without Esther at her side. She felt good – really good.

"Amy, come over and have some cake," she heard Esther calling. "It's my retirement party." Amy looked up to find hundreds of employees crowding the glass conference room. Everyone was chatting, eating and seemed to be having a great time.

"Good morning, Amy, I've been hearing wonderful things about you. How are you doing?" This came from Joseph seconds before he walked up and threw an arm around her shoulders.

"It's great, Mr. Anderson. Thank you again for giving me this opportunity," she said bashfully. The man was still intimidating, but with his gentle smile and friendly eyes, it wasn't hard to relax in his presence. She was growing a bit fond of the gentle giant.

"Nonsense, my girl – you earned this position by studying hard and having an excellent work ethic. Esther said you're fitting right in and doing a fantastic job." He laughed heartily. "Come with me. I want you to meet some other employees." He wrapped her arm in his and dragged her around the room for several minutes, making dozens of introductions, before stopping in front of a well-dressed man. "Mike, I want you to meet Amy. She's the new executive assistant for Lucas," Joseph said in his excessively loud voice, causing several heads to turn in their direction. Amy could feel her face grow warmer, uncomfortable with being the center of attention.

"Nice to meet you, Amy," Mike replied as the corner of his lips turned up into a sexy smile.

He stuck out his hand and took hers, his thumbs caressing her wrist. She may not date a whole lot, but she wasn't unaware of the subtle signals he was sending her way. She felt her face heat a bit more.

"Mike works in the offices one floor down as an assistant. I thought I'd introduce you so if you have any questions, he can answer them. I'll leave the two of you to chat," Joseph said with a chuckle before walking away.

After an awkward moment, Amy found herself enjoying Mike's company. He was a nice guy with a sense of humor and a lot of knowledge.

Mike was far more the kind of man who normally interested Amy. He was average-looking--not someone you'd place on a calendar, but who you'd definitely give a second glance. He was witty and his smile was engaging. He also didn't stir her stomach, or make her cheeks flush. He was safe.

"I know this great little diner right down the road. Can I buy you dinner on Friday?"

Amy looked at the good looking man and wished she felt even the tiniest spark of interest in him, but she didn't. Not only that, but she really didn't want to date anyone at the moment. She was focused on her job and had life goals in mind. She didn't have time to date, but she didn't want to hurt his feelings. She was caught between a rock and a hard place.

◊◊◊◊◊◊

Across the room, Lucas was glaring daggers at his new employee. She never smiled that way when he talked to her. Of course, he was normally barking orders at her, so he could almost understand why. Still, he didn't like the attention she was giving to another male. He really didn't like the interest he saw in Mike's eyes. As Lucas slowly looked at her from her feet, all the way up, he certainly could appreciate that interest.

What did his father think he was doing, introducing her to Mike? Everyone knew he went through women faster than he changed clothes. Many women had been fooled by his act of affection, but Lucas knew the guy only had one goal in mind, and Lucas was sure Amy wasn't ready for the ramifications of a failed office romance.

Lucas was even more irritated that he cared. He consoled himself by thinking he was only concerned because, if she got discarded, her work performance would suffer, which would make him have to fire her. He'd then have to take time away from his busy schedule to hire a new employee.

He was just about ready to storm over there, grab her arm, and drag her away, when his father approached him. "How you doing, boy?" he asked far too slyly.

"Fine, Father. And you?" he automatically responded, not taking his eyes off Amy.

He was thinking the office party had gone on long enough. It was time to get his employee away from Mike, and back to work.

◊◊◊◊◊◊

Joseph had a hard time keeping the satisfied grin from his face as he watched his son throw an internal fit while Amy laughed with Mike. Lucas was already falling for Amy, and the boy didn't even realize it. Joseph may as well push things along a bit more – speed things up. In the game of love, no one could lose.

Joseph could practically feel the weight of his first grandchild resting in his arms. He couldn't imagine a more perfect Christmas present for Katherine and him.

"Don't you think Amy and Mike look good together? She's seemed a little lonely this past week. I've been worried about her, considering she has no family to turn to. She's been tight lipped about her circumstances, but I think she could use a good friend."

Joseph tried keeping his voice sincere as he spoke to Lucas, knowing how to push his eldest son's buttons. There was nothing like a little jealousy to make a man step up to the plate.

"Mike's a cad and I'm going to put a stop to this. You need to quit meddling in people's lives, Father," Lucas said through tight lips.

"I'm sorry, son. I didn't know you were interested in her. You know, as her boss, you probably shouldn't start a romance," he said. He knew his son well and there was nothing Lucas enjoyed more than a challenge. Throwing down the gauntlet and telling Lucas he couldn't have her would make him want her even more.

"I'm not interested in her," Lucas said through clenched teeth. "I just know what kind of a man Mike is. He'll break her heart, and then her work will be affected. I'm only thinking of the work environment."

"Has work been stressful, Lucas? You seem to be tightly wound."

"Work's been fine, Dad. I just don't like it when you come here, cause a bunch of chaos, mess with my employee, then act as if everything is fine. I'm still not thrilled you went behind my back and hired Amy, but she's actually doing her job well, and I don't feel like trying to find a replacement at this time. I have much more important things to focus on. Now, if you'll excuse me, I have work to do."

With those parting words, he started walking in her direction.

Joseph chuckled to himself, feeling downright giddy. Oh yes, his son was falling hard. He had picked out the perfect wife, it seemed. He moved over to Esther and nudged her in the arm so the two of them could watch the show.

"You know, Joseph Anderson, one of these days those boys of yours are going to figure out all the stunts you pull on them, and then the tables will be turned," Esther said with a chuckle.

"Ah, Esther, how you underestimate me. I'm far too sly to get caught."

"You may think you have everyone fooled, but you're not as clever as you believe," she responded, though her eyes were glued to Lucas as he marched across the room.

"We'll just have to wait and see…"

◊◊◊◊◊◊

"Amy, we have work to do," Lucas said as he approached her and Mike. Amy noticed he didn't even acknowledge Mike's presence, and that fact apparently wasn't lost on her companion, either. Mike, obviously not wanting to upset the boss, slunk away without another word. Amy lost a bit of respect for him as she turned toward Lucas.

"Yes, Mr. Anderson. I'm sorry, but everyone was out here, and I wasn't sure what I was supposed to do. I'll get to work now," Amy replied before turning toward her office. She didn't understand why he sounded so irritated with her. It seemed everyone in the building was at the party and it wasn't like she'd been the one who threw it.

Lucas followed close behind her down the short hallway, then stood looming over her as she sat down. She sighed as she lifted her head, knowing he wasn't done speaking.

"I don't like office romances. They cause nothing but trouble, and though it isn't a policy, it's greatly frowned on," he informed her in his most stately tone of voice, which caused the hairs on the back of her neck to stand up.

She had to silently count to ten before responding. "First of all, Mr. Anderson," she said through clenched teeth, "I was simply socializing with another employee. And second of all, who I choose to have a romance with is none of your business." Amy was surprised by the acid in her tone. It was the first time she'd ever spoken back to him, which was surprising, considering he barked at her continuously.

Suddenly, he was inches from her face. "When you work for me, you *will* listen to what I say. Mike's a womanizer, and I don't want to deal with the repercussions when he throws you out like stale bread, and believe me, he will."

Amy leaned back, trying to put a few inches of space between them, her heart beating uncontrollably. She was sure her heart was pounding so hard, it was visible to him, even through her blouse. She forgot about her anger with Lucas as an instant urge to reach out and grab him overwhelmed her.

She wanted Lucas.

Everything about him screamed sex, and if he leaned in a couple more inches and claimed her mouth, she'd welcome it. She knew it was irrational, and she should have her head examined, but she'd been dealing with the heat coming off of him in waves for weeks, and she wondered if her imagination was doing justice to what it would feel like to kiss him.

How bad could one kiss really be? At least then, she'd figure out it was probably all just in her imagination – the sparks, desire, chemistry.

For what seemed like an eternity she couldn't break their eye contact. She felt liquid heat pooling inside of her. She knew she couldn't follow through with her desire, she couldn't lean those few inches and taste his lips.

Look away, look away, look away, she shouted at herself. Finally, she found the willpower to turn her head, having no idea how long they'd been there face to face.

◊◊◊◊◊◊

Realizing how close he'd come to closing that gap and kissing her shocked Lucas into standing up straight and retreating from her office. He slipped inside, his body rock solid, a light sheen of sweat covering his brow.

Lucas leaned against the door and willed his body to return to normal. He hadn't felt such intense desire for a woman since his college days. Even then, he knew he'd possessed more control. If she hadn't broken their eye contact, he knew he would've kissed her. He also had a feeling one kiss would send him over the edge. He couldn't get the picture from his mind of her writhing beneath him on the solid wood desk, her hair finally free from the hideous bun.

It was most definitely time to head to his gym and expend some of his pent up energy. He gathered his bag and slipped from the office, riding down in his private elevator to avoid speaking to anyone. He wasn't in the mood, and was afraid anyone who crossed his path would end up on the wrong end of his frustration.

After a two-hour intense workout, Lucas still found himself wound tight, his frustration banked, but not eliminated. When he arrived back at the office, he pulled up his phone list on his computer. He stared at the names for a solid ten minutes, before clicking the x and shutting it down. He knew the best thing for him to do would be to call one of the women he had an arrangement with, but he couldn't make himself do it.

With a sigh of disgust at himself, he forced his mind to focus. He had work to do and he wasn't going to allow his body to dictate his actions. He turned to his computer and got busy.

He managed to avoid Amy the rest of the day, choosing to communicate through email only. It seemed to be safer that way, for both of them.

Chapter Four

Time flew by quickly for Amy as she became more and more comfortable in her new job. After her intense moment with Lucas the day of the party, she'd been afraid she wouldn't last much longer as his executive assistant. Thankfully, he'd been professional since then, instead of firing her on the spot.

She found that Lucas was out of the office most of the time, and communication was mostly done through email. What she couldn't figure out was why that bothered her. She should be relieved to have him away, not be the slightest upset he wasn't around.

She barely knew the man and he was stirring all kinds of different emotions inside her. Lust was certainly on the very top of the list. She'd always been the good girl, skipping parties to study, putting off relationships because she worked, and saving herself for the right man. Well, she was twenty-four years old and still hadn't met 'the one', so what did that say about her.

She still remembered listening to the girls giggling in the school library about their romantic date the night before. Amy had felt twinges of jealousy that they managed to have time for fun along with their studies, but she'd never felt she was depriving herself of anything. One month in close quarters with Lucas Anderson, and all that was changing.

She suddenly found herself fantasizing about her incredibly good-looking boss, wondering how he'd look if he loosened his tie a little, undid the top button of his fitted trousers. Her imagination was becoming increasingly inappropriate and she had to stop. Having an affair with her boss wasn't part of her future plans.

"Sorry to interrupt you, Amy, but Joseph Anderson is here to see you," Tom said through her phone, startling her.

"I'll be right out," she said after a brief pause.

"Don't bother, he's on his way back, love."

Lucas had fired the blond receptionist, thrilling Amy, as the woman had shot daggers at her every time Amy came in and out of the office. Amy hadn't sent Lucas any longing looks, or tried to flirt with him in any way, and wanted to tell the fake blonde receptionist she could have at him, just to get her to back off. The jealousy that thought inspired irritated her to no end.

The new receptionist Joseph had hired to take her place was a great guy. With the boss gone, when she had spare time, she'd sit with him, chatting about everything going on in their lives. She'd only been working with him for a couple weeks, but he was quickly becoming her best friend.

"Thanks for the heads up," she said, then quickly straightened up her desk before her doorway was filled by Joseph's massive frame.

"Good morning, Amy. I was down here and thought I'd stop in and see how you're doing."

"That's very kind of you, Mr. Anderson, but I'm fine."

"I guess I'm going to have to visit every day until you're comfortable enough to call me Joseph," he said with a chuckle as he sat down, looking intent on staying a while.

"Okay, okay, I'll go against everything I was ever taught and call you by your name. I just want you to know that it sounds disrespectful to me," she said with a laugh. It was hard to argue with Joseph.

"I can be hard when I need to be, but I've found that most people respond to a much friendlier approach. When I was young like my sons, I tended to be a bit of a horse's ass, arrogance radiating off of me in waves. My beautiful wife, Katherine, cured me of that. She never allowed me to get too out of hand."

"Your wife sounds like an amazing and smart woman."

"That she is, indeed. We've been married for over thirty years now, and I thank God for her every day. I only want the same for our sons," he said, looking straight into her eyes.

Amy felt a moment of panic as if he was sending her some kind of message. She finally laughed, shrugging off his comment. He was just being himself, a friendly guy. It's why she enjoyed his company so much.

"I'm sure they'll each meet someone in their own time. I know as I was finishing school, then looking for work, relationships were the last thing on my mind. Your boys probably feel the same way, especially with Lucas taking over your old job, and your other two doing whatever it is that they do," she finished lamely, realizing she had no idea what his sons, Alex and Mark, did.

"Oh, those boys have plenty of spare time. I think they just refuse to marry because they're too busy playing. I'm not worried, though. It will happen," he said as if he was sharing a secret with her.

"That's a positive attitude."

"I've found that life is just too short to be anything other than positive. When something isn't going the way you want it to, then you have to switch gears and make a change," he said. "Look at my youngest son, Mark. He helps out when we need him to, but he was never meant to be a part of this corporate world. He followed in his grandfather's footsteps and became a rancher. Still, he couldn't hide from the Anderson desire for success. He's made the family ranch thrive during his time there. Alex likes to travel the world, and does most of our international business, and he's really good at it, too, constantly bringing in more business. Then, of course, there's Lucas. He followed right in his great-grandfather's steps, and mine, too. Each of us has a driving need to be number one. The one thing my boys all have in common, though, is they have hearts of gold. When they fall in love, it will be for the long-haul. That's why they've been waiting, a bit too long, in my opinion."

His voice was mesmerizing as he talked about his family. He was always louder than the average person, but as he spoke of his children, his tone changed, obviously showing a great love for his wife and boys. Amy had to fight the sudden melancholy wanting to envelope her. One thing she wanted more than anything else was family. It was something she'd been denied, and she knew when she had children of her own, she'd love them as much as Joseph loved his. How much she'd love to have a father like him to be there for her.

She shook her head, pushing the thoughts away. She'd learned long ago not to dwell on what she didn't have. It was much better to focus on the things she could change, and all she'd accomplished. Wallowing in self-pity was counterproductive.

Before Amy realized it, an hour had passed and she found herself laughing at another of Joseph's stories. She felt a twinge of guilt as she realized how much time she'd visited with him instead of working. She shouldn't feel bad, since she was fully caught up, but still…

"I could sit here and talk with you all day long, dear, but I'd better let you get back to your job. Thank you for indulging an old man for a while," Joseph said as he stood.

"The pleasure was all mine, Joseph. Thank you for taking time out of your busy schedule to chat. I could easily forget everything else while you're talking," she told him sincerely.

"You're a true sweetheart, Amy. I'm so glad I was lucky enough to find you," he said, and then to her surprise, instead of shaking her hand, he reached out and gave her a hug. Amy had to fight the sudden tears wanting to spring up as his gentle hands reached around her and the comforting scent of peppermint invaded her senses.

Thankfully, he didn't expect her to say anything further. He released her and walked from the room. She fell back in her chair, not knowing how long she stared at the empty doorway before her buzzer sounded again.

"Amy, darling, it's lunch time. I need to get out of this place before I go insane. Let's head out for some far too greasy pizza and soda," Tom's energetic voice said through her speaker.

"Give me five minutes, and then I'm all yours." Amy knew she should probably just stay there during her lunch break considering she'd spent so much time with Joseph, but she needed to get outside and take a walk. Joseph had stirred a lot of emotions inside her, and being around a very energetic Tom, would help her push them back down.

She came out of her office, smiling when Tom threw his arm around her as they headed for the elevators. The metal doors slid open just as he was leaning into her in what would seem like an intimate moment to an outside observer. Just her luck, it was at that exact moment when Lucas stepped through the open doors.

"What's going on here, Amy?" he asked with ice in his tone and expression. "Have you forgotten this is a place of business? I'm gone a couple of weeks, and you think you can parade your boyfriends in and out of here? What if I'd been a customer?" Amy was too stunned by his behavior to even be capable of uttering a word. What was wrong with him?

Amy caught the slight smile on Tom's face before he turned so his new boss couldn't see. Amy frowned. She wondered if she should just cancel her lunch, and get back to work.

"Hello, Mr. Anderson. Ms. Harper and I were just stepping out on our lunch break. We already set the phones and will be back in one hour." With that, he pulled her into the elevator, and they were gone before she had a chance to blink. Oh, she knew she was going to catch hell for that. Lucas wasn't exactly the type of man who liked to be so easily dismissed. She was slightly afraid of what his reaction would be when they came back to work. It was too late to do anything about it right then, though.

◊◊◊◊◊◊

Before Lucas had time to react, the doors shut, leaving him stunned and more than a little angry. He almost followed them so he could drag her back up to the offices. Only years of tightly managed control had him staying where he was. What he really wanted to do was pitch Tom out a window and haul Amy into his arms. He'd avoided her as much as possible in the hope he'd get over his infatuation with her. It certainly didn't help when her expressive eyes would catch him as they were doing some task or other. He knew it was a mutual attraction, and they both were fighting their feelings for each other.

He made a couple phone calls, figuring out the man she was with was Tom. Lucas had figured his dad would be fine to hire a secretary. It wasn't that hard to find a person to answer the phones. But instead of a nice, sixty-year old woman, his dad had to hire a young, attractive male, who obviously had the hot's for Lucas's new assistant.

He knew he should be relieved, or in the least, not care at all, but he found he did care – cared a whole lot more than he should.

He stayed in his office the entire hour they were gone, not getting any work done. He just paced from one side of the room to the other, waiting impatiently for Amy's return.

◊◊◊◊◊◊

"You know you let him think we were sneaking off for some illicit affair during our lunch hour. I'm going to catch hell for that," Amy tried to say as sternly as possible as she and Tom sat down at their favorite diner only a block from the offices.

"I couldn't resist. He had such a sour expression on his face at seeing you locked in the arms of my beautiful self," he chuckled, obviously enjoying himself. "You were holding out on me, you know. I had no idea the boss was hot for your body," Tom continued.

"He isn't hot for my body," she said emphatically. "He just likes to be in control of everything, including his employees. Just you wait, soon he'll be telling you who you can and can't date, as well."

Amy knew she and Lucas would both end up getting over their shared attraction soon enough and she, in no way, wanted Tom to know she thought her new boss was drop-dead-gorgeous. She really didn't want him to know that Lucas made her breath hitch each time he walked in a room.

"Darling, I can already tell I'm not his type, *unfortunately*," he sighed, being overdramatic. "I would love to change him, but there are some men who only have eyes for the hourglass. Poor me, I'm destined for heartache, seeing that piece of man hunk on a daily basis and never having a shot."

Tom had successfully pulled her out of her melancholy. Even though she'd have to put up with Lucas's bad mood upon her return, at least for the moment, she and Tom were having a great lunch.

They laughed and talked between bites of food and, before either was ready, they finished and walked back to the office, making sure not to have any physical contact upon their entrance. Amy felt no need to press her luck any further that day. She didn't want to lose her job because the boss thought she was the office floozy.

Before she could even sit down, she was getting buzzed into Lucas's office. "Ms. Harper, can you please step in here? We have a lot to go over this afternoon and because of your extended lunch, we're behind," his voice snapped over the intercom.

Amy sighed, knowing her peaceful day was officially over. She gathered her laptop and headed for the door connecting their offices. She did grumble a bit to herself, though, as she'd made sure she didn't take an extended lunch and had, in fact, been back about ten minutes earlier than she needed to be.

Lucas didn't look up as she walked into the room. She silently crossed the floor and sat down on the opposite side of his desk. They sat for several minutes in an uncomfortable silence. She began to squirm, which ticked her off even more. How dare he make her feel like a child sitting in the principal's office because she'd been caught misbehaving.

◊◊◊◊◊◊

Lucas knew the second she entered the room. Her steps didn't make a sound on the soft carpet, but her sensual scent drifted over, slowly surrounding him. Lucas felt the air shift as she quietly sat in the chair across from him; the only sound was that of her legs crossing, the slight hiss of her nylons rubbing together.

His eyes were locked on the computer screen while he blindly punched buttons on the keyboard, having no clue what he was doing. For all he knew, he could've given away millions of dollars in the space of a few seconds. What scared him more than that, though, was the fact that he didn't even care if he had.

He knew he had to make a comment to start their meeting sooner or later, but he was still too close to pulling her from her chair and making her forget any other man but him. His imagination ran wild as he pictured her spread out on his desk as she opened to him and he plunged inside her, finally ending both of their suffering. He could brand her his, and she'd never want another. The clear picture, in his head, of her lips crying out his name almost broke his restraint.

"Did you finish the Nielson report I emailed?" He finally spoke and was satisfied to see her jump at the sound of his voice. For some unknown reason, her reaction relaxed him. Knowing she was just as tense as he was, brought back his control, made him feel like he was in charge. He wondered what else would make her jump.

Lucas stood up, walked around his desk, and sat on the edge of it, his leg nearly brushing hers. He watched as she sat up even straighter, shifting restlessly in her seat.

After what seemed like hours, but was in fact only seconds, Amy handed him the file, having anticipated he'd be asking for it. He took the folder, making sure their fingers brushed. He noticed goosebumps appear on her arm.

His mood immediately lifted as he got comfortable in his element. He was in control – as he needed to be. He pretended to read the file, taking his time, enjoying her close proximity. "Very good." She once again jumped, as if she'd forgotten they were sitting so close together.

He knew she was too strong to admit he was making her squirm, and there was no way she'd cry mercy. He'd learned that much about her from the first day they'd met. If she looked upset in any way, he would've found the willpower to pull away from her. He may be lusting after her, but he didn't cross the line of stalking. He knew it wasn't him she was afraid of, though, it was herself. She wanted him as badly as he wanted her. The passion simmering in her eyes was undeniable, though she tried to hide it.

Her breath was coming in soft pants, making her breasts rise and fall quickly beneath her blouse, and he could see the trace of her hardened nipples pressing against the fabric. He wanted to bend down and feel her pulse pounding beneath his lips. Her arousal was a complete aphrodisiac.

Lucas shifted his weight, causing his leg to press against hers. She remained frozen as her quick breathing hitched for a heartbeat. She could pull away at any moment, but she sat stiffly in the chair, refusing to budge.

It was a game of wills, and he really didn't know which of them was going to break first. He was testing his endurance to the very limit –that was for sure. He knew the smart thing would be to back off, send her from his office, but he couldn't do it. If she asked to leave, he'd let her go, but he hoped she wouldn't. He liked their game. He knew it was coming to an end soon.

He was getting way too hot sitting so close to her, so he gave them both a break and started pacing the room. "Very good work," he finally said, regarding the file. They got into a comfortable routine after that, and worked well together the rest of the afternoon. Time quickly slipped away as it often did when he was with her.

He didn't want to let her leave. He was enjoying the intoxication of her smell. He took pleasure in the way her eyes darted to him before quickly looking away. Her seductive curves made his body tighten, and her voice washed through him.

It was time they ended the torture. A night together, that's all they needed. He tried reasoning with himself that it wouldn't hurt anything. If it was awkward between them after they were both mutually satisfied, then he'd just set her up in another division of the company, so no harm done.

The thought of her leaving the offices left an unpleasant feeling inside him. He struggled with what to do, a first for him. He never moved forward without a plan, and he never messed up.

◊◊◊◊◊◊

Amy fought her own emotions as she spent the day with Lucas. One minute he was barking orders at her, the next pacing the room like a panther, getting a little closer with each pass he made. She really didn't understand her attraction toward him. Yes, he was handsome, but that had never mattered to her before.

Many women liked strong, alpha males, who thought the world should bow to them. She didn't. She'd always been turned off by the He-Man type males she'd encountered during school. So why was she continually having to remind herself she couldn't stand Lucas's type.

She didn't need, nor want, a man to make her whole. She liked her life just fine and wanted no one to step in and tell her how to live and what to do. Lucas was just another guy, like so many other men she'd been around.

If she were to actually break her rules and get involved, it certainly wouldn't be with someone like her egotistical boss. It would be with a warm, caring and nurturing man, someone who wanted a dozen kids and brought her flowers at least once a week. Sex lasted only minutes, a relationship lasted a lifetime. She could live with bad sex; she couldn't live with a jerk for a husband.

Liar. You want excitement. You've been on autopilot since you were barely walking, afraid to disobey, afraid to talk back, afraid to ask for anything. Now, you see this man, this dominating, gorgeous man, and you want him to take control. You want him to force you out of your shell. You want...him. More importantly than that, you want him to want you, to take the choice from you.

Amy sat paralyzed as she fought an internal battle with herself. Her carefully controlled mind fought with her locked up heart. She'd win the fight – she just didn't know how many pieces she'd be in when it was over.

At five that evening, a knock sounded on the door before the knob turned.

Tom bounded into the room. "Hello, Mr. Anderson," he said before turning to Amy. "You ready to head out? I got the phones switched over, and I'm dying for a Bloody Mary and hot wings."

Amy started to rise from her seat when Lucas spoke. "We have too much work to finish tonight, Tom. Amy will have to miss out on happy hour," he said – rather rudely, in her opinion.

"It's okay, Tom, I'll catch the bus home tonight. I appreciate the ride in today, though. I'll see you on

Monday." She gave him an apologetic smile before going back to work on her laptop.

"Okay, darling, see you Monday," he said with a wink.

"Have a great weekend, Mr. Anderson." Tom breezed out as quickly as he'd arrived and, once again, Amy was alone with Lucas. She stared after Tom for a few minutes with longing in her eyes. She'd love to get out of the offices, away from the tension, and sit down to have a drink with her best friend.

Lucas's mood deteriorated after Tom left. "Why didn't you take your own car into work today?" he finally asked, ending twenty minutes of awkward silence.

"I don't have a car. I usually ride the bus into work, but Tom doesn't live too far from me, so the last couple of days we've been carpooling. I have no problem riding the bus, though." She resented having to explain her situation to him.

"I'll give you a ride home tonight since I'm keeping you late," he said, as if the matter was settled. He didn't expect anything but her compliance.

She sat for a moment before replying. "I don't need a ride home. I told you I'm used to riding the bus. I'll be fine," she said between clenched teeth. She knew that wouldn't be the end of the discussion, but she wouldn't let him walk all over her – boss or not.

She was tired of fighting – herself and him. If she didn't get away from him soon she was afraid she was either going to get up and kick him, or even worse, rip his shirt off – preferably with her teeth.

Chapter Five

Her reply angered him. How dare she tell him *no* when he was offering her a ride. For the first time he could ever remember, someone was telling him no, and he found he didn't like it, at all. How could she possibly prefer to ride the bus than accept a ride from him? Was his company so repulsive she couldn't stand to be in his presence for even a moment longer than she had to?

Not wanting to say something he'd regret later, he decided to say nothing. If she believed he was going to allow her to ride the bus, then she wasn't as smart as she appeared.

She may be stubborn, but he could certainly outdo her in that department. He was used to people bending over backward for him. It was a bit of a shock, but not all that unpleasant, to find someone willing to argue with him. He found he liked Amy a bit more each time she challenged him, but there was no way the tiny vixen was going to get her own way on the ride situation, not when it was an issue of her safety.

He could see she was getting tired, but he kept piling work upon her. For one thing, he was still angry she refused to ride with him, and secondly, he just wanted to be in her company.

After his initial anger diminished, he got involved in his own tasks, used to burning the midnight oil as he finished projects. He lost all track of time.

"Mr. Anderson, I don't want to complain, but it's eleven o'clock. Can I come in tomorrow if this really needs to get done that badly before Monday?" she asked with fatigue evident in her voice. He felt guilty he'd let his temper override his good judgment. He would've never normally made her stay so late.

"I didn't realize the time, sorry. Everything else can be done next week," he said as he glanced at the clock. "Let's get out of here." He placed his weekend work in his briefcase and walked her to her office. He stood by the door while Amy placed her work down and gathered her purse and coat. She glanced up, and he could see she was surprised he was still standing there.

"Okay, Mr. Anderson, I'll see you Monday." She tried to make a quick exit by making a beeline to the elevators. He grinned, enjoying the edge to her voice. He found it comical she thought he could be so easily dismissed. Usually women were constantly chasing him. He found it refreshing to be the one doing the chasing and he really liked the cat and mouse game they were playing.

He very much anticipated his capture of her.

Amy pressed the elevator button, and when the doors opened, they both stepped inside for the long ride down. Neither of them spoke, both lost in their own heads.

When they reached the lobby, he followed her out of the cramped space and walked with her toward the front doors.

"Hi, Amy. You're sure working late tonight. There aren't any more busses running. Would you like for me to call you a cab?" the night guard asked.

"That would be great, Paul," she said as she gave him her best smile. "How's that beautiful little girl of yours doing? Did she make the basketball team?"

"Yes, she made varsity and has been prancing around the house for two days now. I'll show you the pictures as soon as my wife gets them developed," he said with a big smile. "Good night, Mr. Anderson. Have a safe ride home," he added, as if just realizing Lucas was there with the two of them.

"Paul, Ms. Harper won't need that cab called. I'll give her a ride home," Lucas stated with the confidence of knowing his word would be taken with no questions asked. Paul looked from her rigid face to his boss's unyielding expression and decided he wasn't getting in the middle of whatever was going on. He was a smart man.

"Okay, then. Enjoy your weekend." He turned and walked back over to his desk.

Lucas pulled Amy through the front doors, gripping her arm. He knew she wouldn't want to cause a scene in front of Paul, so she came with him, without a struggle. He was anticipating the explosion she was sure to give when they reached privacy, though.

He'd been holding back for a month, and the built up tension was at the boiling over point.

As soon as they were outside, she turned toward him, fire in her eyes, obviously ready to unleash on him. Damn, she was amazing in anger. He wanted to rip the bun loose and sink his fingers into her silky hair.

"Look..." she snapped, but he didn't give her time to complete her sentence. He couldn't take it anymore. Reaching out he pulled her into his arms, crushing his lips onto hers.

She stood rigid for about three seconds while he sought access into her mouth. He knew the moment of her surrender, when all of the anger, frustration, and building attraction between them gave way with sweet release. Her arms reached around his neck, and her lips opened in invitation, allowing him full access to her mouth.

Once he had her surrender, his lips softened, began coaxing instead of demanding. His arms slid seductively up and down her back, molding her body to his. He couldn't get close enough to her, their clothing feeling like a wall of separation. He needed more, much, much more.

Lucas was ready to take her right there on the sidewalk. He started reaching below the bottom of her shirt, forgetting they were standing in full view of anyone who cared to walk by. He needed to feel the weight of her full breasts spilling into his hands.

Amy stiffened as she snapped back to reality. Before he could think past the fog of desire in his head, her hand came up and he felt the sting of her fingers as her hand connected with his cheek in a resounding slap, pushing away the last of his lust filled haze.

She stood before him, breathing heavily, her eyes rounded to twice their normal size. Lucas couldn't tell if she was stunned from the kissing, slapping him, or both.

She was flushed and disheveled causing him to take a step back so he wouldn't grab her again. He somehow managed to regain his control, but only because he knew beyond a shadow of a doubt she'd be his. He had to claim her in order to break the spell she had over him.

"I'll allow that one for free, but be ready to face the consequences if you slap me again," he said, while bringing up his hand and rubbing his jaw. She'd really put her body weight behind the hit. She certainly wasn't a helpless female who couldn't hold her own.

"How dare you," she spat. "You don't just go around kissing anyone you feel like. You may be rich and good looking, but you don't own me. I'm your employee, not your whore." With those words she spun around and started walking away.

Lucas allowed her about five steps before he grabbed her arm and spun her around. "I don't know what kind of a game you're playing, Amy, but you gave just as much as you took back there," he snapped.

His body was still on fire, and her hot and cold was playing havoc with his insides. He wanted to throw her up against the building wall and take her in one swift thrust. His unending desire for her shocked the hell out of him.

"I'm sorry about that," she squeezed out, obviously having a hard time apologizing. "I lost my head for a moment, but if you think I took this position so I could sleep with my boss, then you have another thing coming. Forget this night happened – I know I will. I'll see you on Monday, Mr. Anderson." She looked pointedly at where his fingers were gripping her arm.

Her words were escalating his temper. It was like she'd thrown a cup of ice cold water in his face. She'd forget about what just happened? Like hell she would! He was close to reminding her of their explosive chemistry. Somehow, he managed to stop himself.

He wouldn't be forgetting about her anytime soon, and he realized he didn't want her to forget about him either. He was sorely tempted to call her bluff, but he knew he didn't have the strength to stop twice in such a short time period. When they started their next steamy encounter, they'd be somewhere it could be finished.

Instead of kissing her like he wanted, he turned, pulling her along behind him. She fought him each step of the way, but he guessed she knew her words would do no good, because she remained silent. He reached his car and swiftly unlocked the doors with his keyless entry. He wasted no time tossing her in the front seat, and then walking around to get into the driver's side.

He turned the car on and pulled out of the parking lot.

"Where do you live, Amy?"

◊◊◊◊◊◊

Amy was so seething mad she had to count silently to ten before she could speak again. "I told you I didn't want a ride!" she finally spit.

"Whether you wanted the ride or not, you got it, so it would be really helpful if you'd just tell me where you live. Of course, if you'd rather come back to my place and finish what we started on the street, I'm okay with that, too," he offered.

Once again, she had to count in her head. She felt trapped between a rock and a hard place. The last thing she wanted was for her extravagant boss to see where she lived. She planned on getting out of her currently living situation as soon as she had enough money saved up. She thought for a few moments, before giving him the address of a nearby apartment complex.

She knew if he really wanted to find her place, he was perfectly capable, but on the other hand, she didn't see him ever having a reason to go looking for her.

They pulled up to the building, and she saw a car turn on its backup lights. She knew she'd have to move quickly, or he'd insist on walking her to the door. He stopped to wait for the car and she took her chance. She jumped out before he could stop her and then dashed around the side of the building.

She said nothing to him – didn't even glance back to see his expression. She'd assume he was furious with her for getting the upper hand. Once in a while the man surely had to lose a battle; even if she was sure he always won the war.

Amy wasn't taking any chances and, as soon as he was out of her sight, she went into a full blown sprint and hid behind some shrubs. She stayed there for much longer than was probably necessary. Finally, when she figured he was gone, she crept out and snuck to the front of the building, peeking around and looking for his car.

The coast was clear. She sighed to herself. She had about a two-mile walk to get back to her place, and the shoes she was wearing weren't made for it. *Oh well,* she thought, *I may as well get started.*

She said a silent prayer she wouldn't get mugged on the way. The neighborhood wasn't exactly what you'd call "family friendly," and she was usually not out so late alone.

An hour passed before Amy arrived at her place. She sighed in disgust. It was a very weathered, hundred-year-old home that hadn't been maintained. She'd scrubbed her room from top to bottom for two days straight before ever sleeping there.

She'd just needed to stay long enough to finish her college degree. She worked full-time while going to school, but had barely made enough to cover tuition, let alone living expenses. She'd always been willing to do whatever it took to make a better future for herself. She wasn't afraid of hard work and had proven it to herself, and others, throughout the years.

Her single mother had been about the worst parent imaginable and had taken her from one crack house to the next. Amy had always been hungry, dirty, and had to fight her mom's many *friends* off on a daily basis.

Amy was just grateful she'd discovered the local libraries as her sanctuaries at a young age and fell in love with reading. She'd spent hours going through every book imaginable, from opening until closing.

The library had been warm and safe, and it was there she'd figured out she'd go to college, and never live in the unsafe world her mother forced her into, again. Amy's mother died when she was fourteen years old, and she'd been one of the lucky few to be placed in a good foster home. It was there she'd received her first real break in life. Amy had mourned her mother, even though she hadn't deserved to be mourned. She'd felt guilt at her happiness in finally getting to sleep in a warm bed each night with a full stomach.

She'd gone from a drug-infested apartment, to a family friendly neighborhood with a great school, and she'd even managed to earn a few scholarships. She already knew how to survive on nothing and once she graduated and then landed the great job with the Anderson Corporation, her dreams were finally coming closer to reality. In one more month, she'd have a real home of her own.

Amy snapped back to reality as she let herself into her shared rental and looked around her dilapidated bedroom. She lifted her head high, though, because she was soon going to be out of the horrible place, and she'd never once look back.

She crawled into her bed, lying in the dark as she thought back over the past month. So much had changed in her life. She'd graduated, landed the dream job, and developed a strong friendship with a great guy.

Lucas.

She couldn't go a single hour without thinking his name. Even her dreams were filled with her boss. Why did he have to be so stunning? Why did he have to attract her so much? If she were the only one feeling the attraction, it wouldn't be so bad, but obviously after tonight, she couldn't even pretend that he wasn't feeling the same desire.

She wished he didn't want her. It would make it so much easier to keep her distance. With a new resolve, she vowed to keep it professional, no matter how much her body burned. She had to keep her job; she couldn't live in crack neighborhoods anymore. She wanted out.

After tossing and turning for hours, Amy finally fell asleep around the time the sun starting rising in the sky. She was thankful it was the weekend.

◊◊◊◊◊◊

Saturday morning, Tom was getting ready to head out the door and drive to Amy's when his phone rang. "Speak to me," he said in his usual chirpy voice.

"I'm looking for Tom, please," replied the very formal Lucas Anderson. His voice was unmistakable.

"This is Tom. How can I help you, Mr. Anderson?" Why would the boss be calling him on a Saturday?

"Tom, I'm searching for Amy's place. The one in her personnel file appears to be wrong. She left her purse in my car last night, and I need to return it."

Tom almost gave the information to him without thought. The way his boss spoke, it came out much more like a command from a drill sergeant. He felt like he should be saluting, while shouting, "*Yes, sir*!" He stopped himself in the nick of time, remembering Amy had a wrong address for a reason.

"I'll be seeing Amy this weekend, Mr. Anderson. I could take the purse to her. She's meeting me at the bar later tonight," he said. Tom figured this would make all parties happy. He figured wrong, however.

"Tom, I don't hand over one employee's belongings to another. I'll see to it that Amy gets her purse back *myself*. If you'd be so kind as to give me that address *now,* then I can get her the purse." His voice had been formal before. Now it was cold as ice.

Wow, Tom thought, *this guy has it bad. If I want to keep my job, I'd better let him know I'm not interested*. "Um, Mr. Anderson, Amy and I are just friends. She's really, *really*, not my type, if you get my drift. So you don't have to worry about inter-office dating or anything going on between us." He figured Lucas was a smart guy and could put two and two together.

There was a short pause on the end of the line, and then a more pleasant sounding Lucas spoke again. "I still need the address."

◊◊◊◊◊◊

Lucas wasn't happy about having to repeat himself. He was still miffed Amy ran from his vehicle the night before. He didn't like being ignored, and no one had ever felt the need to run away from him. Now he had two employees who didn't seem to want to give him what he needed. He was trying not to throttle them both.

"Look, I understand what you're asking, and why you're asking, but Amy's my friend, and I had to promise not to give out the information. If I betrayed her trust, our relationship would be affected. I'd really love to help you, and I know you may decide to fire me, but I can't give out something that isn't mine to give."

Lucas was barely keeping his temper in check. Figuring out she'd lied to him about where she was living had been easy enough. He'd simply called the management company of the apartments and asked them if she lived there.

They told him she wasn't currently a resident but, at the beginning of the week, she'd put in an application for one of their apartments. They had a unit coming available in three weeks, and she'd reserved it. Her being new to the workforce had been a negative, but they'd spoken to his father earlier in the week and, since Joseph backed her up, they were thrilled to have her for a tenant.

"Sorry, Mr. Anderson, but I have to get going. I know she's in a crappy house right now, but I'm going to offer her a place to stay for a few weeks until she gets her new apartment," Tom spoke quickly before Lucas was able to cut him off.

Lucas was stunned into silence once again, having Tom dismiss him as easily as Amy had done the night before. He was beginning to feel that he was losing his touch.

"I'll speak with Ms. Harper personally." Lucas hung up the phone without bothering to say goodbye. He wasn't getting anywhere with Amy's friend. He'd give the guy one thing, he had guts. It seemed Amy inspired deep loyalty from those who came to love her.

Tom was forgotten about the second the phone touched its base. All Lucas could think about was the next step in tracking down Amy. After about an hour of speaking to various people, Lucas had the information he wanted. He'd grown up with money, but he'd been taught from a young age not to use it against people. Still, there were times when having money made life simpler, and this was one of those situations.

He felt uneasy as he neared her house. The neighborhood wasn't anywhere he'd hang out comfortably during the daytime, let alone at night. By the time he saw the actual house she was living in, he was appalled.

What was she doing there? How could she so casually risk her own safety? He wouldn't wish his worst enemy to reside in the house, or the neighborhood, for that matter. When he saw places like the home she was staying at, it was a humbling experience for him, and he knew he needed to make more time for his volunteer work, because there were so many people who needed help.

He'd been volunteering since he was a young boy, as had his brothers. The busier he got in his day to day life, the easier it was for him to forget about people in need, but as he looked upon the sad excuse for a house, he made a vow he'd make the time, no matter what else was going on.

Lucas carefully walked up the steps, afraid he was going to fall through the rotten porch. The door looked no better, and he would've been grateful to have some Lysol on hand after placing his hands anywhere near it. He reluctantly raised his fist and knocked loudly so he could be heard above the screeching of animals, which seemed to be coming from every direction.

The distinct smell of urine, which he hoped belonged to animals drifted up through the rotten porch rails. The longer he stood there, the angrier he became.

Amy had been with their company for a month, too much time for her to still be residing in the slums. She brought home a work computer with confidential information on it. If it slipped into the wrong hands, it could cause massive hours of work.

She should've asked for an advance, done something to remove herself from the place. Even foolish pride had its limits.

Chapter Six

After waiting a good five minutes, the door was finally answered by a man reeking of alcohol, who was wearing nothing but a pair of dirty boxer shorts. Lucas found himself having a hard time keeping the disgusted look off his face as he stared into the face of the filthy man, who didn't seem to know what a hairbrush or razor was.

"Hey dude, you sure don't look like the pizza boy. Did I win something?" the man blubbered.

"I'm looking for Amy Harper." Lucas wasn't going to chat with the man. He'd pick up Amy and get them both out of there.

"It figures the first person to visit that snob is a suit," the intoxicated man mumbled. He looked Lucas up and down and then muttered, "I should've been charging her more rent. She's obviously doing better than me if she has someone like you showing up. What is she? A high priced call-girl? I bet someone like you enjoys the illusion of innocence, and she has that in spades. I knew it was nothing more than an act. I guess I just don't make enough money to pay for her services." The man continued to mumble, making Lucas want to slam him against the wall. He had to find Amy before doing anything rash.

"Amy, you have some high and mighty guy here to see you," he yelled before walking away from the door. Lucas hoped that was the last he'd see of the man. The guy was crazy, and Lucas had to get her away. He couldn't understand how she felt safe with him anywhere near her.

Lucas heard the creaking hinges of a door opening, and then Amy was standing before him. There were no other words to describe the look she gave him other than horrified. She looked like a deer caught in the hairs of a crossbow, and he knew she'd rather sink through the floor than stand in the filthy house while speaking to him.

Lucas would've found humor in Amy's expression any other place, but watching her standing in the grimy house with the disgusting man nearby washed any traces of humor away. He was real close to just throwing her over his shoulder and physically removing her from the home.

"Aren't you going to invite me in?" Lucas asked between clenched teeth.

"Mr. Anderson, how did you find this place? I'm only here temporarily, I swear. I'll be moving into those apartments in just a couple of weeks." She sounded anxious.

"I made a few phone calls. You were in such a hurry to get away from me last night, you left your purse in my car," he replied. She looked down and noticed him holding it.

Amy reached out to take the purse, but he held it back before stepping through the doorway. She backed away from him, avoiding physical contact.

"Mr. Anderson, there's really no need for you to come inside. I appreciate you bringing my purse by, but I was just getting ready to leave." She wouldn't make eye contact with him, and he could barely stop himself from grabbing hold of her chin and forcing her head up to meet his gaze.

"Let's get your coat. We need to have a talk," was all he said in response. Those words finally made her look up, and some color came back into her washed out face. *Good*, he thought, *I'd much rather see her angry, than embarrassed or defeated*.

"You may be my boss Monday through Friday, Mr. Anderson, but the weekend is mine to do as I please," she heatedly stated. "You can see yourself out." She turned toward her room, apparently expecting him to obey.

Obviously, she was getting the wrong idea about him, if she thought he'd leave. Her dismissive attitude was starting to really get on his nerves. He quietly followed her and shut the door to her room behind them. She turned around at the sound of the door closing. Fire lit in her eyes as she looked back at him.

"You just don't listen, do you?" she snapped. "I told you, I have things to get done today. I'm more than willing to let you be the boss during the week, but my personal time is my own, and I don't owe you any explanations." Her hands were on her hips, her lips pursed, and her foot tapping the threadbare floor.

She was truly a sight to behold.

He finally managed to turn his gaze from her as he looked around her small space. Her room was almost…homey. He didn't think there was a single speck of dust in sight. It was small – very small. His walk-in closet was bigger than her room, but he was impressed with how neat and tidy everything was.

Her clothing was hanging from a wire against the far wall, some of which was guaranteed to give him more sleepless nights. She also had a bucket in the corner with laundry soap next to it. On the other wall was a small dresser with a mini-fridge and small burner sitting on top.

In the middle of the room, just a couple feet in front of him, was her twin-sized bed. It was made up with a very appealing quilt on top. The bed seemed to be sitting on some sort of blocks.

He could see she'd put real effort into her little area, but unfortunately, placing a china bowl into a sewer didn't make the sewer any better. You wouldn't see the beautiful bowl, only the muck covering it.

Lucas finally seemed to realize they were standing alone in her small space, an inviting bed right before him. His gaze took in Amy in all her enraged glory, and his fury suddenly diminished, need taking its place.

Lucas took a step toward Amy. He was losing his will to resist her for even a minute more. He'd sworn he wasn't going to start anything until he could finish it, and as disgusting as the house was, there was a clean bed in front of him, which would work just fine. Suddenly the door was thrust open and in walked her drunken, mostly naked roommate. Lucas was ready to punch the guy, something he hadn't done since his college days.

"Well, Amy, since it looks like you've been lying to me," he slurred. "Your rent just tripled, and I want it all right now or you can get your rich ass out of my house. Obviously, you have a rich clientele, so you should have no problem with cash on hand."

"I don't have that kind of money…," she began.

He quickly interrupted her, "You're always walking around here like you're so much better than the rest of us. You're picking things up and have that look of contempt on your face. Seeing one of your boyfriend's, I know you have plenty of dough. That car he's driving is worth more than three of these houses. I want my money, now!" he shouted and took a menacing step in her direction.

Lucas quickly stepped in his path, and the look in his eyes stopped the man from coming any closer. Normally, Lucas would've stopped the guy from speaking to her that way, but things were working out better than he could've hoped for. He'd been planning on demanding she leave the place, but now he wasn't the one who had to look like the bad guy. The worthless piece of trash was turning Lucas into the hero. He'd be getting her out of the house and the drunken slob was the responsible one.

"You drunken bastard, I've never once put you, or this piece of crap place, down. I've always paid you on-time each month just so you could take my money and get high. I've stayed here only because I've had no other choice, and for your information, I was leaving here in a couple of weeks, anyway. I'm sick of your stench!" she finished with tears in her eyes.

"Get out now you snobby whore…!" he shouted before he was interrupted by Lucas.

"That's enough. She will be leaving, but until she does, get out of her room. If you speak to her that way again, you'll deal with me," Lucas said. The man stepped back and made a quick retreat. Even he knew better than to disobey Lucas.

"Amy, you don't need to take anything from here. I'll replace it all. Let's just leave." Lucas was trying to be kind, something knew for him, with her, but it came out sounding like he didn't think her belongings were worth keeping.

"You may make more money in one day than I've made in my entire life, but I still take pride in my possession," she snapped.

"Amy, I wasn't trying to put you, or your belongings, down. It's just that your roommate is really unstable, and I want to get you out of here as quickly as possible."

She finally broke down into tears. "I don't take handouts!"

Lucas moved toward her and pulled her into his arms. She tried to push him off, but it was like moving a two-ton boulder. She stopped fighting him and gave into the hopelessness she felt right then, sobbing against his chest. He quickly called his brother for assistance to empty out Amy's belongings.

When her sobs had quieted and she was able to recompose herself, he helped her begin packing. By the time they finished, his brother, Alex was there with his truck.

"Hey, Lucas, am I interrupting?"

Amy looked up when Alex entered the room. "Is it a rule in your family that all children are born better looking than the Greek gods?" He could see she'd spoken before thinking about it. Lucas watched her face turn bright red right after the words escaped.

Lucas suddenly grinned, his first smile in a while. He liked Amy comparing him to a God. It was pleasing to know she found him sexy. She certainly wasn't as immune to him as she was trying to lead him to believe.

◊◊◊◊◊◊

"You must be the famous Ms. Harper who's causing my brother sleepless nights," Alex spoke as he walked up and immediately lifted her in a huge bear hug. Amy was too stunned to say anything.

After Alex finally released her and gently placed her back on her feet, she looked at him, shocked, and a bit dismayed, to find she felt not the slightest stirrings of desire for him. He was as good-looking as his brother, with a body to match, and yet there were no fireworks going off from his touch.

The fact didn't please Amy. If she was attracted to him, then she could explain her attraction to Lucas, too. He was hot, so any woman would be attracted. As she stared longer than she should at Alex, she realized it was hopeless. It seemed the only Anderson her traitorous body was responding to was the one who was scowling at her.

"Alex, if you could stop manhandling her, I'll introduce you. Amy, this is my obnoxious younger brother, Alex. He was the only one available with access to a large truck so I couldn't pass up his help," Lucas grumbled.

"Thank you," Amy murmured, not really knowing what else to say.

"My pleasure, Amy. I'm always willing to help out a damsel in distress," he said with a wink, causing her cheeks to heat.

"Yes, Alex, we get it, you like to flirt. If you can put your hormones away for five minutes we can get this room cleared out, and get the hell out of here. I don't know how long until the crazy guy comes back, and I really don't feel like getting shot today," Lucas muttered.

"Yes, sir," Alex said with a mock salute, before chuckling. Lucas sent a glare his way before the two men started moving.

Before Amy knew what was happening, they had her room completely cleared out and loaded into Alex's truck. She was standing at the curb looking back at the house she'd been forced to live in for a couple years. Looking at it through Lucas's eyes, she was a little horrified she'd managed to last so long in the dump.

Amy was pulled out of her musings, when Alex's words shocked her. "I can't wait to steal you away from my big brother, Amy. You're stunning and way too good for him. Don't break my heart." He finished talking, gave her a quick kiss on the lips, then turned and trotted over to his truck.

She stood rooted to the cement for several seconds, her hand lifting to her lips. She'd never been around such confident men before and was finding it hard to figure out how she was supposed to act. Guys she associated with didn't normally kiss her on the cheek, let alone the lips.

Finally, she gave in to her natural good humor and started laughing. How could you not enjoy the company of such a fun guy? She found that she kind of liked his harmless flirting. It made her feel much better about her day.

Lucas, on the other hand, didn't look so amused. "You need to ignore my brother. He lets hormones run his entire life, and he likes pretty women, but he's harmless." He took her hand and led her toward his car.

She saw Lucas was irritated, but not furious. It looked to her like the brothers cared about each other. It also appeared they liked to get a reaction from the other if they could. She didn't want to get in the middle of that. She wasn't strong enough for it.

◊◊◊◊◊◊

Lucas wouldn't admit to her how he'd wanted to smash his brother in the face for daring to kiss *his* woman. He also wouldn't admit how jealous he was at that moment that she hadn't slapped Alex in the face after he'd kissed her.

He made himself calm down because he knew Alex was just trying to get a rise out of him.

It had worked.

When they reached the passenger side of his car, Amy suddenly hesitated. “Wait a minute. Where’s all my stuff going? I don’t even know where I’m going, yet. This happened so fast, I haven’t had time to think about what happens next.”

Lucas could see she was starting to panic. “Amy, you’re alright. I’m going to take you to my parents’ house for now. My brother told my father what was happening, and Dad wanted to speak with you.” She started to shake her head no when he looked into her eyes. “Amy, it’s not wise to tell my father no.”

Amy’s eyes were wide as she tried to swallow the rising panic in her. She said nothing further as she climbed into the vehicle and buckled her seat belt. Lucas chuckled as he walked around the car. He knew how she was feeling. When his father beckoned, you came. You didn’t come because he was the head of the family. You came because the man earned respect. You obeyed because he was the type of man you’d bend over backwards for.

He’d been an exceptional father, never placing work ahead of his family, and he was always the first one any of the kids came to with a problem – or with good news, for that matter. He was already aware of Amy’s situation because the family always told him everything.

Lucas and Amy didn’t speak on the ride to the family mansion. He knew she needed time to compose herself. She’d been through a lot the last few hours and he was happy to know he wasn’t the bad guy in the current situation.

Amy needed time to gear herself up because she was about to be thrust into the chaos of his family.

Everyone was at the manor this weekend for his mother's birthday. Any holiday was cause for the family to celebrate together, but his mother's birthday was a huge bash.

His father always said his wife's birth was a great cause for celebration. She was the light of his life and his world would've been empty without her. He felt her birthday should be a national holiday. Amy interrupted his thoughts when she finally spoke as they approached the house.

"Mr. Anderson, it looks like you have company right now. This probably isn't the best time for me to be here. Will you please just let me use your phone so I can call a cab and get out of your hands?" She spoke barely above a whisper.

"Not a chance," was his only reply.

Amy looked down at herself and then back up at him. "I'm wearing old jeans," she pleaded. "Please don't make me go in there looking like this."

He just laughed at the panicked look on her face and her horrified voice. His family had been blessed with more than most, but they weren't who she thought they were. They'd never treat someone badly because of the way they were dressed, or because they didn't have as much money.

"Amy, you act like we're a bunch of snobs. We're normal people, like anyone else. So what if we like nice things. You're the one being a snob right now, judging my family on what we have," he said accusingly.

His words worked like a charm. Her eyes widened as she thought about what he said, then the fire he liked seeing entered her eyes. Good. He liked her defenses up, her confidence in place. He didn't want a mouse of a woman sitting next to him. He wanted a strong, stubborn woman, who challenged him and fired up his blood. One thing Amy needed to learn about him was that he always got what he wanted, and at that moment he wanted her with him. Lucas came around the car and helped her out. He placed her arm in his and half-dragged her up the walk.

She'd come to the mansion for her job interview, so at least she didn't have to be quite as intimidated now. Even though she'd been there before, he noticed how her breath was taken away by the beauty of it all. He was used to his childhood home, but he knew what it looked like to a stranger. It was stunning.

Lucas led her through the foyer and into the back where laughter could be heard down the halls, carried on the background music. As he continued down the hallway with Amy by his side, Lucas felt the last of his tension ease. He liked being with her, even though he knew he shouldn't. It didn't matter, though, he was home and Amy was safe. He was feeling pretty good.

"You finally made it. What did you do, take the scenic route? I've been here for a half hour already, and I wasn't the one driving the race car." Alex came up and nudged his brother in the ribs. "All is forgiven, though, since you brought my beautiful future bride. How are you doing, gorgeous? We've been apart for too long already. Do you want to run away with me to Vegas and get married?" he joked. He threw his arm around her and dragged her across the room for a drink.

Lucas shook his head while rolling his eyes. He knew his brother was even more afraid of marriage than he was himself. He was still going to keep an eye on her, though, because if anyone could change his brother from committed playboy to a happily married man, it would be Amy.

He was going to make sure and stake his claim, so both his brothers knew that Amy wasn't on the market. He was amazed at the jealousy coursing through him. He'd never felt that way about any other woman he'd dated. If someone he was dating wanted to run off with one of his brothers, he would've gladly said goodbye.

It never would've been an issue, though, as neither of his brothers would ever trespass on the others' woman. They had a code between them and would never break it. You just didn't try and steal your brother's girl. On the other hand, making one of said brothers jealous was a whole other issue, and each of the guys loved to push buttons.

He started to walk over to take his woman…um, employee…back, when Esther saved him from doing just that.

"Alex, you leave this girl alone. You're flirting shamelessly and embarrassing her. How are you doing, Amy?"

"I'm great. I'm really getting that computer program down, and I don't think I'll have to call you at all on Monday. Today is just another speed bump. Nothing to worry about," Amy told Esther with a brave face.

Lucas could see that Amy wasn't used to having people worry about her, or love her, for that matter. She'd have to get used to both. Employees of the Andersons were considered family. They took care of their people. Her days of bearing the weight of the world on her own shoulders had ended.

◊◊◊◊◊◊

"I know you're doing great at work. I meant, how are you doing with your life? I heard about your place," she said sympathetically. Before Amy knew what was happening, she was engulfed in a hug. She found her throat tightening as Esther embraced her.

"Now, don't be afraid to ask for help once in a while. We'll be getting to know each other well because this family takes care of the people they love," she said.

"Thank you, Esther. It's really nice to have such amazing employers," Amy finally managed to get out.

"Yes, it was difficult at first for me to retire. I so loved working in the offices with Joseph all those years. I watched all three boys grow up as they ran around the hallways at work. Then I became very close to Katherine. The best part of retirement, though, is they're my family now, so I don't lose them, I just get more days I can sleep in."

"I'm a bit overwhelmed by all of this. I'm not used to people being concerned about me. It feels a bit surreal, like I'm going to wake up at any moment. I really hope that's not the case," Amy admitted.

"You can relax, Amy. You're in good hands now," Esther promised.

"Amy, I'm so glad you're here. We have much to talk about, but that will come later. I'm sure you've noticed all these people milling around." Joseph snuck up on them and his enthusiasm caused Amy to jump a bit. He continued speaking before she had a chance to reply.

"Today is my amazing wife's birthday, and we all come together to celebrate this beautiful woman's entrance into the world. Come, come, I want you to meet her, along with some other people. I've told her all about our newest employee," he finished.

He placed her arm in his, and she had to jog a little to keep up with him. He may have retired from being president, but he'd run the company for many years and was still very much invested.

"Katherine, I'd like you to meet Amy, Lucas's new executive assistant. She's doing great things over there. I didn't think it possible to replace Esther, but we got real lucky on the first try," Joseph said as he approached an elegant woman, who didn't look like she could possibly be in her fifties.

Her medium length white hair was styled perfectly against her slim shoulders. She was about the same height as Amy, though her heels put her at about five-four. Her sparkling brown eyes had small lines around them, making it apparent she smiled a lot.

"It's wonderful to meet you, Amy. I've heard so much about you. I'm so sorry about your circumstances, dear. Don't you let this crowd overwhelm you too badly. I know there's a lot of testosterone in this room, but all these boys only talk big. When it comes down to it, they're nothing but gentle giants," Katherine said as she leaned forward.

Before Amy could speak, Katherine pulled her in for a hug. Amy was realizing the Anderson's were an affectionate bunch and that it wasn't just the boys. Everyone seemed quite comfortable giving hugs, or even kisses, for that matter. As Katherine pulled her in for a tighter squeeze, she held her for a moment longer than was typical and Amy had to fight off the tears at the gentle encouragement she felt, and melted into the embrace. Katherine's sweet cinnamon fragrance filled Amy's nostrils, solidifying the moment to memory.

Amy's birth mother had never hugged her. How could she when she was so busy getting her next fix? Holding her family tight was something Amy vowed to do every day when she had her own children. She found herself wanting to savor the continuous flow of acceptance the Andersons offered.

Most of the time she thought she was fine with having no family ties of her own, but seeing the large, affectionate Andersons all in a room together was making her realize what she was missing. She longed for a similar family bond.

"Thank you for having me at your party," Amy managed to say when Katherine released her.

"The pleasures all mine, dear. I love my birthdays because it's always wonderful to have my family and friends close. We'll be seeing a lot of each other with your new job. That's why Joseph has always been so picky about who he hires in those positions - he knows they're not only becoming employees, but a part of our family, too."

Amy didn't know what to say. She'd been told the Andersons treated their employees very well, but she just couldn't understand the concept of them bringing people into their home, treating them as equals. No wonder their turnover rate was so low. Amy's heart swelled with gratitude again for landing her job.

With even more resolve, she knew she had to fight her attraction to Lucas, because she in no way wanted to lose her position with the Anderson Corporation. Even more important than her paycheck, which she desperately needed, she loved the idea of being a part, no matter how remote, of their family.

"I'll take you to meet more people, Amy. There are a lot of executives from the offices you'll probably recognize, but I know it always takes me a while to learn names. This is a good place to do it. Some of the people here have been retired for some time, but you'll often see them in the offices helping out the new generation. Once you're a part of the fast paced world of business, it's hard to let go of it, even if you know it's time to hang up your suit," Joseph said with a chuckle.

For the next twenty minutes, Joseph dragged her all around the enormous room – making so many introductions she knew she'd never remember everyone.

Even though the people were dressed casually with their crisp polo shirts and newly pressed kakis, she still felt uncomfortable standing among them wearing her old jeans and a sweatshirt. No one was looking at her in disgust, at least not that she'd noticed, but she was still self-conscious about her appearance.

As they made their final rounds, there was a stir in the room. She looked up to see what caused the commotion, when suddenly standing in front of her was another Greek god.

Seriously, did they grow them on trees? She saw the family resemblance and knew that this must be the last brother. Holy smokes, he was sexy as sin in his skin tight, worn out Wrangler jeans and black cowboy hat that had seen better days. The grin stretched across his face completed his devastating look.

Even though his clothes were just about as worn as hers, *he* pulled it off – and pulled it off incredibly well.

"Hey boy, what took you so long? You know your mom's been crying, wondering where her youngest son was. She figured you forgot all about her birthday," Joseph said, before leaning in and giving his son a hug.

"Ah, Dad... Isabelle was birthing and I had to make sure she was okay. Chad's with her now, so I hurried on over," he said sheepishly.

"I suppose we can forgive you. At least you got here before we cut your mother's cake."

"Where's Lucas? I need to talk to him," Mark asked, before his eyes connected with hers. Dang, he looked like his big brother, but a little more rugged. The three of them together must make women's knees give out.

"Your brother is across the room, and if I'm not mistaken, he's shooting you the evil eye," Joseph said with a wink at Mark that she didn't understand.

Mark looked over at Lucas, got a huge grin on his face, then turned back to her. She thought her own knees may give out. The guy had unrefined sex appeal written all over him, and she had to admit that it didn't hurt her eyes to look at him.

Amy had no way of knowing that the look Lucas was giving his brother was clearly telling Mark that Amy wasn't just his assistant. Lucas was making it clear to him, and all the other men in the room, that Amy was his.

"Who's this gorgeous woman you have on your arm? Did Mom finally come to her senses and kick you to the curb?" Mark asked, his eyes holding her own captive.

She immediately turned scarlet, then looked down, not wanting him to notice her embarrassment.

"Mark, quit embarrassing our guest. This is Amy Harper. She's the newest executive secretary for your worthless brother over there," Joseph said with a chuckle.

"Well, Ms. Amy, it's truly a pleasure to meet you. I have a real job opening available if you get sick of working for that stuffed shirt brother of mine," he said, adding a flirtatious wink.

Before Amy could blink, she was whisked into his arm and immediately dipped backward, looking into his humor filled eyes. His lips connected with hers in a chaste kiss before he quickly whipped her back up and threw his arm around her shoulder. "That job offer's open anytime you want it. You're one hell of a good kisser," he said with a wink.

Amy feared her face would remain scarlet the entire time she was around the Anderson men. With their good looks and confidence, she had a feeling they each had a take-the-world-by-storm attitude. She should be offended she'd been kissed by all three of the brothers, but she didn't feel like complaining. Neither Alex, nor Mark, had tried to deepen their kisses. Even though she knew it was about getting under their brother's skin, she could've saved them some time and let both of them know nothing was going on between she and Lucas.

As Amy compared the three separate kisses she'd received by each of the Anderson boys, she was dismayed to find, that only Lucas's touch had caused a burning flash inside her. She wasn't drawn to Lucas because he was the only eligible man around; she realized she was actually drawn to *him*. This was an extremely unpleasant epiphany.

She knew Lucas's brothers were harmlessly flirting, but usually when a woman was kissed by a man as suave and downright handsome as both Mark and Alex were, she couldn't control her body's natural response. She was pondering what she should do when Lucas approached them.

"Okay, Mark, you can quit putting your hands all over Amy. I'm going to take her to get some food." Lucas said as he pushed Mark's arm from her shoulder. She hadn't even noticed his arm was still around her until Lucas pointed it out.

"By the way, she's not available," he finished. With that, she was pulled away from Mark, and instantly had Lucas's arms in the same place. She was beginning to feel like a shiny new toy being passed around the room. She'd definitely have to remember to correct him on telling people her availability. It was none of his business, and certainly not his right to tell anyone about her love life, or more accurately, lack of one.

As his hand rested on her shoulder, his fingers dipping low and rubbing against her collarbone, Amy felt the familiar tug of heat begin sliding through her. His thumb brushed against her neck, and instant goosebumps surfaced on her skin. Why him? Why did it have to be Lucas who seemed to have awakened her sleeping libido?

"I'm sorry about my brother – both of them, for that matter. They're just trying to get a rise out of me, but they shouldn't be pawing all over you to do it," Lucas grumbled as he led her to the food area, where unlimited dishes were sitting out for the guests to choose from.

"I guess the positive to the whole situation is now I can tell everyone I've kissed three out of three of the hottest brothers I've ever seen. It will make me seem much more worldly than I am," she said with a laugh.

Amy figured she had two choices in the matter. She could either get irritated or she could find the humor in the situation. It wasn't every day a girl got kissed by three amazingly hot guys so she decided she'd take choice number two and laugh.

"You like playing with different men?" he questioned, his voice quiet.

"Your brothers are harmless," she replied. Lucas glared down at her and she didn't understand why he was so upset.

"You weren't laughing when I kissed you."

Amy was stopped in her tracks by that comment. No, she hadn't been laughing when he'd kissed her, but then, her body had been on fire the entire time, making her forget where she was. Lucas scared her – made her forget she didn't want a relationship. She couldn't kiss him, it was too dangerous.

“Didn’t you say something about food?” she asked, trying to change the subject, hoping he’d just drop it.

He stared at her intensely for a few moments before he resumed walking. She breathed a sigh of relief as he let the matter go. An awkward silence surrounded them as they each reached for a plate.

Amy lost all appetite as she stood next to Lucas, wondering exactly how she was going to continue working for him. If he’d just leave her alone, she was sure she could get over her infatuation of him, but with him touching her, she wasn’t sure she’d last even a month before she was begging him to finish what he’d started in the dark street.

She tried pushing it from her mind as Lucas led her to a table and they sat down. It didn’t take long for others to join them. Soon, they were surrounded and Amy was surprised to find she was enjoying the evening as the party continued long into the night.

Amy let go of her problems and even forgot she was technically homeless for the moment. She relaxed and took the time to get to know other people from the office, even making a few lunch dates later in the month. Everything would work out. It had to, because she was starting to feel secure for the first time in her life.

Chapter Seven

Amy had no idea how late it was getting until she was sitting comfortably in the swinging chair on the back deck and noticed the party was starting to thin out.

Her problems came crashing to the forefront of her mind, now that she had a moment to herself to consider them again. She didn't have much money saved. She had her first two paychecks, which were impressive, but that money was supposed to be for the down payment on her new apartment. If she dipped into those funds to stay at a motel it would take longer to get into her place.

Oh well, she thought. She had no choice but to do that. It delayed her plans by a month or two, but that was a minor setback – one she could handle. She was so close to her goals that nothing was going to stop her. In the large scheme of things, it was not a big deal.

"There you are, Amy. I sit in this swing quite a bit, myself," Joseph stated, startling her out of her thoughts. "The party has finally wound down, so let's step into my office and take care of business."

"Okay, Mr. Anderson," she replied without thinking until he raised his brows at her in question. "Sorry, Joseph," she said with a small smile, getting more used to using his first name. She was just nervous and her first instinct was to panic at the thought that he wanted to talk business. She was worried she wasn't qualified enough for the job and he'd be letting her go any day. She knew logically that he wouldn't invite her to a party, only to fire her afterward, but living the way she always had, made fear a natural instinct.

"Now that we have our names established, come with me," he said with a chuckle. She couldn't help but smile at his good humor.

Amy stood up and quickly followed Joseph through a maze of hallways, wondering how he didn't get lost in his huge palace of a home. It had to have taken Katherine years to decorate the entire thing. Amy looked around thinking that was a job she'd really enjoy.

She'd considered taking interior design in school, but knew good jobs were hard to come by in that market, so she'd been smart and taken business instead. Even though she wished she had the luxury of having a job she truly loved, she didn't. Her first priority was to secure her future. She'd never live in an unsafe environment again.

She wanted a family and she couldn't do that until she had her life situated. She had to remind herself she was young and had plenty of time.

As they got closer to his office, she ended up stopping without realizing it, as she came across a particular painting. It was a piece by her favorite artist, Thomas Kinkaid.

A beautiful cottage sitting on the side of a stream, one of Amy's favorite paintings. It was stunning, as all Kinkaid's work was. The way he painted made it look as if the water was actually moving, and the lights in the cottage were on, beckoning her to come inside. She could easily imagine herself sitting on the rustic front porch while watching her worries drift away, down the stream. She smiled at the appealing thought, feeling a sense of peace at the site of the beautiful image at a moment in her life when stress was at its highest.

◊◊◊◊◊◊

She missed Joseph's smile at her look of rapture from seeing the art. The more he was around Amy, the more he knew he'd made the right decision. She wasn't awed by the million-dollar statues or fancy cars. She was impressed with the real works of beauty. She really would make a great addition to his family.

He took pride in his ability to read a person in a short amount of time. It was how he'd been so successful all the years he'd been a CEO. He'd figured Amy out very quickly. She was lonely, in need of family, and scared to trust people. She also had a heart of gold.

He'd watched her most of the evening, how she interacted with the people in the room. She was always doing what she could to make them more comfortable, even though she had to be stressed over her life at that moment. He couldn't imagine how it would feel to not have a safe home.

She'd make a wonderful wife for his son. They were both searching for something more in their lives, it was just that neither of them realized it, or were willing to accept the fact.

Joseph could already see that Lucas couldn't keep his eyes off Amy. It was obvious she was developing strong feelings for Lucas, as well. Joseph hoped for a spring wedding. That way he may get a grandchild before Christmas. It just didn't get better than that.

◊◊◊◊◊◊

Amy snapped out of her daydream, mumbled an apology, and continued following Joseph into his home office. As with everything else in Joseph's life, the office was enormous, but surprisingly inviting. A huge fireplace dominated half of one wall, a fire blazing inside, the wood crackling, sending the smell of sweet pine into the air. There were several comfortable chairs arranged close to the fire, and a floor to ceiling bookcase lined one two-story wall. She wandered over to the bookcase and found some of her favorite titles sitting on the shelves.

She caught herself, just in time, before grabbing one of the copies. She could picture herself curled up on the sofa, reading until she fell asleep. That sounded just about perfect at that moment.

Lucas stepped into the room, immediately drawing her eyes as she drank in his impeccable form. She forgot about Joseph, who was comfortably sitting in one of the lounge chairs near the fire, quietly watching the silent exchange between the two of them. Heat spread through her at the sight of him, though she'd been with him only an hour earlier. Something about the intimate setting of the office immediately turned her thoughts to sex.

She pulled her eyes away only to glance at the soft rug placed in front of the fire. She envisioned herself entangled in his arms as his head slowly lowered to take her suddenly straining nipple into his mouth.

Stop! What are you doing? she demanded of herself. *You will not fall for your boss.* She repeated the statement to herself ten times. She finally gained a tiny bit of her willpower back and slowly lifted her eyes and focused on Joseph, instead.

After an uncomfortable moment of silence, Joseph offered her a comforting smile. For a moment, it was as if he could read her mind, which frightened her. She'd be mortified if he knew the kind of thoughts she was having about his son.

"Come sit, Amy, so we can chat."

Amy immediately moved forward and took a seat on the couch across from Joseph. She tried to relax, but her hands were a bit shaky, so she gripped them tightly together in her lap and sat ramrod straight as she waited for him to continue.

"Amy, we like to take care of our employees. We believe if we treat our employees well, then they'll remain happy in their job and, therefore, happier in their lives. It all comes around full circle. A happy employee equals happy clients," Joseph began.

"I'm very happy in my job, sir. I know I'm struggling a bit with the computer system, but if you give me a little more time, I'll have it down. I'm more than willing to work weekends and stay late so I'm not using your time while learning the system," Amy said as she found her voice. She'd do whatever it took to keep working for him.

"You're doing an amazing job, dear. I have no complaints with how your work performance is going. Esther and Lucas have both said you're a real asset to the team. This conversation isn't about any work problems," he comforted.

Amy took a deep breath of relief.

"I brought you in here to let you know about your benefit package while working for the company. You've passed your probationary period so we're offering you a permanent position," he said.

Amy had been worried she may be losing her job, and instead she was gaining security. As elation surged through her, she found herself having a hard time remaining in her seat. She wanted to jump up and do a little dance. Relief flooded her veins.

"Thank you so much for your confidence in me. It truly means a lot. I promise to not let you down, and I'll still be spending all my extra time making sure I'm giving you one hundred percent. This is the best job I could've ever hoped for, especially right out of college," she said with real gratitude.

Joseph chuckled at the enthusiasm in her voice. "Amy, you're a breath of fresh air, but wouldn't you like to hear about your new salary and benefits before thanking me so much?" he asked.

"Yes, of course, sir," she said.

"You know that officially I'm retired now, and my son runs the company. He's doing a damn fine job of it, but I like to be slightly involved, and working on employee benefits is a good way for me to keep busy. Our company takes great pride in offering more benefits than your average corporation. I don't disclose this to new hires because, first of all, I want them to take the position because they want to work here, and secondly, if that employee doesn't work out, then no harm caused."

"We take care of all employees, from the top of the chain, all the way to the bottom. Our executive positions get a few added bonuses, though. Since you work for the president of the company, you get the executive perks not many others receive," Joseph said before pausing.

Amy waited to hear what he was talking about. She figured she'd get a medical and retirement package, but didn't know what else large corporations offered.

"First of all, you'll receive a company car. Lucas will take you down to the dealership to pick it out tomorrow. Esther's favorite was always the Mercedes LX, but we have several options for you to choose from. You'll be doing a lot of driving for us, and we want you to enjoy the ride. We always consider safety a number one factor, as well."

Amy knew many companies offered vehicles for work, but she hadn't even thought that may be a benefit of her job. Esther had warned her she'd be doing a lot of running around once her training was complete, but she hadn't had time to worry about how she was going to do it. She was almost giddy with excitement. Did she get to take the car home with her? She didn't know if it would be rude for her to ask.

"You will keep the vehicle with you and can use it for personal use, as well," he said, as if reading her mind. "Unless there are performance issues with the car, we trade them in every two years."

"That's incredibly generous, thank you," she mumbled, feeling a bit too awed to say much.

"We aren't quite done yet. We also provide you with cellular service. Here's your new cell phone," he said, handing it over with a piece of paper. "Your number's on it. You have unlimited minutes, so you may also use this as your personal cell and can turn off your old one. Communication's key to a good business, and we need to be able to reach each other at all times…well, that's except in the middle of the night when work should be the last thing on anybody's mind," he added with a laugh. "Unfortunately, in the corporate world, time is forgotten, and there will be some extremely late nights and long weekends."

Amy had no issues with working hard. She would've been willing to do it without all the added benefits, but with them, there was nothing she wouldn't do for the corporation. If she had to work twenty hour days, she'd do it with a smile.

"My dearest wife threw a couple of my company phones into the lake when we were on vacation. She always told me there was a time for work and a time to relax." After meeting Katherine, Amy could absolutely see her doing that and the thought made her lips twist in a smile.

"Of course, you'll have the finest medical insurance, which starts on Monday, and all the other benefits, which I've listed here. You can read through them later. The material will help you fall asleep."

"Now, for the biggest benefit, which I think is fitting, considering your current situation, which Lucas has relayed to me," he added without any condemnation in his voice. "All of our executive officers are offered housing. We have a terrific apartment complex reserved for our company personnel and visiting businessmen and woman. We do a lot of work with people overseas and have found they prefer the apartment suites to a hotel.

"There's low rent, and all utilities are included. Several of our board members stay in the complex for years, while saving up and buying their own homes. There's no time limit on how long you stay. It's yours for the duration of the job. If you're out on sick leave, the apartment's still yours. I want you to feel completely at home and safe in your new place."

Amy had a feeling he knew a little bit about her past. Of course, he'd know about her past. She figured he did extensive background checks on the people working for his company, especially at such a high level.

"Your new apartment will be ready to move into by Monday. We had to do some painting and cleanup, as that's where Esther was living for quite some time. I think you'll find it very comfortable if you want it. It's already furnished, but Lucas will take you out tomorrow so you can pick your own decorations. Your belongings have already been moved in, except for a few clothes, which are sitting over by the door for you to use tomorrow."

"I'd love to accept the apartment. The building I got approved for a couple weeks ago is quite a commute to work. The closer complexes were too out of my budget," Amy said with embarrassment.

"Perfect, then you'll be ready to go by tomorrow. That takes care of all the business I had for now. Do you have any questions for me?"

Amy was stunned. She didn't know what to say. She had her own apartment. Her own apartment! It was even furnished. She also wouldn't have many bills. As excitement washed through her, she forgot who she was for a moment and jumped up, throwing her arms around Joseph. "Thank you so much," she said, finding herself near tears.

When she realized how unprofessional she was acting, she leapt back. "I'm sorry about that, Mr. Anderson. It's just…I never imagined any of these things could be a part of my job, and…," her voice became thick as she tried to hold back her tears, then realized she couldn't continue.

Joseph rose from the couch and pulled her back in for a bear hug. "It's all right, dear. I never turn down a hug. You're a good person and highly intelligent. You've earned all that you're receiving. Don't forget that, young lady." He patted her back before letting go.

"As for tonight, I understand you don't have a place to stay, so I'd like to offer you the guest house on my property. Now, don't shake your head. We enjoy having people stay there. That's why it's called a guest house. There's no need for you to go stay in some cheap hotel when I have a perfectly comfortable place you can use," he said, sounding like his son, leaving no room for argument.

"You look as if you're about to fall over, so I'll have Lucas walk you out there. I noticed you were eyeing the books when you first came in. Would you like to take one with you to read this evening?"

Amy knew there was no point in arguing with the man. She'd lose, anyway. "That would be great."

Amy couldn't say anything else, or she was going to burst into tears. Her eyes were red from unshed tears and she knew she wasn't hiding it well. She'd never had anyone do so much for her. She'd never had someone have faith in her, or show so much caring. It was amazing how wonderful Joseph was. She understood why he'd been given so much.

His family deserved everything they'd been given because they gave back tenfold. She'd overcome her attraction to Lucas because there was no way a cheap affair was worth losing all she had.

Yes, she had a feeling it would be hot, but a night in bed with him would lead to years of regret. There was no way she'd find a job as great as the one she had, and she knew her job would be over if they slept together.

Being a couple just wasn't an option. He was too far out of her league, so she'd just have to make sure and keep her distance. She knew he wanted her, it was obvious. He most likely gave the same look to all women between the ages of twenty-one and fifty, though. He was just an incredibly sensual man. She was most likely reading far more into the glances between them than what was actually there.

Her mind replayed their explosive kiss.

She could even justify that. It had been late at night and they'd been arguing. Anger had a tendency to turn to desire, that was all.

Amy realized she was just standing there, so she forced herself to move and headed straight to the huge bookshelf and grabbed the paperback she'd been eyeing earlier. She couldn't wait to get lost in the story.

"Thanks again, Mr. Anderson. I hope I don't let you down."

"You know, I'm going to get you to call me Joseph, eventually without having to remind you," he teased her. "I have complete faith in you, Amy. I have a feeling you'll be with us for many years to come. I'm going to leave Lucas to take you out to the guest house. I need to find Katherine and say goodbye to the last of the people here. Enjoy your night, dear."

With those words, Joseph turned and left the room. Suddenly, the once comfortable office seemed smaller than a closet with just she and Lucas standing there. She finally realized he hadn't said a word for the entire conversation. She really wished she knew what he was thinking.

Chapter Eight

Lucas watched the entire transaction between Amy and his father. He'd waited to see the same look of greed enter her eyes that all women usually got when around his family. Surprisingly, what he saw on her face was only shock, mixed with gratitude.

Could she really not care how much money they were worth? He was going to find out. Lucas knew he was cynical when it came to women, but he'd yet to find one who didn't prove him right. That's why he didn't date, and certainly didn't enter into relationships.

He only went out with women to satisfy his needs, and as he treated them well, he felt no guilt over it. They got what they wanted out of him – expensive jewelry, the occasional trip, and attendance to the highest publicized functions in town.

He was able to get his needs met and they were able to get five minutes of fame and expensive gifts. It worked for him – or at least it had been working for him before he met his assistant.

She seemed innocent, but he knew if they went to bed together, she'd turn, like all the other women did. He couldn't understand his fascination with her. He got it, at first. She was new, seemingly untouchable, which was like a red flag to a bull. He wanted to conquer and stake his claim. Those feelings should've ebbed by now, not grown stronger. He was sobered by the thought that she could be the one woman who could bring him to his knees.

Pushing aside the ridiculous journey his mind had taken, he forced himself to concentrate. The sooner he got her settled, the faster he could get away before he did something stupid, like kiss her again.

"Come with me, Amy. I'll show you where you'll be sleeping the next couple of nights," he said as he took her arm.

As they stepped from the office and started walking down the long hallway to the back of the house, Lucas felt as if his fingers were seared. Only his stubborn determination to conquer his desire kept him gripping her arm. He wouldn't let lust control him.

When they stepped outside and were hit by the cold night air, he took in a large breath, hoping the chilly wind would somehow cool him down. To his great disappointment, it didn't work.

By the time they arrived at the guest house, he was grateful she couldn't read minds because in his he was slowly undressing her, piece by piece, tugging her hair loose from the ponytail she had it in, and spreading it across his pillow, gripping the silken strands in his fingers, pulling her head closer…

"Oh, this is beautiful," Amy gasped, jerking him from his thoughts.

He looked at the small cottage surrounded by trees and flowers. A stone path led up to a small covered porch that had a couple of rocking chairs sitting near the wall.

He remembered spending hours running in and out of the cottage with his brothers as they played. One week they were Robin Hood and his merry men, the next G.I. Joe, battling to save America. The cottage was either enemy territory, or their refuge, depending on the game. They'd gotten in trouble more than once for scaring guests as they'd popped out of the bushes to ambush them.

Lucas almost smiled at the memory. He and his brothers hadn't wanted to actually attack the guests, they'd just been pretending like they were going to capture them. Some of the people hadn't found humor in the masked boys chasing after them.

Amy sighed, pulling him back from his visit with the past. He looked at her quizzically, but she refused to meet his eyes.

"Come in, Amy. I'll show you where everything is. My parents had the kitchen stocked so you'll have plenty of food. There's fresh linen on the bed and clean towels in the bathroom. It's a small place, so I don't think you'll get lost. Please help yourself to anything in the house. It's for guests, after all," he said, though he didn't think she heard him. She was too busy wandering around.

He tried to see it through her eyes, noticing the fresh cut flowers that were sitting on the small kitchen table, the variety of soaps and lotions lined up on the bathroom counter, and the oversized garden tub he could picture her crawling into.

With that last thought, Lucas knew it was time to go. He in no way needed the image of her in his mind covered in bubbles.

"I'll get out of your way so you can relax," He said before he made a quick escape out the front door. He stopped on the front porch and took a deep breath. If he hadn't walked out that second, he would've caved in and thrown her on the bed, making love to her until they were both incapable of walking.

As he stood on the quiet porch, he decided maybe it was better if he just slept with her. He could make it work, he reasoned. He'd simply tell her up front that it was obvious they were highly attracted to each other, and it was the smart thing to do. She seemed reasonable, like she'd understand.

It was the only way he figured he'd get her out of his system. Once they had sex, his sanity would return to normal. If she hadn't kept glancing at him with her own smoldering looks, then he may have been able to maintain a bit more control. Her face was an open book, though, only complicating the matter. Knowing how much she wanted him was fueling his desire.

He slowly walked back up to the big house to speak with his father. He took his time going inside, not wanting his father to see him until his body was under control. It took much longer than was acceptable for him to cool down.

Finally, he walked inside, finding his dad sitting in the den with a glass of whiskey in his hand. That looked like an excellent idea.

"Did you get Amy settled in?" Joseph asked.

"Yes, Dad. She loves the place," he answered, while striding over to the liquor cabinet. He poured himself a triple shot of bourbon and downed it in one gulp. He felt his nerves start to calm as the fire burned down his throat and his eyes watered. The pain of the drink was well worth it, though, if it could calm his frayed nerves.

He tipped the bottle again, and poured a smaller amount into his glass before turning around and walking to the seating area. After sitting down, he forced himself to sip the drink, instead of guzzling it. He didn't need a buzz on top of everything else.

Lucas didn't see the knowing grin on Joseph's face. Maybe if he would've, he'd be more prepared for the upcoming conversion. He had no clue what lengths his father would go to in order to have grandkids and ensure his boys weren't alone the rest of their lives.

"Where did you find Ms. Harper, Dad?"

"We had a job fair at her college a few months ago, and I got her resume then. I did some research on her and knew she was perfect for the job. You know, it takes someone special to work for the president of our company," Joseph answered.

“Yes, she’s working out much better than I thought she would. She’s a little mouthy, but I’m sure she’ll settle down the longer she’s with us.”

“A little mouthy? Did you honestly just say that?” Joseph asked, surprising Lucas. He gazed at his father with an expression of puzzlement. Slowly, he realized what he’d said. His lips turned up in a smile. Well, he was just calling it like he saw it.

“I’ve heard mom talk about some of the things you’ve said yourself, old man,” Lucas said, the smile on his face taking any sting from the words.

“I grew up, boy, and so should you. You aren’t getting any younger, you know.”

“I’m only thirty. It’s not like I have one foot in the grave,” Lucas said with exasperation.

“By the time I was thirty, I had two boys already, and another just around the corner,” Joseph countered.

“Are you kidding me? You think I should get married?” Lucas said the word *marriage*, like it was a foul word.

“You’re the oldest, Lucas, the one who should be setting an example for your younger brothers to follow. You know, your mother and I aren’t getting any younger. We may only have a few years left…” Joseph trailed off, slumping a bit in his seat.

“Oh, please, Dad. You’re one of the strongest men I’ve ever known. Don’t even think acting frail will make me feel guilty that I’m not knocking women up, left and right, so you can have grandchildren. Besides, you don’t have a foot in the grave, either. You and mom still go skydiving,” Lucas said as he threw his hands up in frustration.

"You never know what could happen tomorrow. I have a great girl I think you should meet. She's the daughter of a dear friend of mine and I think you'd hit it off."

"I'm stopping you right there, Dad. I don't need for you to set me up on dates. Contrary to what you may believe, I have no problem finding my own women. If you really want to do some matchmaking, you should be focusing on Mark. Out of all of us, he's most likely to settle down and give you a brood of grandchildren," Lucas said as he glared at his father.

His dad had started grumbling about grandkids a couple years ago, but Lucas hadn't been worried. If Joseph was going to try and set up blind dates for him, he'd go into panic mode. He had no desire to walk down the aisle – not ever.

"I'll drop it for now, but you need to start thinking about your future," Joseph said as if he was doing Lucas a favor. Lucas decided it was best if he just let it go.

The two of them chatted for a while longer about business and Lucas started to relax. His day had been long and he was ready for bed, though he hated cutting his time short with his dad.

"I need to go home, Dad. I'll see you in the morning, okay?"

"That's fine, I'm getting a bit tired, myself," Joseph said as he turned. "Hold up, Lucas, Amy forgot to take her papers. Can you run them down to her before you leave?"

Lucas's stomach clenched at the thought of seeing her again that night, but he didn't have a good excuse to give his father as to why he wouldn't do it. Maybe luck would be with him and she'd be asleep and he could just leave them by her front door.

"Sure, Dad. Tell Mom I love her, and I'll see her tomorrow." He gave his dad a quick hug before walking from the room.

He quickly made his way to the cottage, only seeing a dim light shining through the front window. He knocked on the door, but there wasn't an answer, so he checked the knob. It was still unlocked. He would have to speak to her about that. He stepped inside and was about to call out her name when she turned the corner.

Lucas stood frozen in place as his eyes consumed her. She was standing before him with nothing on but a small towel barely covering her body. He could see all the way from her toes to the top of her creamy white thighs. The top of the towel was dipping so low the swells of her ample breasts were calling to him. As if her barely clad body wasn't enough to push him over the edge, her entire body was still glistening from her bath.

Her sweet fragrance drifted over to him, filling his nostrils with some sort of spice, like cinnamon. Whatever it was, it made him want to take a few bites out of her. One more inch of movement in either direction and he'd be able to see all of her secrets.

Lucas told himself to turn around and walk out the front door. Logically he knew that's what he needed to do, but somehow he couldn't get his feet to obey. He began moving in her direction, suddenly standing in front of her with his arms wrapping around her waist.

He pulled her damp, nearly naked body against his own, and then he was devouring her lips. He felt her stiffen for less than a second, before she was grabbing him back just as hungrily. He'd never wanted a woman so badly, to the point he felt he'd die if he didn't take her.

For half a second his brain tried to regain control, but when he heard a soft moan escape her lips, his restraint completely snapped. If she would've pushed him away, or told him no, he would've somehow been able to release her, but she was straining closer to him, moaning as he tangled his tongue with hers. She squirmed in his arms, neither of them seeming able to get close enough together.

With one swift movement, he ripped the towel away, allowing his hands to freely run up and down her body. He caressed her curves, relishing the smooth feel of her skin as his hand drifted over the curve of her hip, then upward to the side of her breast. Without breaking their kiss, he picked her up and walked the short distance to the bedroom. Gently laying her on the bed, he stripped his own clothes off, feeling a void in the few seconds apart from her.

His gaze was drawn to the beauty of her body, causing his arousal to swell even more, blood rushing through him, focusing on one area, urging him to take her.

Lucas saw Amy's eyes round in excitement and awe as she gazed at his naked body. He was suddenly afraid that she'd change her mind if he gave her too much time to think about what they were doing. He was sure he'd implode. Although taking his clothes off took no longer than half a minute, he was already aching to touch her again.

He joined her on the bed, his body covering hers. She leaned toward him, her mouth seeking his. He gladly accommodated, biting her bottom lip before sucking it into his mouth, urged on by the sounds of desire coming from her throat. Finally, he broke away to move his lips downward. He gently and, ever so slowly, licked a path down her neck, before slightly nipping at the sensitive skin, causing another moan to escape deep within her throat.

As he explored her delicious body, he lost all remaining doubts and lost himself in the intense pleasure of touching her. She began moving beneath him, spreading her legs in invitation for him to thrust deep inside her.

Lucas could feel Amy's body begging for completion, but he refused to make her his until he knew she was ready. He knew he wouldn't last much longer, especially with her rubbing against him, but he'd regret it if they ended too quickly. Even though he was doing this to get her out of his system once and for all, he still needed her to feel the same pleasure and satisfaction as him – to make the night complete.

When his hands slid over her rounded breasts, his thumbs pulling and elongating her nipples, her back arched off the bed, her body shaking. She wrapped her hands around his neck, pulling him back to her, her eyes unfocused as desire consumed her. Grabbing a fistful of her hair at the base of her head he crushed his lips to hers, sinking his tongue deep inside her mouth. He couldn't get enough of her – her taste –

scent – sound. Everything about her turned him on like nothing before. The more his tongue stroked the contours of her mouth, the more she twisted with need.

He ended the kiss to explore the rest of her body, causing her to cry out in frustration. His own body was begging him to end the torture he was bestowing on them both. He was going to sink deep inside her and make her his own.

He tasted the soft silky skin of her stomach, feeling it quivering beneath his mouth. As he moved his head lower and ran his tongue along her inner thigh, her entire body responded, trembling. He'd never been with such a responsive woman before, and he was finding it impossible to maintain even a semblance of control.

His mouth followed her thigh up to her most secret place, finally tasting her, causing her hips to arch off the bed as she cried out in pleasure. Her moans gave him the strength to keep going. He tasted her sweetness, feeling her tremble beneath him. She suddenly tensed, and then her entire body jerked and she cried out as a powerful release overtook her. She was shaking beneath his skilled mouth as he flicked his tongue against her moist heat one last time before slowly making his way back up her body.

She was slightly limp in his arms as he began kissing his way up her stomach. He felt like he could worship her body the rest of the night. He trailed his tongue up her swollen breasts and gently took one of her tight buds into his mouth.

She began trembling again as her body stirred back to life. He took his time moving from one sensitive peak to the other until she cried out for him again. The deep cry of pleasure snapped the last bit of control he had left. He quickly moved his body over hers, pressing the tip of his solid erection against her opening.

His mouth took hers again as his hand slid down to make sure she was ready. Easily sliding his fingers over her swollen womanhood, he slipped them inside. Her entire body arched off the bed, pressing into him as she groaned in pleasure.

"Please!" she cried. She was more than ready.

"Open your eyes. I want to see into them when I make you mine," he whispered. Slowly, as if weights were holding them down, her eyes lifted halfway open.

In one thrust, he buried himself deep inside her. He almost exploded with the first contact of her tight heat gripping him. He felt her body stiffen, and a sound of pain escaped her lips as she adjusted to him. Her eyes snapped wide open, while her mouth formed a look of shock.

Lucas's entire body stiffened as he realized she was a virgin. How did a woman – especially one as attractive and sexually alluring as her – reach the age of twenty-four still a virgin?

The shock was bringing back some of his lost control. He had to stop. He didn't sleep with women who didn't know the score. He wasn't a *happily ever after* kind of guy, which meant virgins were strictly off limits.

He started to pull out of her when her face relaxed, and she sighed in ecstasy as her body adjusted to his.

He knew he should do the right thing and stop, but when her hips moved up, gripping him even tighter, he ignored his better judgment. Moving in a steady rhythm, her breathing became heavier, and he felt her body quivering around him, he couldn't take any more and started thrusting quickly. Her hips pushed up to meet him, and she tightened in pleasure. As she cried out and her body began shuddering around him, he flew over the edge, spilling inside her, shaking with the power of his release.

He lay on top of her, not moving for several moments as his breathing became more regular. Realizing he was most likely crushing her, he turned, taking her with him. He didn't know what to say, so he remained silent. He just stayed still while rubbing her back until he heard her steady breathing, indicating she'd fallen asleep.

He remained where he was for an hour, watching her sleep peacefully in his arms. In sleep, she couldn't get close enough to him. Her leg was wrapped around his lower body, and her head rested on his chest. She was the most stunning woman he'd ever seen, and she was now his.

Suddenly, Lucas's head snapped up. He'd been about ready to fall asleep when the realization that he hadn't used protection hit him. What had he been thinking? He'd never had sex with a woman without wearing a condom. He wasn't so stupid as to get caught in the baby trap.

His thoughts took on great speed in a million different directions. He knew there was no way she could've planned the unprotected sex. How could she have known he was coming back to the cottage that night?

There was also no possible way she could've faked her intense reaction to him. He'd been with women who'd simply gone through the motions, pretending to be into the sex. He'd figured it out real fast and walked away. He wanted a woman to be hot and willing when in his bed, not acting as if they were performing a chore.

He was angry with himself, but he turned that anger on her. He in no way wanted to be forced into marriage, but if their night of passion led to a child, he'd never walk away. Family was everything to him, and a child wasn't a mistake – ever.

He glared at Amy, suddenly feeling trapped. He'd been determined to purge her from his system, but it could end up costing him everything. She'd be the first woman who'd managed to catch him off guard.

As he slipped from the bed and got dressed, his eyes kept returning to her, such innocence on her face as she slept, a small smile playing across her lips. She shifted, her arm reaching out as her body moved toward the center of the bed. The blanket slipped, exposing one beautiful breast, and his body instantly reacted.

With illicit frustration at himself for still desiring her, he quickly and quietly exited the cottage, rushing down the entry steps. What he wanted to do was go back inside and climb into the bed next to her. He had to get out of there and cool down, figure out what he was going to do next. He felt completely lost for the first time.

Chapter Nine

Amy woke up in the middle of the night and stretched. *Ouch!* She was incredibly sore. It took her a minute to fully awaken, and as she became more aware, it only took seconds for her to be sitting straight up in bed. What had she done? She had sex with her boss.

She had sex with her boss?

How stupid could she have been? Did he now think she'd be at his beck and call anytime he felt like getting his needs met? He probably thought he could just come around, have sex with her, and then slink off in the middle of the night.

There was no way in hell he was going to use her and discard her. How was she going to handle it? She had a couple of options. She could make a big scene, yell at him, and quit her job, though that didn't sound appealing. Her other option was to pretend as if nothing had happened. She liked that option a whole lot better. She'd just make sure she didn't place herself in any more compromising positions.

She wouldn't have him in her place alone – ever.

She knew that one simple touch from him made her forget all her careful planning and any idea of resistance. She couldn't allow herself to be in situations where he'd be touching her.

She'd make up a boyfriend. That would stop him from thinking he could take advantage of her. She'd just tell him she was in a long-term relationship, and she'd slipped up. She felt a little bit of regret, knowing she wouldn't get to repeat such an extremely satisfying experience.

For her first time making love, the experience was unforgettable. She had no idea her body could give and receive so much pleasure in so many places. She was certainly and most deliciously sore, but it had been oh-so-worth-it. She now understood what all the fuss was about. She'd read that sex for the first time wasn't a good experience. Those people must not have been making love to someone like Lucas Anderson.

She had to smile at the irony. The man looked like a Greek god, had more money than anyone needed, and made love like every girl's fantasy come true. None of that mattered, though. It was a mistake, and one she wouldn't be repeating. One mistake wasn't going to change her life plans.

Amy went into the bathroom and cleaned up. She was lying back down when it finally hit her that they hadn't used protection. She bolted upright in bed again. She was dismayed to think of the stupidity of having unprotected sex. She wasn't prepared to be a mother yet. She'd always dreamed of having her own child, but not made this way. She wouldn't give the child up if she did get pregnant, but how would she be able to manage it all?

She'd have to sleep on it and figure everything out later. She didn't know anything yet. She was most likely overreacting. They'd only had sex one time. The odds were unlikely she'd make a baby the first and only time she had sex.

Amy slept fitfully the rest of the night. She dreamt she'd just delivered the most beautiful little girl. She was holding her close to her chest, bonding with her newborn. The baby was perfect in every way. Suddenly, Lucas stepped into the room with three men, all in designer suits.

They started speaking legal jargon, and suddenly she looked down and she was no longer holding the baby. Lucas had her. Then in walked a tall, blonde bombshell of a woman, and he handed the baby to her. "Here you go, sweetheart. I told you I'd get a baby for you. Anything you want is yours," he said as they walked out together, leaving Amy crying for her baby in the cold hospital room.

Amy woke up in terror. The dream had seemed so real. She was surprised to find real tears falling down her cheeks. She considered herself a strong woman, but there was one thing that could bring her to her knees. She couldn't survive it if someone were to take away the family she so desperately wanted.

She gave up on sleep and got out of bed to fix herself breakfast. She tried to read for a while but couldn't concentrate. Each movement she made awoke the foreign soreness she felt and had her body remember the sizzling encounter with Lucas. She decided she'd take a walk around the grounds and focus breathing in the beautiful, clean morning air. It was exactly what she needed to clear her head.

She wandered around for a couple hours when Joseph snuck up on her and nearly made her jump out of her own skin.

"How are you doing, young lady? I hope you slept well." She wondered how such an enormous man could so easily sneak up on her.

"I slept very well," she automatically replied. The circles under her eyes gave away her lie, but he was too much of a gentleman to call her on it.

"You seem a little anxious about something. If there's anything I can help with, all you need to do is ask."

"Everything is great, Mr. Anderson. I'm just thinking about the move and work. You've been too kind already, and I don't want to take advantage. I felt a bit guilty about even staying in the cottage last night," she replied.

"Now, Amy, don't hurt my feelings. I thought the cottage was pretty comfortable. I've slept there myself a time or two when my wife got sick of my attitude," he chuckled.

"Oh no, Mr. Anderson, I love the cottage. It's just very difficult for me to take handouts. I do appreciate a place to stay, and I have to tell you, I've already fallen in love with the cottage. It's perfect in every way possible," she quickly responded, not wanting to offend him.

"Katherine's still sleeping. She must get her beauty rest," he chuckled. "Please come join me on the terrace for breakfast. I love having a beautiful young woman to eat with. It makes the food taste so much better." He then held his arm out for her and she took it. They walked arm in arm to the main house.

They were laughing while eating breakfast when Lucas strolled in. Amy could see he was instantly on alert.

"Good morning, Dad," he said while sitting down. "Ms. Harper, I hope the accommodations were to your liking," he added formally.

Amy looked at him for a moment, trying to figure him out. It took her about ten seconds. The man had already gotten what he wanted, and now he was letting her know it was back to business and nothing more. She already knew this was how he was, so why did his attitude sting so?

Well, she thought, *two could play the game of "cold as ice"*.

"I slept perfectly, Mr. Anderson. The beginning of the night I had this bad nausea and a nasty headache, but then it went away, and the rest of the night was flawless," she said in a voice even colder than his.

His eyes turned into slits and if eyes could kill, she figured she'd be a pile of ash. She decided she'd push her luck just a bit more and smirked at him before turning away and ignoring him completely.

Joseph watched their little byplay, both of them thinking they were being so sly. He wondered what had gone on last night. It looked to him like the kids might have gotten close and were both running scared, now. Well, he wasn't going to let them avoid each other, not when it looked like things had finally started heating up.

"Eat up, Lucas. You have a busy day. You need to take Amy to get her car and help her shop for the apartment. Better to get an early start, so it will be ready for her to move into." He then looked at Amy. "I think you'll be happy there."

"Mr. Anderson..." she began, but he stopped her.

"Now, Amy, you're a guest in my home. Don't you think it's time you started calling me Joseph?"

"Um, okay, Mr.…I mean, Joseph. I was thinking. Mr. Anderson," she nodded toward Lucas, "is really busy, and I don't mind doing this stuff on my own. If it's a matter of a signature, they could fax you the paperwork. I could just take a cab to the car lot. I really, *really* don't mind," she pleaded with him.

Joseph watched the steam practically rise from his son's ears at her statement. It seemed Lucas could dish out attitude, but didn't like getting it back. He quite enjoyed watching his son squirm.

He'd been impressed with Amy from the moment he'd met her, but as she put his son in his place, he liked her even more. She was good for Lucas. He needed a woman who wouldn't allow him to walk all over her. She reminded him a lot of his Katherine.

Joseph had been a fool when he'd first met his wife, but luckily she'd forgiven him. He couldn't imagine what he would've done had she not. He loved her more each day they spent together.

He didn't mind pushing his son's buttons a little, especially if it hurried him along.

"If Lucas is busy this afternoon, I could always give Mark a call and ask if he wouldn't mind escorting you around. I don't think that would be a problem. He's my one child who actually enjoys shopping," Joseph said, watching Lucas out of the corner of his eye.

He thought the boy may actually upturn the table as bright as the fire was burning in his eyes. Good. He needed to be pushed.

◊◊◊◊◊◊

Lucas hadn't wanted to spend the day with her, but her trying to get out of it just plain ticked him off. How dare she not want to be with him? They had some talking to do, and she was damn well going to spend the day with him.

Plus, there was no way he was going to sit by while his brother whisked Amy around town. He could easily see Mark falling in love with her. His little brother had a heart of gold. He vehemently denied he ever wanted to get married, but Lucas saw the longing in Mark's eyes when they got stuck watching a sappy movie, or an affectionate couple were nearby. Mark may say he didn't want to get married, but Lucas knew it was all talk.

Lucas quickly sat up and addressed his father.

"Of course I'm not too busy to take out Ms. Harper," he said, his voice dripping with venom. He finally faced her with a smirk on his face. “Why don’t you go ahead and get ready so we can take off right away?” he said, looking her up and down. He knew she was already dressed for the day, but he just wanted to be an ass.

He smiled as he watched the fire enter her eyes. He could practically hear her screaming at him in her head. As much as he didn’t want to react to her, he instantly hardened, everything in him wanted to lift her over his shoulder and cart her to the nearest bed.

He’d thought one night would purge her from his system. He’d been dead wrong and he had a feeling, a month straight wouldn’t be enough.

◊◊◊◊◊◊

He had some nerve looking down his nose at her! Amy was fighting to keep her emotions in check. She looked just fine, and she wasn’t trying to impress him, anyway. She’d go with him, just to show him she could be in his company without being affected by it.

The only thing keeping her from telling him what she truly thought about him was the fact that she was sitting at his father’s table, and she respected Joseph. As far as Lucas went, he’d better be careful, cause her foot may slip on the gas pedal and run him over when she was test driving her new car.

“I am ready, Mr. Anderson,” she said in a voice of honey, dripping with vinegar. “You may want to get ready yourself, though, and clean the jam off your face,” she added with satisfaction.

His eyes narrowed even further before he got up from the table and walked into the house without another word. She quietly chuckled, enjoying the victory of winning their little battle. It felt kind of good to knock the all-powerful Lucas down a notch.

"Well, you kids seem to be getting along rather well," Joseph said with complete sincerity. She couldn't tell if he was serious or not. He seemed to be. Maybe the two of them hadn't been as obvious as she'd thought. She figured you could've sliced the tension between them with a knife, but it was good Joseph hadn't noticed.

"He's a great boss," was all she said before looking down and picking at her breakfast. She didn't see the amused grin on Joseph's face.

"I'm happy to hear that, as the two of you will be spending a lot of time together. I used to love my business trips. Esther was invaluable at keeping everything together for me when we were away. I couldn't have done my job nearly as well without her. Katherine often accompanied us, especially when we went to the tropical places. That's how the two of them became such close friends."

Amy felt a moment of pure panic as Joseph talked about her traveling with Lucas. How could she possibly keep herself together if they were locked alone together on his jet, or in a hotel suite? She didn't even hear the rest of what Joseph was saying. Something about Katherine and Esther. It didn't matter – all that mattered was that she may end up on some tropical island with a boss who she couldn't seem to keep her hands off of.

She tried to relax, thinking back over their conversation. He wasn't interested in having sex with her, anymore. He'd already gotten what he wanted. She could deal with his sarcasm, even his rudeness; she just couldn't deal with his touch – at least not without melting.

◊◊◊◊◊◊

Lucas came back out and stood by, impatiently waiting, as Amy deliberately took a few more bites of food, chewing as slowly as she possibly could. He glanced at his watch pointedly, trying to get her to pick up the pace.

"Now, Lucas, quit being so impatient. It's never polite to rush a lady," his father scolded.

"We have a lot to do today, Dad. I just want to get going because I have plans with Vienna tonight," he added, lying about having a date.

He noticed Amy tense in her seat. *Good*, he thought. She wasn't as unaffected as she wanted him to believe. He was surprised with how good the thought made him feel. He didn't take rejection well, even if he didn't want the woman. However, that wasn't the case with her at all. He still wanted her – even more now than ever before.

She stood up and grabbed her purse off the back of the chair. "I wouldn't want to make your date wait on you," she said in a perfectly calm voice. "Thank you so much for breakfast, Joseph. It was delicious. Your company was the perfect way to start my day," she said and then calmly walked through the door, leaving Lucas to catch up to her. To Lucas, if felt he'd been chasing after her way too much since their first meeting.

He smiled to himself as he watched the sway of her hips, and the snug jeans that were molded to her luscious backside. He had to admit he didn't mind the view from behind. Chasing her wasn't bad – not bad at all.

"Have a good time, kids." Lucas heard his father call out to him, but he didn't bother responding. He was too busy keeping an eye on his incredibly sexy and frustrating assistant.

◊◊◊◊◊◊

"Joseph Anderson, what are you up to?"

"Good morning, Beautiful. I was just having breakfast with a beautiful young lady and your grumpy son." Joseph looked up as Katherine walked through the door. Even with a scowl on her face, she was absolutely exquisite.

"We both know that's bull. You're matchmaking, and from the looks of things between those two, it's going very well," she said with disapproval in her tone. "When that boy figures out what you're up to, he's going to stop speaking to you. Just know that I've warned you."

"By the time he figures it out, he'll be very much in love with his wife and thanking me," Joseph said with the same cocky attitude Lucas had inherited. Joseph certainly hoped that was the case. Because, otherwise, his wife would be right, and his son would be none too happy with him. It was a risk he was willing to take.

"Let's go for a drive," he said rising from the table and pulled Katherine into his arms, leaning down and giving her a good morning kiss.

He meant for it to be short, but by the time he pulled away, he was a bit out of breath. He smiled at the sight of Katherine's cheeks flushed and her eyes a bit glazed over.

Was it so wrong for him to want his sons to have a love of their own, like what he had with his Katherine? He didn't think there was anything wrong with that.

He decided today was going to be a great day. It had started off wonderfully with Lucas and Amy on their way to a passionate relationship. It would end even better, with Katherine by his side.

"Joseph Anderson, you're just trying to get on my good side by distracting me," she said a bit breathlessly.

"Is it working?"

Katherine's face softened as she looked into his eyes. She never could stay mad at him for long, which was a very good thing, considering he did a lot of stupid things.

"I really shouldn't let you get away with your scheming, but I suddenly just don't care. Let's go for that drive," she said, her face softening even more as her hand lifted up and cradled his cheek.

"Nothing would make me happier," Joseph told her before bending down and kissing her again.

Yes, there was definitely nothing wrong with him wanting his boys to have the same thing he did. They'd come to appreciate his meddling when they had a good woman by their side.

Chapter Ten

Amy got in the car with Lucas, immediately engulfed by his scent. Why did he have to smell so good? She could feel a stirring in her stomach as she sat motionless next to him. How could she want to be with him after the things he'd said and done? She was trying not to see the good in him because it was so much harder to maintain her distance when she let down her guard.

They rode in silence for several minutes, until he turned into a parking lot. This wasn't the car dealership. What was he doing? Maybe he was going to drop her somewhere and hope she got abducted.

"We're going shopping first. That way the items can be delivered and the crew can finish your apartment," he explained. He didn't wait for her to answer. He stepped out of the vehicle and came around to her door to open it. When he did the small things, such as treating her as a lady, it made her see the more human side of him. She didn't want to see that side – it was much harder to resist him. She'd rather he act like an arrogant ass so she could justify her own distance.

She got out of the car and walked next to him into the vast store. "I really don't need any decorations. I'm sure the apartment is fine as it is," she tried telling him. She was uncomfortable as it was, with all the Andersons had done for her. It felt too much like assistance.

"Let's get this done," he stated in a voice that said, *Deal with it, it's going to happen.*

She soon found it was much easier to go along with him than argue. He took her through each department, asking her preference on colors and styles. His mood seemed to lift as they progressed through the store. She'd never have guessed it, but it looked like Lucas enjoyed shopping much more than she did.

She'd never had the money to frivolously spend, so shopping had been a chore, never something fun.

When they finished in the store, Lucas made arrangements for the items to be delivered to her apartment immediately. "We're ahead of schedule, Amy. I think you'll be able to move into your place tonight," he said as they exited the store. "I'm hungry. We'll have lunch before going to the car lot."

He didn't ask if she was hungry. He didn't ask if she wanted to share a meal with him. He simply stated they were going to lunch, and so in his mind, that's exactly what they were doing. If she hadn't been so hungry she would've refused to eat just to prove a point, but she knew he wouldn't even notice, and then she'd be the one suffering for the rest of the day.

He pulled up to a small diner and again came around to open her car door. As they began walking inside, he placed his hand on the small of her back, sending chills all the way to the souls of her feet.

Once inside, the waiter left them chips and salsa, and then quickly returned and took their order. As they waited for the food, Amy thought it had to be one of her most uncomfortable moments.

"You and my father seem to be getting awfully cozy," Lucas said, his tone sounding more like an accusation.

"I like Joseph. He's always been very kind to me. He's spent some time in the offices while you've been gone, and I feel like I can honestly talk to him for hours on end," she answered.

"He's got a big heart. I don't want *anyone* taking advantage of that fact."

Amy snapped her head up and looked at Lucas incredulously. Did he really just accuse her of using his father? That's what it sounded like to her. She wanted to knock him off his high horse so badly her hands were practically shaking, but instead, she took a calming breath before opening her mouth.

"You may think the whole world is out to get you, and everyone wants something from your family, and that may even be the case with a lot of people you know. However, you don't know me even kind of close enough to make a jackass accusation like that. I have nothing but the deepest respect for your father, and would never even imagine doing anything to hurt him. Just because you're jaded and bitter with the world, for some unknown reason, doesn't give you the right to speak down to me. You have two choices, either apologize right now, or I'm walking from this restaurant. I love my job, but I won't be talked to this way. It's unacceptable."

She looked him in the eye, fury boiling inside her. She saw the shock on his face as she gave her speech. She had no idea how she wasn't crying. She knew he may terminate her employment right then, and she'd probably regret her words by the time she found herself sleeping in a hotel room later that night, but at the moment, she was too ticked to care.

After several moments of silence, the edges of Lucas's lips lifted and small lines appeared around his eyes. The smile then turned into a chuckle. Amy watched him in shock. He was now laughing at her?

She pushed her chair back and stood up. A person could only take so much.

"Amy…stop," he said between chuckles as she quickly made her way through the restaurant. No way was she turning around. She knew she had less than thirty seconds before her rage simmered down and the tears started. She wanted to be far away from him before that happened.

She made it outside and started running, managing to make it to the alley next to the building. She took a few steps inside, then leaned against the wall, her legs shaking as reality began setting in.

She heard footsteps quickly following her and she wanted to scream. Lucas caught up to her as the first tear slipped down her cheek.

He slowly approached as if he was dealing with a wild animal, which wasn't too far off the mark. She felt very unpredictable right then.

"I wasn't laughing at you, okay? I'm sorry. I know you're not using my father. I don't know why I even implied it. I'm just…you're just…I don't know!"

He took a step back, running his fingers through his hair as he paced in front of her. A few more tears slipped as she watched him. Agitation was clear in his movements, but she was still mad, feeling no sympathy for his frustration.

"Look, you're driving me crazy. I don't know what the hell is wrong with me right now, but you don't help the situation when you look at me with your lust filled eyes. You don't exactly hide your emotions well," he snapped as he turned and stood right in front of her.

Amy's tears dried as he towered over her, his body only a foot away. Even wanting to throttle him, he still turned her on. He'd opened the floodgates inside of her and a tidal wave of desire had raced through. Now she had sex on the brain constantly. She wanted him, even if she didn't like him very much.

Their eyes locked and she saw his blue depths dilate. Her breathing grew heavy, as pulling in oxygen suddenly became a workout.

"Screw it," Lucas muttered before his hands pushed against the wall on either side of her and he quickly caged her in. Before she had time to blink, his lips came crashing down on hers. Need – anger – frustration – desire. It was all in his kiss. His mouth crushed hers as he pushed his tongue inside, forcing her submission.

She had no choice.

She couldn't fight what her body longed for with such intensity. She tried to remain stiff against the solid brick wall, but as his hand lifted, sliding up the front of her blouse, she gave up. She kissed him back as his palm captured her breast, massaging the soft flesh, pressing against her hardened nipple.

The kiss deepened as his hips pushed against her, pressing his arousal into her heat. She pressed back. She knew it was wrong, knew they shouldn't be doing this, but she didn't care.

A horn sounded close by, startling Amy. Lucas pulled back, his eyes hazy with desire. Suddenly, a siren went off, and they both turned, watching as a police car flew by the alley entrance.

Lucas stepped back and swore as Amy stood rooted to the spot, wondering what the heck she'd just done.

"That shouldn't have happened. It seems I once again need to apologize to you. It's becoming a nasty habit, one that I don't like. Let's forget about my earlier comment, forget about this kiss, and just finish our lunch, then get on with the day."

Lucas faced her, his eyes challenging as he made the offer. She could accept his apology and let it go, or she could walk away from everything – her job, security, and new friends.

It was an easy decision.

Without saying a word, she stepped away from the wall and walked toward the restaurant. She refused to think about what the staff was imagining they'd been doing. She knew her hair was tousled and her lips had to be swollen. It was obvious she'd just been kissed to within an inch of her life.

With as much grace as she could muster, she resumed her seat and picked up a corn chip, taking a bite. It tasted like sawdust, but she forced herself to chew and swallow, then repeated the process.

The rest of their meal was eaten in an awkward silence until, thankfully, he received a phone call which occupied him until they were finished.

The pressure from the day was beginning to settle on her shoulders, and she just wanted it over with. The sooner she got to be alone, the better off she'd be. Then she would have time to think.

They silently made their way to the car lot after lunch. She'd never owned a car before – never even priced one. She knew she'd get one after college, but she hadn't had the money yet. She'd taken a driver's training course in college, so she knew how to drive, but she still wasn't real comfortable behind the wheel.

She didn't want Lucas to know about her insecurity, though, so she decided to suck it up and brave the situation.

"Do you want a manual or automatic?" was the first question he asked.

"I'd prefer an automatic."

"If you want my opinion, I think you should go with the Mercedes ML450 Hybrid SUV. We have about ten choices for you, but I've done the research on this one, and it's highly rated in safety. It gets excellent fuel mileage and is recommended on the consumer reports," he offered, sounding like a car salesman.

"I really don't know anything about cars, Lucas. I wouldn't know where to begin," she answered.

◊◊◊◊◊◊

His head spun around to look at her, but she was staring at the car lot like a lost child, so she didn't notice her slip. It was the only time she'd ever used his first name. He found he liked the sound of it on her lips.

He knew she didn't realize what she'd said. In her nervousness at being so out of her element, she'd temporarily let her guard down. He liked this side of her. Amy, minus the armor, seemed much sweeter, and more innocent, and he wanted to wrap her in his arms – protect her. He wanted to take her back into his arms so badly, his fingers clenched at his sides.

He stopped himself – barely. He was in no way ready to open his heart to anyone. He'd remain in control of himself, and he'd be able to forget about what they'd done the night before and earlier in the afternoon. Neither of them needed to enter into an affair that would end with her losing a job and him with regrets. He'd figure things out when he had more time to think.

"If you don't know much about cars, then I hope you'll take my advice, but the choice is yours. You'll be the one driving the vehicle."

Lucas walked her into the building and skirted around the salesmen, heading straight to the manager's office. "Lucas, it's good to see you again. You're early, but I've already pulled out the car you asked for," said the man behind the desk, who had a genuine smile and stood to shake hands with both of them.

"Thanks, Frank. I appreciate it." Lucas grinned and was already turning to lead Amy back through the showroom and out the side doors.

As they walked outside, they saw a beautifully polished, crimson vehicle sitting at the curb. Lucas led her to it and opened the driver's door. She looked at him with surprise and delight in her eyes.

Lucas couldn't take his eyes off her face as she fought back tears while looking at the car in front of her. He suddenly realized what it must've been like for her growing up. He knew she'd never had a real home, going from a crack house to foster care. She must not have gotten gifts too often. The vehicle must seem like a shiny new toy. He looked at it through her eyes, and felt humbled.

Suddenly, her face broke out into a huge grin as she climbed into the seat and started looking for the ignition. "Where's the key. I don't even see a place to put it in?" she asked, looking at him with a confused, yet ecstatic, expression. Lucas laughed and explained it was a push button start.

"One of the new features of the hybrid cars is that they run on electricity when you're traveling at slower speeds. The gas will kick on when it's needed."

She pushed the button, and the lights came on, but there was no sound. She looked at him again with confusion. "How do you know it's on if there isn't any noise?" she asked, genuinely puzzled.

Lucas couldn't help himself. He laughed out loud, really enjoying himself. She was so unlike the women he normally dated, not that they were dating, he reminded himself.

His open laughter wiped the smile from her face. He knew enough about her to know she didn't like being mocked, and it probably seemed like that was what he was doing. "I'm not laughing at you. I just find you to be a breath of fresh air," he continued, chuckling. "Place the car in gear. Trust me. It will drive for you," he said.

"What is this, a space car?" she muttered under her breath. He managed to keep his laughter inside and pretended not to hear the comment. He had a feeling he could laugh often with her in his life. He tried to stiffen his resolve, knowing he didn't want to get too comfortable around her. That was a dangerous road to take.

◊◊◊◊◊◊

Amy drove around the back roads of Seattle for about an hour. Lucas led her out of the city, not wanting her first ride to be stressful, which she was grateful for. She loved the vehicle. It drove like it was on glass. Even once the engine kicked on, there was only a purr that could be heard. It was wonderful, and she didn't want to stop. She almost forgot Lucas was even with her, which was a pretty amazing feat in itself.

"Amy, it looks like you love this car. Why don't we head back to the lot and sign the papers so you can take it home?"

She was a little disappointed the ride was over, but she nodded and turned back toward the dealership. She reluctantly got out of the car when they arrived, her eyes turning back to the car, almost afraid if she walked away, it would be taken from her.

"It's all yours, you don't have to worry," Lucas said when she was still rooted to the spot.

"Sorry," Amy muttered, as she felt her face heat. She turned away and followed him inside. She forced herself not to turn around again.

The paperwork only took about twenty minutes, since Lucas was a preferred client, and they had everything prepared for him. The lot had to do a final cleanup, so they told her it would be delivered to her place that night. She was extremely disappointed she couldn't take it with her right away, but she didn't argue with them.

Lucas led her to his car, and she slumped a bit in the seat after they pulled out of the lot. She knew it was ridiculous, but she hadn't been like most kids, getting loads of gifts for the holidays, and new clothes anytime she wanted.

The first time she'd received a Christmas present was when she was in foster care, and though they were good people, they didn't have much money, so the kids each got only one small item. She still had those treasured gifts, and cherished each one of them. The car, though… the car was nice. It was something she'd never expected to have. Even if it wasn't really hers, it was hers to use for as long as she had the job. That was pretty exciting.

"We've finished all we need to today, and you're apartment's ready. Do you want to see your new home?" Lucas asked.

"Yes, definitely," she responded, feeling her mood perk right back up. She had a hard time sitting still as they made their way through the busy city. They passed the Anderson Corporation, and then went about another mile before turning off the road.

As they pulled up to a large building, she was taken aback. It looked more like a fancy hotel than an apartment complex. A huge water fountain with colored lights sat centered in the circular driveway, surrounded by colorful, lush flowers. The drive was paved with multi-colored stones, looking like a path out of a fairy tale book. She watched as they passed the front doors, which were adorned with gold trim with brass fixtures. A doorman in a tuxedo stood just inside and waved as Lucas drove past.

She peeked out the window and looked up at the overhead roof, where three chandeliers hung, shooting rainbows of color as they drove beneath the canopy. It was an overwhelming thought that she'd be living in such a sophisticated place.

They pulled inside an underground parking tunnel, where he used a card to enter, before he parked in front of a reserved sign.

"You'll park here," he said, while pointing out another reserved space near the elevator. He came around the car before she managed to unbuckle, then opened her door – something she was getting used to. She couldn't admit to him how much she liked it.

She was silent as they walked into the plush, dark wood elevator and he pressed the only button available. "This elevator only goes to the lobby. It's another safety precaution we have in place. We take the security of our tenants very seriously."

When the doors opened to a huge lobby area that would rival the best hotels in New York, Amy couldn't stop her surprised gasp. There was a large desk sitting against the far wall with a security guard eyeing the monitors in front of him.

"Good evening, Mr. Anderson. You're in early tonight," he said before smiling at Amy.

"Hello, Fred. How are you?"

"Good. Good. I can't complain."

"Fred, this is our newest tenant, Ms. Harper. She'll be living in 19-A."

"It's a pleasure to meet you, Ms. Harper. I hope you'll enjoy living here. It's a great place. I work the evening shift Tuesday through Saturday, but I live here, in apartment 2-A, if you ever need me. I already put a list of numbers in your unit, so don't hesitate to call me, anytime."

Amy liked Fred instantly. He seemed to be in his early fifties and had one of those welcoming smiles, putting one instantly at ease. With the added security measures she felt safe, like the rest of the world couldn't get to her if she didn't allow it. Living in Seattle, and always the slummier parts, had made her very aware of safety issues. She'd been too afraid to sleep, on more than one night, throughout her life.

"Come with me and I'll give you the grand tour before showing you to your place," Lucas said.

He led her down a hallway to the left. The first door they entered led to a state-of-the-art gym, which they quickly walked through. She wanted to pause and look at the equipment, but he seemed to be in a hurry, so she quickly followed his fast pace. The next room housed an Olympic-sized pool. Her heart accelerated. Could it be real? She not only got a place, which she didn't even care if it was the size of a shoe box, but she also got a swimming pool, gym, and more.

Her head was spinning as he showed her a hot tub and sauna, and several other spaces, such as a game room. Amy felt Lucas watching her as they toured the facility, and she made an attempt to control her expression. She failed miserably at hiding the pleasure on her face

He showed her the private backyard garden with several benches hidden in different locations. As they passed by one of the shrub covered areas, she spotted a young couple too busy kissing to notice their intrusion.

Her pulse started racing, seeing the couple, so obviously in love they couldn't keep their hands off each other. She didn't notice if Lucas had spotted them or not, but she wanted to get back inside before she had any further erotic thoughts about her boss.

"What do you think so far?" he asked. Amy tried to keep a cool expression, tried acting as if she was used to living in similar places. It wasn't like he didn't know about her previous home, though. She finally gave up pretending and spun in a circle as she laughed aloud. She almost grabbed him in her excitement, but at the last minute, she pulled back.

"I can't believe I get to live here. I know I should act all cool and collect, but I just don't care. I love this place, and don't think I'll ever want to move out," she said, a huge grin splitting her face.

"Well, you may want to reserve judgment until you see your actual apartment," he said, while leading her back into the lobby.

Lucas pressed the elevator button and stepped inside when the doors opened. They rode to the nineteenth floor in silence. Amy had to fight the rising giggle of disbelief in her throat at her good fortune. As they stepped off and she looked around at the extra wide hallways with beautiful paintings strategically placed, Amy finally realized the enormous size of the complex.

When she was told it was a corporate apartment building, she'd assumed it only had a couple floors, with minimal units. But, from what she was seeing, there must be several hundred units.

As they walked down the hallway, she noticed there were hardly any doors. They came close to the end when Lucas stopped and placed a key in the door to their left.

"There aren't many doors up here. How many apartments are on each floor?" she asked, almost afraid to see how big her place was.

"This floor only has two living units. We have four floors with three-bedroom apartments, six floors with two-bedroom, and the rest are all one-bedroom. The first two floors house our temporary units, where traveling business associates stay. All the rest are permanent residences," he replied. "This floor is also used for conferences and has several rooms available for meetings. We conduct business here, often."

"Oh," Amy replied, not really knowing what else to say.

They walked inside, and Amy's breath rushed out. The apartment was enormous. There was a vast entryway, tiled in comfortable earth tones, leading to a beautiful living room. The furnishing looked new, and the room was even equipped with a large screen television.

"Esther left you this gift basket she thought you'd enjoy as a welcome home gift," Lucas said as she gazed at a large package on the table overflowing with popcorn and chocolates. A note said to enjoy her new home, and was signed simply, Esther.

She was touched Esther would do something so nice for her. She'd have to make sure and send her a thank-you card, then take her to lunch. Lucas stood back and let her wander through the apartment. There was a nice-sized room set up for a guest, should she bring anyone over. The main bathroom was decorated in her new linens, with a few added touches of bath and body washes from nice boutiques.

She opened the door at the end of the hall and was stunned by the master bedroom. There was a huge four-poster bed in the middle of it, covered with the purple comforter she'd picked. It was the kind of bed she'd always dreamed of owning. She walked over, jumped into the middle of it, and let out an infectious giggle.

"I don't know what to say. I've never known a company to be so generous. It makes me feel guilty having all this when so many people don't have even a third of it. What if the corporation hates me in another six months? What if I'm a complete failure and can't do the job, after all? This is so much pressure."

"Amy, we wouldn't have done this for someone we didn't have full confidence in. You've been doing fine, and I hate to repeat myself, but we offer this to all executive officers."

Amy smiled as Lucas stepped out of the room. She wasn't receiving any treatment they didn't offer anyone else, which made her feel better. She didn't want to stand out. She didn't want to feel guilty for what they'd given her. She wanted to simply just enjoy what she had and for now, at least, it was all hers.

Amy walked back into her living room. Lucas was standing with his back to the wall, watching her. *Here goes*, she thought. He didn't look as if he was planning on leaving anytime soon, and she just wanted to de-stress and enjoy her new place. If things were different, she'd be able to imagine the two of them snuggling up on the couch, watching one of her romantic comedies, but that would never happen. She needed to let her excitement come out, smile hugely, and dance around her new living room. She couldn't do that until he was gone.

"Thank you for taking time out of your busy schedule to do all you did today. This place is amazing. It's better than I could've ever imagined, or hoped for, though I really don't need all the space. If you want to move me into a smaller apartment and save this one for an employee with a family, I'm fine with that." She was talking quickly, so he couldn't interrupt.

"I'm not saying I don't love the apartment – because I do. It's seriously more amazing than any place I've ever even seen, let alone lived in, but it just seems to be such a waste of space for only me," she continued, rattling on.

Amy figured if she spoke first, he wouldn't make the demand she was thinking he was about to make. She wasn't going to sleep her way to the top, no matter what he thought of her after the way she'd behaved the night before. She wasn't that hungry for success.

Well, she was hungry – it was just a much, much different hunger. She'd get over it as soon as she had some alone time to really think. She kept telling herself that, but she was having serious doubts about her own reasoning.

Uncomfortable silence drifted through the room as she paused. It looked like he wasn't leaving until she made him.

Chapter Eleven

Lucas knew Amy was babbling so he wouldn't have time to speak. He figured he'd let her talk herself out and then get his say.

When she finally stopped and looked at him, their gazes locked. He saw her chin rise slightly, and she visibly firmed her shoulders. She seemed angry all of a sudden, and he couldn't figure out why.

"I think you should go now, Mr. Anderson. I have a lot to do tonight, and I'd like to get settled in," she said tightly. She stood across the room from him, her arms crossed, looking like she wanted to say a whole lot more.

Lucas finally stepped away from the wall and started walking to her. He was taking his time, in no hurry for the conversation they were about to have. She took a step back as he got closer.

"Mr. Anderson," she emphasized his name, "last night was a mistake. It shouldn't have happened, and there won't be a repeat performance. I'm sorry if you think you deserve it or that I'm going to roll over on my back in appreciation of your family's generosity, but I'm not some cheap hooker," she finished.

He knew the look in his eyes had to be terrifying, because she staggered back a step, which inflamed his temper even more. He'd never before hit a woman, and he never would, though if anybody could push him close, it would be her.

Lucas was angrier than he could ever remember being. He had to stay where he was because he feared he might strangle her if he got too close. How dare she think he expected her to pay back his corporation's generosity with her body! *She* was the one who was out for the ultimate prize – *him*! She hadn't been innocent when she was crying out his name in pleasure. She'd wanted him just as badly as he'd wanted her.

He stood glaring at her for a couple of minutes before he was finally calm enough to speak. "I told you earlier we had to talk about a few things, which we still need to talk about. But right now, let's straighten out those comments you just made. I have never paid for sex, in any form, in my life. Any woman I've taken to my bed has come *willingly*, and when she left, she was still begging for more. Last night you were just as willing to jump into bed with me, as I was to be there with you. There were two of us entwined in those sheets, and I refuse to take all the blame."

He saw the fear drain from her eyes as anger took its place. As his words continued slashing at her, she reached up to slap him, but he caught her hand before it connected. "I warned you, I'd only let you get away with that once," he said with a smirk.

He then yanked her into his arms and crushed his lips to hers. He was so angry the kiss was almost bruising in its intensity. He wasn't gentle as he willed her to surrender to him. He grabbed her hair and yanked her head back so he had easier access, his body pulsing with unleashed desire.

She fought against him for a few seconds and then she was kissing him back just as passionately. When he knew he had her full surrender, he pushed her away, though it took every ounce of control he had, to do it. Her eyes were glazed over with passion, and her anger had turned to need.

They stood at a standstill, panting heavily, each fighting extreme emotions. "Sit down, Amy," he finally said, a bit calmer as he walked over to the sofa. She didn't want to face his wrath if she continued to defy him.

◊◊◊◊◊◊

As reality started setting back in, Amy berated herself. She told him she wouldn't be doing anything with him and then, with only one touch of his lips, all rational thought ceased, and she could do nothing but pull him closer. She was beginning to realize there was a thin line between love and hate. She wasn't nearly as antagonistic toward Lucas as she wanted to be.

The more she was around him, the more she noticed the attractive things about him, not just his great looks. What was even more attractive than his looks, though, was the way he talked with other employees and how willing he was to lend a helping hand. Maybe she'd pre-judged him too soon and that was what had caused them to be so unfriendly toward each other. She knew she'd been giving off a negative attitude from the first day she started. She was willing to make a change. She didn't want to get involved with him in a relationship, but she could respect him as a boss.

She finally figured she may as well get this over with, so she sat in the chair opposite him. "I'm physically attracted to you. It doesn't mean anything, though; I meant what I said earlier. Last night shouldn't have happened. It was just a moment of weakness for me. I don't want to lose my job, and I don't want to have a cheap affair with my boss. We need to remain professional from now on," she stated in what she hoped was a professional tone.

He looked at her like she'd lost her mind. "I agree with you, Ms. Harper," he said, reverting to her last name. "Last night shouldn't have happened. But we need to deal with the consequences of the night. I forgot to use protection, which is a first for me. I know you were a virgin and most likely not on birth control," he finally stated. "I don't neglect my responsibilities, so if you're pregnant, I need to know as soon as you do. I won't have a child of mine raised without me. We would marry immediately. Do you understand?"

Amy was so stunned by Lucas's words, she didn't reply for several heartbeats. She wouldn't have thought it was something he'd even consider. She would've assumed in the case of an unplanned pregnancy, he'd ask her to have an abortion. She never would, but she knew many men wouldn't want the responsibility. The more she thought about it, though, the more it made sense he'd do what he considered the right thing – to take care of his child. He came from a loving family, who'd never deny one of their own.

Amy took a few deep breaths before speaking to Lucas. She repeated to herself that she couldn't afford to lose her job, and if she was pregnant she couldn't afford for him to know about it. He could easily prove he could take better care of the child. She didn't need, nor did she want, a man in her life. She needed to focus on herself. She'd watched her mother go through more men than anyone could count. She'd also watched those men abuse her mother on a daily basis. It was only her will for survival that had spared her from the same abuse. She'd learned at a young age to hide when her mother's many friends came over. She hadn't yet met a man who could be trusted.

"Are you going to just stand there and glare at me, or are you going to behave like a grown-up and talk?" he snapped.

"First of all, just because I'm an employee of yours doesn't give you the right to speak to me the way you are. Secondly, I'd never marry you, for any reason, especially not to torture any child of mine," she said coldly.

"If there's a child, you damn well…" Lucas began demanding of her again, but she interrupted him.

"If there was a child, it would be mine and mine alone. This isn't the old days where a woman has to do a man's bidding. But a child isn't something you have to worry about. I've already checked my calendar, and there's nothing to fear. Last night was a mistake. I've been dating a man for about a year and have been reluctant to take that last step. Since being with you wasn't too uncomfortable, I can now cement our relationship," she lied.

There was a stealthy look on Lucas's face as he walked slowly toward her. She remained firmly planted, not backing away again. She'd show strength, even though she was shaking uncontrollably on the inside.

Without any words, Lucas bent down and her head back, moving his face to within an inch of hers. He remained frozen in place until she began quivering with need. "So, last night was just a test run for you and your boyfriend," he said in a voice so quiet it was far more frightening than if he'd been yelling. She could feel the coiled power running through his arms.

She wasn't afraid of him hitting her. She was far more afraid he'd kiss her again. Her resistance was at an all-time low, and if he took her lips again, she'd end up begging him not to stop. The heat kept pooling in her body in anticipation of just that happening.

"I don't appreciate being used, Ms. Harper. Not at all. I really don't appreciate you lying to my face. Last night may have meant nothing to you, but while I was hard and deep inside your body, there was no other man on your mind. You were quivering for me and only me. When you lay with this boyfriend of yours, my face will be what you see. He won't make you quiver the way I did. He won't make you scream out in pleasure. He certainly won't have you so satisfied, your body will just give out." He paused for a long moment as her heart thundered and her legs squeezed together, trying to relieve the unbearable ache he was causing with nothing but his words. "You can think about that."

He pushed away from her and walked out of the apartment.

Amy waited until she heard the door shut before she allowed herself to lose her composure. Once she heard the click of the latch connecting, she slumped against the wall, her knees giving out as she slid down it. Then, she allowed herself a good cry.

Why had she let this happen? If she'd just taken her bath later and not been standing there in only a towel…If only she could've been able to say no, then maybe – just maybe – they'd be able to occupy the same room without snapping at each other, or trying to rip each other's clothes off. They could've even possibly stayed professional. Even as she thought it, she knew it was a fantasy. The fierce attraction was just too strong, even from the first day.

She remained in the same spot on the hardwood floor for more time than she should, crying and feeling sorry for herself. Finally, she got up. She wouldn't let this affect her any longer. She'd go to work with her shield of armor on. It was the smart thing to do.

She'd been smart for the first twenty-four years of her life. She'd have to forgive her one lapse in judgment. Everyone was allowed to make a mistake once in a while.

Chapter Twelve

Amy had mixed feelings going into work on Monday. She was floating on clouds because her new car had been delivered the night before, and she loved driving it. It was an exhilarating feeling – controlling the beautiful machine and knowing she'd never have to fight the crowds on public transportation again. There'd definitely been a few times of terror on the bus when she'd been approached by some less than respectable people.

She was terrified, on the other hand, of the work environment when stepping through those double doors. Was Lucas going to cause a scene? Was he going to send her packing? Could he fire her? He couldn't let her go just because of their physical relationship.

Lucas could, however, fire her for not being good enough at her job. She was already nervous about how well she performed in the position. She parked the car and headed inside. She'd just have to see how the day went. There was nothing she could do about it, so she'd have to do what she could and go from there.

The elevator doors chimed and opened to Tom's smiling face. "I was wondering when you were going to get here. I've been bouncing in my seat for a half hour," he said with no time for hellos.

Amy sighed. "Hey, Tom. If you've been bouncing in your seat for a half hour, then you were here an hour early because I'm a half hour early," she replied. He threw an arm around her shoulders and led her to his desk.

"Okay, Amy, time to spill. What happened? You totally ditched me this weekend. The way the boss was acting on Friday night, I didn't even know if you'd be here this morning," he whined.

"Everything's fine, Tom. The boss and I just had a little misunderstanding. I promise I'll fill you in later, but I need to get started on my work before the aforementioned person walks in and has a reason to fire me for being a slacker," she said while walking to her office.

Tom trailed along with her. "You're here early. You can't get into trouble for chatting with me on your own time."

"I don't think any time we're in these offices is our own. Please, just let me get to work, and we'll go out for happy hour tonight, I promise," she said pushing him out of her office.

Amy was busy at her desk when Lucas came in two hours later. *It must be nice to be the boss and show up when you feel like it*, she thought with attitude, and then regretted it immediately. She wasn't some high school ex-girlfriend who was going to think petty thoughts. What he did on his own time was his business – definitely not hers.

"Ms. Harper, I need you to come in here, please," he said over the intercom, making a cold sweat break out on her brow. She wiped her forehead and grabbed her notebook, locking her knees tight so they wouldn't tremble.

With as much composure as she could fake, she stepped through their connecting doors and approached his desk. He was on the phone, with his back to her, as he peered out his window at the spectacular city view.

She waited several minutes, too nervous to sit down, but very unsteady on her feet, as her entire body wanted to shake.

Finally, he hung up the phone and turned in her direction, his face a blank mask. She blinked as their eyes connected. She thought she detected a surge of fire in his eyes, but he blinked and it was gone, making her think it was nothing more than her imagination.

"Have a seat. I need to dictate some files for you to type up," he said in his most professional tone.

She shakily sat as she got ready to take notes. He started speaking, and soon she was engulfed in work, not having time to worry about anything other than correctly jotting his words.

"Thank you – that will be all. I'll be out of the office the rest of the day, so send them to me through email by closing tonight."

Lucas sat in his chair and turned back to his computer to type something, dismissing her. She sat a moment longer, then finally got back up and walked to her office.

She slumped in her chair, then let out a relieved breath. It looked like he really was going to act as if nothing had happened. She was both relieved, and irrationally, a bit hurt.

She immediately began typing his letters, and the day quickly passed. He left before lunch, finally giving her a chance to breathe. It wasn't easy to do when he was only a thin door away from her.

The rest of the day passed with no more incidents. Lucas communicated with her strictly through email and by the time five o'clock rolled around, her mood had considerably lifted.

"My computer's shut down, the phones are switched over, and if you don't do the same, I'm going to be forced to physically carry you from the room," Tom said as he walked into her office and sat on the desk.

"How do you ever get a job when you're more interested in running out the door than doing actual work?" she teased him.

"Honey, I get the jobs because of my bubbly personality. Everyone wants me to answer their phones," he replied with a suggestive wink.

"You're just what the doctor ordered, Tom. I need loud music, deep fried food, and lots of soda," Amy said as she turned off her computer.

Tom jumped off the desk, and took her coat before she could. He held it out, and she smiled as she slipped her arms inside. He was such a great guy. It really was too bad he was gay. She'd love to have a man like him in her life.

Well, if she was dating, that is.

"Thank you, Tom. You're a peach."

"Tell that to my ex. He said I was flirting way too much. I told him there was a big difference between flirting and being friendly. Some people are just over the top jealous. Who has time for all that drama?"

"Amen. Now, let's go before Mr. Anderson shows up with an all-night project," she said with a laugh, but she wasn't far off from the truth. The man seemed like he could work day and night, not even stopping to eat or sleep.

"Honey, the only all night project Lucas would have in mind wouldn't involve me, unfortunately. You, on the other hand, could probably burn his midnight oil, anytime," Tom taunted.

Amy smacked his thick bicep before resting her arm in his, and following him to the elevator. It opened quickly and they made their way from the building.

They arrived at their favorite place, early enough to still find a seat. After putting in an order, Tom stared at her expectantly.

"What?"

"Don't play stupid with me. I've been waiting all weekend long. You conveniently had to eat lunch in the office today, so now I want all the gory details. Don't you dare leave a single thing out," Tom demanded.

Amy contemplated lying to him, but since she couldn't lie worth beans, she knew she'd be wasting her breath. Besides, she really did need someone to talk to, and she knew her secrets would be safe with him.

"Okay, but be warned, it's a long story…" she said. He just raised his brows expectantly and rested his chin on his folded hands, letting her know without words but nonetheless dramatically, he had all night.

Amy finally spilled it all – from the fireworks between them, starting the very first day, to the exceptional sex, and finally to the scene in her apartment. Tom's eyes were wide as he stared at her in shocked delight.

"Say something," she demanded when he continued sitting there with his mouth hanging open.

"Oh my, my, that was hot with a capital H. I'd have killed to have been a fly on the wall when all those sparks were going off. How in the world did you make it to the ripe old age of twenty-four without losing your innocence in the backseat of some teenager's muscle car?"

"Out of everything I just told you, *that's* the question you have for me?"

"Well, yeah. I can't believe you were a virgin. Did it hurt?"

Amy may have found the conversation weird with any other person, but she was already used to Tom's no-holds-bar attitude. He didn't hold anything back – not ever.

"Yes, for about two seconds, then it was just…I don't even…well, incredible," she sighed.

"Oh my," Tom answered, picking up the drink menu to fan his face. She couldn't help it – she laughed, really laughed, for the first time in weeks. She should've called Tom on Sunday and had him come over. She would've felt much better coming into work the next day.

"Thanks, Tom. I needed to get that off my chest, and I really needed to laugh," she said as her eyes stung with emotion.

"I love you, Amy, and I'll be there for you anytime, day or night. Now, you have to remember that for when I show up on your doorstep at three in the morning with my own broken heart."

"My door will always be open," she promised.

"Apparently, you slut," he said with a laugh, taking any sting from his joke. "I'd give a million dollars if Lucas would press me against a wall."

"You don't even have a hundred dollars, so you're out of luck."

"You like to crush my dreams, don't you?" he said as he flopped back in his seat.

Their food arrived and they continued to banter. By the time they left, it was getting late, and Amy arrived home in a much better mood than when she'd left that morning. She began feeling optimistic that her world would smooth out. She fell asleep with a smile still on her face.

Chapter Thirteen

Amy stepped into the elevator, fear and some unnamed emotion constricting her chest. She needed to talk to Tom. She couldn't tell him over the phone, so she'd been edgily waiting since the night before, making it impossible for her to sleep.

She was in her fifth month as Lucas's assistant, and she loved her job, well the work part of her job, at least. She knew what she was doing, and was confident in her abilities, now. Esther had stopped by several times over the months and praised her progress, saying it was as if Amy had been with the company for ten years instead of a few short months. The two of them had grown close, and Amy never turned her down when she wanted to go have lunch or watch a movie.

She had two great friends now. Three, if she counted Joseph, who stopped by at least once a week to see how she was doing. He insisted on taking her to lunch, telling her she was too skinny and needed some meat on her bones before she was blown away by a strong wind. He was a wise man – it was never a bad thing to tell a woman she was too skinny. He'd obviously been happily married many years, and not only that, but listened to his wife.

Lucas was strictly professional with her. He'd give Amy her work-assignments, with very little talk between them, and then he'd leave her alone. He never lingered but was always courteous.

She often found her gaze following him as he left the room, more often than it should, and she was in no way over her crush on him, but she was doing great at masking it. He'd been nothing but professional, which was what she wanted – at least what she should want.

Her disappointment each time Lucas left the room, was a big give-a-way in how she truly felt. She'd even tried going on a date with a guy from accounting, but that had been a disaster. He'd bored her to tears, and when he'd kissed her at the end of the night, she'd felt not even the tiniest smidgen of passion.

It seemed almost nightly that she'd wake up in the early hours of the morning with Lucas's name on her lips – her body wet and ready. She was grateful he was keeping his distance, because she'd never have the willpower to push him away if he made a move.

Her hormones were all over the place – at least she knew why now.

She had no other man to compare Lucas to, but she couldn't imagine lovemaking to be any better than what she'd had with him. She seemed to be in a constant state of aching, her body desiring what her mind said she didn't need. Why couldn't it just be easy? Why Lucas?

If she was going to take the plunge into the relationship world, work past her fear of men, then why couldn't it be a guy like Bob in accounting. Sure, he was boring, but he was safe, secure, and easy. He wouldn't make her blood pressure spike. He'd be easy, mellow – so why not him?

She knew why not. She may think she didn't want passion, but one taste was all it had taken to change her. One taste and it was like a drug – she had to have more. Some days were easier than others, and she knew today was just going to be one of those hard days.

Amy had put off taking a pregnancy test for too long because she already knew the answer. She'd been dealing with morning sickness for two months, and there were subtle changes in her body. She was naturally small, so most wouldn't notice the tiny bump on her lower stomach, but she did. She finally broke down and took the test, then threw it in the garbage. She'd already known the answer was *yes*.

The doors to the elevator opened and she stepped out, making a beeline to Tom's desk. He was on the phone, so she impatiently tapped her foot while waiting for him. He held up a finger and silently mouthed her an apology. He could obviously see she *really* needed to talk to him.

"I'm glad you're here early, Ms. Harper. Can you come to my office?" Lucas asked as he approached the desk.

Amy sent Tom a panicked look, but he was busy on the phone. There was nothing he could do to save her anyway. It wasn't like Lucas knew anything. She didn't know what she was going to do, but she couldn't tell him – even though she knew how wrong that was.

"Yes, of course, Mr. Anderson," she finally replied just as Tom hung up the phone. She mouthed 'traitor' at him as she walked behind Lucas.

Tom sent her a questioning look, but now she'd have to wait even longer to talk to him. There was no way she was taking a chance of Lucas overhearing their conversation.

"Let me stop in my office and grab my notepad," Amy said as they came to their doors.

"You won't need it. Go ahead and put your purse and coat away, then come in," Lucas said as he went through his own doorway.

Amy took her time putting her belongings away. She knew Lucas wasn't patient, but she was running on barely any sleep, and her heart was racing. She needed to speak to her friend, get some perspective, not sit in front of Lucas, taking in his scent, looking in his bright blue eyes, and fighting the urge to jump in his lap.

Amy slowly walked in Lucas's office, hoping the conversation wouldn't take long. She wasn't ready to face him yet, not after taking that test. She never should've done that during the week. What was she thinking?

She was surprised when she found him standing by his window. He was just staring out of it, his hands behind his back as he looked down on the morning fog blanketing the Seattle lights. She stood near his desk, not knowing if she should say something or not.

"I have a business trip next week and I need you to come with me," he said, still not turning around.

Amy's heart started thumping. She hadn't gone on any trips with him yet, and he'd left many times over the last few months. She wondered what this one was all about, and why he needed her there all of a sudden.

"Where to?" she finally asked, not that it mattered. All that really mattered was the fact that she'd be alone with him, completely alone.

"It's in Australia. We have a vineyard there, and we've been having problems. It seems someone's purposely trying to sabotage our crops. It's taken many years to develop our great reputation for exceptional products, but one bad shipment could destroy all that," Lucas said as he finally turned. Amy could see the frustration he was feeling, but she still didn't see why she needed to go with him.

"This could take a couple of weeks and I need an assistant. I've been taking Esther on trips with me, but she's finally put her foot down and refuses to travel anymore, so I need you to go," he said, obviously figuring out she was confused.

At his words, she felt red-hot anger boil up inside her. He'd been going behind her back and not allowing her to do her job. She'd thought she was doing so well, when all along, he hadn't trusted her.

She felt betrayed, which was a strange emotion to be feeling over a job.

She still hadn't said a word when he spoke again.

"Look, Amy, none of this had to do with your work performance. Let's just leave it at that," he said as he ran his fingers through his hair.

"I see," she replied stiffly, though she didn't see at all.

"You are so unbelievably naïve. I can see you're angry and hurt that I didn't ask you to come along. Do you really want me to spell it out?" he practically bellowed.

"No, I'm fine," she responded, thinking it was time to leave. She was obviously ticking him off.

"I didn't take you, because I knew the minute the jet got in the air, we'd end up in my very large and comfortable bed…and we wouldn't be sleeping," he said, looking right into her shocked eyes.

Amy gasped at his boldness. It didn't get any more black and white than that, she figured.

"Well, I…uh…see," she stuttered as she took a step back.

"I have a meeting to go to. We'll finish this conversation later," he said, dismissing her. The way his words were spoken, were uttered like a threat, though. She had no doubt they were getting closer to a confrontation.

She couldn't figure out if she was more afraid or excited by the prospect.

She quickly retreated to her office, where she spent the rest of the day on her computer. She didn't get a moment alone with Tom as Lucas sent her more and more work. She plugged along until Tom came in and jumped on her desk.

"Amy, it's late, and I'm more than ready for happy hour. Come, girl. Let's whisk you away from here."

"I'm sorry, Tom. I didn't realize what time it was. It's been an unusually stressful day. I've been trying to talk to you since this morning, but then I got swamped," she said as the stress of the night before came crashing back down on her.

"Well, never fear, the day is over, and I'm going to take you out to paint the town," he said, practically bouncing in his seat.

"First off, Tom, it's a weeknight, and not all of us can stay up until three in the morning and then function the next day. More importantly, though, I really need to talk with you somewhere quieter than our usual hang out," she said, trying to keep her voice low.

"If intimacy's what you want, then that's what you'll get. I know this incredible club I haven't taken you to before. We'll go there, have a few drinks and then we can both browse for hot guys. They come in right out of the office, and look fine in their business attire," he said with a whistle.

Amy couldn't help but laugh. It was impossible to stay worried when she was in Tom's presence. He was just so full of life, and he had a way of easily making her see the positive side of things.

"I'm game. It couldn't hurt to meet my future prince charming," she joked, not meaning it in the least. Her thoughts tried to turn to Lucas, sitting only one room away, but she refused to let him creep into her mind.

She had to vent to Tom, and the reality was that she wouldn't be dating for a very long time, if ever, because in about six months, she'd have a newborn baby.

◊◊◊◊◊◊

Lucas was in his office, with the connecting door cracked open, and heard the exchange between Amy and Tom. He was surprised at the jealousy coursing through him. He didn't like how easily she laughed with Tom, and he sure as hell didn't like the idea of her picking up on other men.

He'd never felt jealousy before meeting Amy, and he was stunned by the tugging in his gut. He'd already convinced himself there was no way they could be a couple, so why would it matter who she went out with. He shouldn't feel anything toward her, but even after months, he couldn't stop thinking about her – nonstop, it seemed.

He sat a little straighter in his chair. He was going out of his mind, which would amuse his brothers to no end. He laid his head in his hands and waited for her to leave. He had no complaints with her work. She'd learned more each day and was doing an excellent job.

He'd entertained the idea of firing her, but had thrown the thought out immediately. He couldn't let her go, not yet. Maybe he'd be able to eventually. He'd get over the strange turmoil his body was going through, and then be able to work with her just fine. If he didn't soon, he'd have no choice but to move her to another division.

Even the thought of her going to another part of the building made his muscles tense.

Lucas got up and decided to go out for a drink. He'd find himself a nice distraction for the night. Any woman would be happy to come home with him. He was Lucas Anderson, after-all. He'd bet there were several messages for him already. He just had no desire to call any of the women he normally did when his body was alerting him he'd put off pleasure too long.

Even though the thought of any woman besides Amy, wasn't even slightly appealing, he'd just have to work through it. He knew, once he stepped out, he'd begin to feel better, and he was sure some pretty thing would catch his eye – at least enough for one night.

Lucas went to a club he hadn't been to for a while and sat down. He ordered a drink and was there no more than five minutes when an exceptionally attractive redhead sat next to him. She gave him the look that said, *Buy me a drink, and you can take me home.*

He threw back his drink before turning to give her his full attention. "Can I buy you something?" He placed all the charm at his disposal in his voice.

She rubbed her finger up his arm. "I'll have a dirty martini, Sugar."

He bought her several drinks and listened as she tried to charm him over an almost endless hour. He knew all he had to do was crook his finger and she'd be in his car, going home with him. He was trying to will himself to do just that, but he knew it wasn't going to happen.

Lucas felt zero desire for the woman who's curves were on display to anyone wanting a clear view. "Thank you for your company this evening," he said as he threw several bills on the table. "Goodnight."

"In case you haven't noticed the signals, baby, I'm offering to go with you. Trust me, you won't regret a night, or more, with me," she said with a voice of utter seduction.

Lucas just looked at her for a moment, and then turned and walked away. He'd felt nothing. Normally, he would've taken her home and accepted what she was offering. A no-strings-attached night of great sex.

He would've loved to do just that, except for the fact that the entire time he'd been sitting there, the only woman he'd been able to think about was Amy. She was soft and feminine, not trampy and brash. She was also the greatest sexual experience he'd ever had. He wasn't getting over her.

He walked out of the club and stood next to his car, breathing in the almost icy air. When his body was still burning several minutes later, he knew nothing was going to sate it, nothing but a curvy blonde, who'd somehow, turned his world upside down since meeting her.

He quickly pulled away from the club and made it home in record time. He parked and immediately noticed Amy's car. He was surprised by the feeling of relief washing through him at knowing she was home. Of course, that was short-lived when the thought occurred to him there could be a man with her. She *had* been going out looking for someone.

Suddenly, he had to know if she was with someone, or by herself. He knew if he was with her one more night he could get over his strange infatuation with her. He needed to take her again.

Lucas was in a rush to get to her apartment. She still hadn't figured out the other unit on their floor was his. He'd been very careful about when he came and went. He hadn't wanted her to know he was that close.

The doors opened, and Fred looked up from his paper. "Hello, Mr. Anderson. How was your day, sir?"

"It was great, Fred. Do you know if Ms. Harper is in her apartment?"

"Ms. Harper is currently in the pool, sir."

"Thank you, Fred. Have a nice night." Lucas quickly changed direction.

If she was already swimming, she must've only been out for about a half hour. That was a quick night. Maybe the pickings had been slim with it being a weeknight.

It was either that, or maybe she was planning to go out later when the real nightlife began. Well, she could put those thoughts on hold, because he'd decided she was spending the night with him.

He went into the men's locker room and changed.

Lucas came out of the locker room and stood unnoticed for several minutes as Amy swam in the pool alone. She looked phenomenal in her bright red bikini. It showed her curves off to perfection. He wanted to take her right then, but anticipation was part of the fun. When she was swimming away from him, he dove effortlessly into the pool.

He made little noise, and Amy didn't notice his entrance. She turned around and was making her way back in his direction. He waded in the water, making sure he was in her direct line, anticipating the impact.

She didn't disappoint as her body hit up against him. She went down for a second, then quickly came up sputtering water. "Oh, excuse me," she said as she started to look up. When she noticed who she'd run into, she froze. "What are you doing here?"

"I thought it was a great time for a swim," he replied and took off at a fast pace across the pool, his body energized. He felt better at that moment than he had in months. He smiled all the way to the other side of the pool, hoping she'd accept his challenge. He'd see if she ran away, or stayed and sparred.

Chapter Fourteen

Amy stayed in place, holding on to the edge of the pool, trying to decide if she wanted to finish her laps or get out. She was about to exit the pool when she decided she wasn't letting him chase her away. She started her laps again and finished her set amount. When Amy climbed out, Lucas was still swimming.

She went over to the hot tub, which was a part of her routine. She sat down and let the warm water wash her worries away.

Amy knew the moment Lucas joined her. Her head was back and her eyes closed, but she could feel him. She didn't say a word. She pretended he didn't exist. If he wanted to make her uncomfortable he was doing a great job, but she wasn't going to show it.

At least, she thought she was doing a great job concealing all trace. Her body could hide nothing in her swimsuit, though. If she would've known he was eyeing her nipples at that moment, she would've melted into the water.

She stayed in the tub for a few more minutes and then decided enough was enough. She climbed out quickly and wrapped herself in the towel she had nearby. She didn't say anything, just headed to the locker room to change.

After taking her time changing and pulling herself back together, she finally emerged from the locker room. When she saw Lucas standing at the front desk, she sent him a glare before practically stomping to the elevators. She didn't even care if she looked like a child throwing a tantrum. She certainly couldn't get over her infatuation with him if he was in her face at work and home.

"How was the pool, Ms. Harper?" Fred asked.

"It was just what the doctor ordered," she answered. "I'm bushed, though. I'll see you tomorrow," she told him as she pushed the elevator button. No matter how much Lucas was irritating her, she'd never take it out on Fred.

The second the doors opened, she stepped inside and quickly pushed her floor's number. When it started to close, she breathed a sigh of relief, until Lucas jumped in at the last second.

"Is there something you needed to speak to me about?" she threw at him. "Or do you just follow all employees to their homes and act like a stalker?"

"Stalker?" he questioned. "I happen to live here too, Amy, or did you not notice my parking place?"

"You live here?" she asked, dumbfounded. Why in the world would he live in the apartments when he could live anywhere he wanted? She looked at him without knowing how to reply to this latest information.

She hadn't seen him around the building, and she'd assumed he had his own parking place because he did a lot of business there.

"Yes." It took her a moment to realize he'd answered her question.

"Why would you live in an apartment when you can have a house?" She let her curiosity overrule her need to not speak to him.

"I prefer the apartment because I'm a busy man, and here I don't have to worry about anything like house maintenance," he answered.

She snorted. Like he'd have to worry about the upkeep, anyway. He'd hire minions to do any of his grunt work. He wasn't the type of man who'd pull the lawnmower out of the garage and take it for a spin around the yard. She shrugged and went back to ignoring him.

The door opened on her floor and he stepped out with her. It was at that moment she realized he was who lived in the other apartment on her floor. How had she not figured that out in the months she'd been there? They worked and lived in the same place, and she had no idea he was living a few feet away.

She was going to have an even worse time sleeping now, knowing how close he was, and yet how very far away.

She picked up her step and almost ran to her door. She was having difficulty with the lock when he stepped up and took the key. His body brushed hers, and she just about jumped out of her skin.

He felt so good against her, if only for a moment. He took her key and slipped it into the lock, rubbing against her the entire time. His scent was intoxicating, making her body long for his touch.

The door finally opened, and she slipped inside, turning, with her hand out for the key. He looked at her for a moment and slipped in, shutting the door behind him. How much was she supposed to take? Her willpower was slipping quickly.

"May I use your bathroom? Then we need to talk." He didn't wait for an answer. He just headed to her bathroom. She leaned against the door and tried to strengthen her willpower. She could handle this. She handled the stress of being in the same room as him, fine at work. Her apartment was no different, she tried to convince herself. She really, really wanted a stiff drink right then. She knew she couldn't, but she could wish.

◊◊◊◊◊◊

Lucas took a deep breath while walking to the bathroom. He could be civilized. Maybe they could even start some kind of relationship. He wasn't good with being in a commitment, but he was willing to give it a try. He couldn't stop thinking about her, so there had to be something there worth pursuing.

He may have jumped to conclusions about her, anyway. She wasn't anything like he'd originally thought her to be. He smiled sheepishly. He didn't normally admit to being wrong about anything, not even to himself.

The two of them would have a nice, reasonable, adult conversation, and then he could take her to bed without feeling guilty about it.

Lucas was feeling good with his decision as he finished up and washed hands. He turned around to leave, and that's when his world suddenly stopped spinning.

He almost missed it.

In her garbage can was a pregnancy kit box. *What the hell?* He'd never felt as scared as he did while reaching for that box. He looked inside and found the little stick. There were two lines on it. What did that mean?

He quickly read the back of the box. His entire world changed in an instant. She was pregnant. Holy hell, she was pregnant! Had she planned the pregnancy? How could she have? He couldn't even think, as he stood staring at the pregnancy test. A few of his ex-girlfriends had tried to trap him into marriage by claiming they were pregnant by him, when he was already onto their game. He'd deftly avoided them. Somehow, though, his assistant had gotten pregnant the one and only time they'd had sex. He was angry with himself and even angrier with her. He knew it wasn't logical, but his emotions ran higher than his logic at that moment.

Many women had tried to trap him into giving them his name, and all the money that came along with it, but none had succeeded until now.

Well, I better get out there to the future Mrs. Anderson, he thought bitterly. Lucas took a few extra moments to compose his face before walking back out to her.

Amy was sitting on the couch when he entered the living room. She didn't look at him, which he was grateful for because he was having a heck of a time composing his features.

"I'll be right back. There are a couple of phone calls I need to make," was all he said as he walked past her and through the front door. He picked up the phone as soon as he sat down in his home office.

"I need to speak with my father?" Lucas asked without any preambles.

"One moment, Lucas." He was put through a minute later.

"Hello, son, how are you?"

"I'm getting married, and I want it done this week, next at the latest. I'm busy with work, so can you take care of the arrangements? Normally, I'd have my assistant do it, but since she's the bride, I need someone else."

"You're getting married to Amy? I'm so happy for you, son. She's a real keeper. I'll take care of all the arrangements. We'll shoot for Friday then, either this week or next?" he said with no surprise in his voice. Lucas was taken aback a little by his father's attitude. He was in too much shock to be suspicious, though.

"Friday will be fine. Amy's pregnant, so I want to keep this discreet, please. Just you and mom, and Amy and me," he said cautiously. He knew his father's love of throwing parties, and he didn't want a mass of people there to witness the charade.

Lucas finished speaking with his father and then called his attorney to draw up a prenuptial agreement, making sure he was protected.

The phone calls took him an hour. He finished and then drank a shot of bourbon. “Okay, Amy, let’s get this over with,” he mumbled out loud. He knew he was in for a fight once he told her they were getting married.

He walked back down the hallway and used the key he hadn’t given back to let himself in. Amy was still sitting in the living room. At first it looked like she hadn’t even moved, and then he noticed the bowl sitting on the table.

Well, he guessed her pregnancy hadn’t ruined her appetite. He took a closer look and didn’t see any differences at first. She was only a few months along, after all. The more he allowed himself to *really* look at her, the more the subtle changes became apparent. After all, he had seen her naked and knew every curve of her body. Her breasts seemed to be fuller, although she hid them well in her loose clothing. Instead of looking like she’d gained any weight, though, she seemed a bit slimmer. He didn’t know how that was possible.

“Why haven’t you told me you’re pregnant?” he asked.

She hesitated a few moments as she looked at him, her face losing all color. It was obvious he’d shocked her. She broke eye contact and quickly looked to the floor.

“I didn’t see that it was any of your business. My job performance hasn’t been affected by it, and in this day and age it’s nobody’s business if you’re a single mother or not. You can’t fire me for being pregnant.”

He stared at her, open-mouthed. None of his business? How the hell could she say that carrying his child was none of his business?

"You won't be a single mother, Amy, and you know that. I won't allow my child to be raised as a bastard. He'll have my name." His voice told her his way was the only way they were handling the situation. If she didn't like it, then too bad.

"This isn't your child." Amy looked directly at him as she spoke those words. There was no emotion in her voice. He stared at her, dumbfounded. Not his child? What was she talking about? He knew she'd been a virgin when he'd had sex with her. The timeline fit. Of course it was his child.

"If it's not my child, then whose is it?" He decided to see what she'd say. He was watching every move she made. There was no way she'd be able to come up with a story out of the blue.

"I told you I was in a relationship. It progressed, but he didn't want the baby, so we split up."

He saw the tiny flicker in her eyes as she lied. He knew she wasn't telling him the truth. He knew the baby was his, but he couldn't figure out why she'd tell him otherwise. What if he allowed her to convince him the baby wasn't his? He couldn't figure out what she'd gain by that.

"What kind of game are you playing, Amy? I don't get it. We both know the baby you carry is mine, so why would you lie to me about it?" In his confusion, he let down his guard and spoke softly to her, puzzled instead of angry.

"I'm not playing games with you, Lucas. This is my baby, and no one will take him, or her, from me."

She said almost pleadingly. “I’m telling you the truth. The child isn’t yours.”

Lucas finally understood why she was denying he was the father. She thought he’d actually take the child away. He was furious she thought so little of him – that he could rip a child from his mother. If she wanted to believe him a cold-hearted bastard, that’s what she’d get.

“Don’t worry, Amy. You’ll get to be a mother and *wife*. We’ll be married within two weeks, hopefully one. I’ve already made the arrangements.”

Lucas suddenly leaned down, trapping her between the couch and his arms. “Don’t get me wrong, though, my dear fiancée. If you try to cross me, or run away with my child, you’ll never see him again. Do I make myself clear?” he whispered in a deadly calm voice.

“Lucas, I’m sorry, but she isn’t yours. That night we had together was great, but…I moved on. I don’t know what else to tell you…”

“Fine, if you say the child isn’t mine, we’ll have a DNA test done tomorrow. The procedure will be somewhat painful for you, but will cause no harm to our child,” he said, calling her bluff.

Amy turned stark white at his words. He could tell she had no idea such a test existed. She probably figured he’d have been glad not to be the father. She obviously didn’t know him.

She started to speak, and then just gave up.

Game.

Set.

Match.

He smiled without humor. He knew getting married wasn't what either of them wanted, but there was no possible way he'd ever let another man raise his son or daughter, or even that he'd be a weekend parent. Amy was carrying his baby; therefore, the only solution was for them to wed. He'd never understood how a man could walk away from his family.

It wasn't something he'd do.

Lucas had enough for one night. "We'll finish this business tomorrow. Enjoy your last week as a single lady," was all he said before walking out the front door.

He calmly walked to his apartment and let himself in, discarding his jacket on the back of his couch, then heading straight to his liquor cabinet.

The night had begun with such promise. He should've been in her bed right then, with her calling out his name, not him downing a triple scotch.

He turned out his lights and walked into his bedroom, discarding his clothes wherever they fell, then climbed into his shower and stood beneath the hot spray.

What scared him the most about the entire situation was how calm he felt. He was getting married in a week, yet, he wasn't afraid. He was angry with her for not telling him – angry that he hadn't followed through and made sure she hadn't gotten pregnant.

What he wasn't angry about was making her his wife. The thought of lying next to her every night should terrify him, but instead, it sent a strange euphoria through his body. He couldn't get the image out of his head, of her body trembling, her head thrown back in ecstasy, as she shattered around him while he was buried deep inside her.

As the spray continued raining down on him, he became instantly hard, his body still in desperate need of release. He was tempted to march back down to her apartment and give them both what they really wanted.

A few more nights. You can wait a few more nights.

With a groan of frustration, he switched the water to cold, and then stood under the spray as a thousand tiny drops of water hitting his skin felt like razors. After a couple minutes, the water did its job and he climbed from the shower, shaking, but with his body under control – at least for a few minutes.

Chapter Fifteen

Amy collapsed on the sofa and allowed herself a good cry. How could she have ever fooled herself into thinking he'd believe her child wasn't his? Why hadn't she gotten rid of that test? If only she'd emptied her garbage, she could've kept her secret for a few more precious months – maybe even longer, if she'd found the right clothing.

After an incredibly long and trying day, Amy was done. Feeling defeated, she dragged herself back to her room and cried herself to sleep. Oblivion couldn't come soon enough.

The next morning, Amy awoke, feeling miserable. She ran to the bathroom and emptied her stomach's contents and then some. In the shower she threw up again. She was just starting into her second trimester. The morning sickness should have been subsiding.

She knew she was losing weight, as her clothes were hanging on her. She hadn't worried too much about it, as everything she'd read so far had shown morning sickness was a normal part of the first trimester.

She weakly sat on the floor of the tub as the steaming water washed over her. She threw up more, and when there was nothing left, she continued to dry heave. Amy turned off the water as the last of the liquid from her stomach washed down the drain.

She sat in the tub, shivering, but her body felt too exhausted to climb out. She was frightened by her sudden fatigue. "Please, God. Let nothing happen to my baby. I'll bear nine straight months of sickness, if you'll just spare my child," she quietly whispered.

With all her energy gone, climbing from the tub wasn't an option. In a last attempt, she reached deep inside for a small burst of strength and grabbed the nearby towels and draped them over her in an effort to keep warm.

She couldn't even get up to call into her job. She'd get fired for sure, as Lucas would assume she was a no call/no show in an attempt to avoid him.

She fell asleep as pure exhaustion washed through her entire body. She thanked the blackness, as she wouldn't have to feel the overwhelming cold and achiness anymore.

◊◊◊◊◊◊

Lucas paced his apartment, once again glancing at his watch. He'd decided to wait until Amy left, before going into work, himself. He'd put his guard on alert to notify him during the night – at any time – if she left the building. The employees of his company were loyal to him, as they were treated well. No questions were asked. They simply assured him he'd be notified.

When it was past the time they should've been to the office, and she still hadn't left the building, he was furious. So, she figured now that she was pregnant she could skip work. Over his dead body! She wasn't avoiding him to try and come up with more lies.

He marched over to her apartment and let himself in. She wasn't in the living room or kitchen. He was even more furious. *She hasn't even bothered getting out of bed*, he thought. Well, she'd gotten the husband, so he figured she didn't want to work any longer. Why work when you could get all you wanted for free?

He walked to her bedroom and swung the door open, ready to pull the covers off her and have a rip roaring fight. He needed to vent his anger, and she was the expected target. He was angry about everything, and he desperately needed something to take out his frustrations on.

When he opened her door and the bed was empty, he began to feel his first stirrings of unease. Had she left without him knowing? That wasn't possible. He had a secure building. She wasn't a prisoner, but his staff would've told him if she'd left. He double-checked his phone to make sure he hadn't somehow missed a call.

He turned to go into the living room when he noticed her bathroom door was shut. He walked over and listened for a moment. There was no sound from inside. Without thinking of her privacy, he opened the door and walked in.

Lucas was terrified when he saw her small body lying on the floor of the tub, covered by only a few small towels. Had she taken her life?

No!

He ran to the tub, dropping to his knees as he bent over the side. When he saw the slight movement in her chest, showing she was breathing, he felt his heart slow a bit, and released the breath he'd been holding. She was shivering, even in her sleep, and she had dark purple smudges underneath her eyes.

He took a good look at her and noticed how small she looked. She'd dropped significant weight. Weren't pregnant women supposed to gain weight? How hadn't he noticed the changes in her body?

That was an easy question to answer. He hadn't noticed because he'd done all he could to avoid looking at her too closely. He'd avoided her as much as possible so he didn't take her right there on her desk.

As he sat frozen beside her, shame consumed him. He knew no one could fake this kind of illness. He'd put her through too much the night before. She was in no condition to be yelled at, or threatened. Thinking back, he could see where she'd looked exhausted, and he hadn't cared. He'd only cared she was trying to fool him.

He could've handled the situation differently. That didn't mean he'd changed his mind on them getting married, it just meant, he possibly should've gone about it a different way. He'd learned often in life, though, that the only way to get what he wanted was to demand it.

Lucas wrapped his arms under her body and stood, lifting her from the tub. She immediately snuggled closer against him, seeking warmth, even in her sleep. The towels fell away, and his gut clenched in shock.

She'd lost even more weight than he'd first thought. She obviously wasn't having a good pregnancy. He should've been paying attention. He laid her on the bed and covered her, while her body curled into a tight ball. He noticed the slight bulge of her stomach for the first time just as she let out a soft moan of pain.

Wow, he thought, *that's my child*. The realization that he was going to be a father in six months slammed into him with such force, it took his breath away. Now that his anger had fled, the idea of a son was amazing. In six months, he'd be holding his baby. He'd be bouncing him on his knees and then later throwing balls with him.

Lucas was shocked to find he already loved his unborn child. He loved the precious baby growing inside her. He wouldn't let anything happen to him, or his mother.

Lucas called his family doctor, and then climbed into the bed and pulled Amy close. He simply wanted to warm her up. He needed to protect both of them. As long as he lived, he'd never forget the moment of terror at seeing her lying in the bottom of the empty tub. She was a part of his family now, her and the child she carried.

Nothing and no one could make him let go of them.

She curled around him and let out a sigh. After a few minutes, her shaking subsided. He continued to engulf her in his warm embrace and rubbed her back, willing her and his child to be fine.

When Lucas heard the doorbell ring, he let the doctor in, then stood back and waited while he pulled out his tools. Lucas was sure it was nothing more than morning sickness, because he couldn't imagine an alternative.

◊◊◊◊◊◊

"Amy? There you go. Open up your eyes. That's good. My name is Dr. Scott, and I'm going to check you over, okay? Do you know what happened this morning?" Amy awoke to the gentle voice and questions of the doctor. She had no idea how she'd gotten into her bed, but the warmth felt so good that she didn't even care to ask.

"I was throwing up all morning. It just wouldn't stop, so finally I climbed into the shower, hoping the spray would help. Then, I got light headed, and lost all my energy and couldn't get back out," she mumbled in a cracked voice. She finally looked around and noticed Lucas standing nearby.

"I don't know how I got here, or really what happened. I was just so cold and tired," she finished.

"Save your energy, Amy. We're going to make sure you and your child are okay," said the doctor, comforting her. Amy's eyes felt like they had a ten-pound weight on each lid and without another word she let them slowly close.

She felt him touching her and then felt a slight pinch, but the worst part of the whole exam was being uncovered periodically. She faded in and out of sleep. Finally, she heard the doctor quietly talking to someone. It felt more like a dream. Maybe it was.

"She'll be fine. She needs to be on bed rest until I get these tests back, but it looks like severe morning sickness, leading to dehydration. There's no bleeding, but she's undernourished. The baby seems to be fine. Your child takes from Amy what he or she needs, but Amy hasn't been able to eat enough to nourish herself. I'll want her to come to the offices in a day or two for an ultrasound, but it seems she's about three months along. Get a lot of fluids into her today, especially soup broths and juice. The more calories, the better."

"That's great, Scott. I appreciate you rushing over here so quickly. I'll see you on Friday." She heard fading steps as they left the room and finally the faint sound of a door shutting. She faded back into the blissfulness of sleep.

◊◊◊◊◊◊

Lucas paced the apartment after he called in and cancelled all appointments for the day. He wanted to shake Amy awake and force feed her, but the doctor told him the rest was just as important as food. Scott had given her sleeping aids and anti-nausea pills and told Lucas to keep an eye on her to make sure she ate and drank whenever she woke.

Each time she partially came to, Lucas practically force fed her. She mumbled complaints, but she took his administering.

By the time darkness hit, Lucas was exhausted. He went into the room and climbed in bed next to her. He pulled her close and fell into a deep and exhausted slumber. He felt that he could sleep an entire week with her in his arms.

Chapter Sixteen

Lucas was woken from a deep sleep by something stirring next to him. He slowly opened his eyes to find Amy next to him, bringing the events from the day before to the forefront of his mind. The two of them were facing each other, and she was staring at him with shock, embarrassment, and a bit of panic.

"Morning," he mumbled. "Did you sleep well?"

Her eyes opened wider at his casual words. He knew she was confused. He could see it. She was most likely wondering how they'd gotten into bed together, and more importantly, wanting to know if they'd done anything.

"Don't look so panicked - all we did was sleep. You were freezing all day and night until I climbed in bed and shared my body heat," he said lazily. It felt so natural waking next to her. He couldn't remember ever having slept so well. He hadn't woken up once during the night.

"Excuse me," she said as she tried to untangle herself from his body. "I…um, need to use the bathroom, please." Her cheeks turned red. He let her go, and she quickly jumped from the bed.

Lucas was glad to see some restored strength in her and was grateful he'd dressed her. He wouldn't have been able to handle watching her walk naked from the bed. Not after her body had been molded to his the entire night.

He continued lying there, not able to get out of the bed. He was wearing nothing but a pair of boxers that would show her the restraint he'd used in letting her go if she happened to walk out of the bathroom when he was still not dressed. When he heard the shower start, he finally moved, a bit disappointed she wasn't coming back to join him.

Amy was in the bathroom long enough to make Lucas worry. He was about to go in after her when the door finally opened. She was wearing the robe he'd seen hanging off the back of the door.

She took his breath away.

Even pale, underweight and makeup-free, she was spectacular. He was beginning to think it wasn't going to be a hardship, in the least, to wake up next to her every day. He thought they could actually make the marriage work.

As his gaze traveled down her oversized robe and rested on her covered belly, he was once again sobered to think his baby grew there. They were going to be a family. The thought scared him enough that he swiftly brushed past her and shut himself in the bathroom.

What was he doing? Yes, they needed to get married, but why was he getting so sentimental? They had an arrangement, one she hadn't technically agreed to yet, though he knew she would. She didn't have a choice.

Lucas turned the shower on and stood under the spray for ten solid minutes, not moving, just letting the hard jets ease the ache in his shoulders.

He was used to dealing with a great amount of stress, but since meeting Amy, his levels had tripled. It was either from his constant state of arousal, or the fact that he wanted to strangle her. She was…exasperating.

None of that mattered anymore, though, because she'd soon be his wife. He had to smile as he realized his life would never be dull again.

Lucas finished his shower, then strode from the steam filled room with only a towel covering him. As he walked into the bedroom, he found Amy sitting on a chair, lacing up a pair of her tennis shoes. She looked up and their eyes met, and Lucas instantly hardened, his towel not doing much to hide his desire.

"Um…I'll…um…let me get out of your way," Amy gasped as her eyes dilated. When her head dipped down and she looked at his predicament, then licked her lips, he nearly dropped to his knees.

Slowly he made his way to her chair, standing in front of her, his chest dripping water. She slowly leaned back, her head level with his stomach, causing a myriad of ideas to flash through his mind.

"If you weren't on strict orders to rest today, I'd take you over to that bed, slowly strip off the clothes you just put on, then lick your body from head to toe. Even the thought of doing that is causing me intense pain right now," he said, watching her reaction. She wasn't unaffected by the power pulsing between them.

Why he was torturing himself even more, he didn't know, but he was almost past the point of no return. It had been too long since he'd felt her in his arms, sunk inside her flesh, satisfied them both.

"I want you so badly," he whispered, his throat so tightly closed, it was hard for him to even speak.

Amy said nothing as her eyes moved down to the tent his erection was making of the towel. Tentatively, she reached her hand out, then ran a finger across the stiff point in the towel, making his knees almost buckle. Her hesitant touch was the biggest turn-on of his life.

He realized they'd made love so quickly the only time they'd been together, she hadn't even had time to see him, let alone do any exploring.

"We can't have sex, Amy, but we can lie in bed together," he said before ripping the towel from his body. His confidence soared as she gasped, her eyes never leaving his manhood.

He knelt before her, and started undoing the shoes she'd just put on, pulling them off, before running his hands up her legs to grip the soft curve of her hips. He pulled her to a standing position, her stomach pressing into his face.

He breathed in her scent as he slowly hooked his thumbs into the waistband of her sweats and began pulling them down her legs. Her hands moved to his shoulders and he felt tremors rack her body as he slid his fingers down the inside of her thighs.

He could touch her, taste her, explore her beautiful body, without hurting her. He had to do something, anything to relieve the pain he felt.

Her pants bunched at her feet, and he carefully lifted one foot, then the other, and tossed the pants somewhere behind him. She stood before him in a t-shirt that just barely skimmed the top of a pair of tiny lavender panties, barely covering her from his view.

His hands moved to her rounded backside, then tugged, making her stumble into him. He pushed his hands up and moved the t-shirt out of his way, so he could press his face against the tiny swelling of her stomach. His seducing tongue trailed her silky flesh, and a soft moan drifted to his ears as her hands tightened on his shoulders, and her knees began to shake.

He moved his arms down, supporting the back of her thighs as his mouth traveled across the curve of her stomach and he bit the elastic at the top of her panties. Moving lower, he carefully ran his tongue along the outside of the delicate lace, dampening the material as his hot breath drifted over the thin fabric.

"Lucas," she moaned, her entire body trembling. Slowly he moved back, getting to his feet, his arms supporting her the entire time.

When their eyes met, and he saw the intense lust pooling within them, he almost forgot he had to be careful with her – almost forgot his own name.

He lowered his mouth and gently kissed her, sliding his tongue along her lips, before slipping it inside the recesses of her mouth. Before he let the kiss go too far, he again stepped back, then lifted her into his arms and carried her to the bed.

He crawled in next to her, his hand immediately drifting to her stomach, then running down the outside of her thigh before coming back up on the inside. He stopped at the junction between her thighs, her moist heat already soaking her panties.

"I have to stop," he said as his finger slipped inside the fabric and he circled around her swollen flesh.

"Please don't," she sobbed, making him look up to see a tear falling down her face.

"Am I hurting you?" he asked as he immediately began pulling his finger away, terrified he'd gone too far.

"No, I need…please…so much pressure," she begged, her hands gripping the blankets.

Though he knew he may actually explode, he knew what she was asking. He pulled away long enough to grip her panties and remove them, then he pulled off her t-shirt and tossed it aside.

He took a moment to enjoy the view of her stretched out naked in front of him, her beautiful body glistening in the dim bedroom lights, her thighs open for his pleasure. He wanted so badly to sink inside her silken folds, but he wouldn't risk hurting her.

He could certainly pleasure her, though. He bent and took one of her pert nipples into his mouth, making her cry out his name.

Then he moved his hand down her body and started rubbing a circle around her swollen flesh. Her hips rose, pressing harder into his fingers as they worked her body.

Within a minute, she fell apart, her body shaking as she climaxed, her cries echoing across the bedroom. He slowed his rhythm, making sure to draw out her pleasure, as he lifted his head and swallowed the rest of her cries with his mouth. His erection was pulsing with its own need for release, but he tried to ignore it.

After several minutes she stopped shaking and her body relaxed. He was on his side, facing her, as he ran his hand upward and into her hair. She turned into him, pressing her hips against his, causing his throbbing member to press into her thighs.

He brought his lips back to hers, his kiss gentle, telling her everything he couldn't admit out loud. He was coming to the realization he cared about her, way more than he ever possibly imagined.

"Can I…I want to…um…touch you?" she tentatively asked, her face turning red at her request. His shaft jumped at her hesitant words.

Not able to speak past the desire clogging his throat, Lucas nodded his head, and then turned onto his back. He gripped her hand and placed it on his chest, then slowly pushed it lower.

He watched her face, as her eyes focused on their joined fingers, slowly moving across his quivering stomach. He took a deep breath, then guided her hand to the head of his arousal and then up and over it.

As she slowly moved her fingers across his skin, he gritted his teeth, chanting in his head that he could handle it. He didn't know how, but he had to.

He removed his hand from hers, letting her explore on her own, as he fisted his fingers into the sheets, holding on as if his life depended on it. He was too afraid he was going to grab her if he didn't hold himself down.

Her fingers softly trailed up and down his thick shaft, over and over again, circling around his stiff flesh as she became braver.

When his pleasure glistened on the tip of his erection, she ran her finger against it, then used his own fluid as lubrication as she tightened her fingers around him and started moving up and down his flesh.

"You're so soft, like satin, but so hard at the same time. It's…well, really beautiful," Amy whispered, her eyes not straying from his lower body.

The only reply he could give was a deep moan of pleasure as his body began to prepare itself for release.

His sound seemed to spur her on, because she shifted, getting a tighter grip on him as she quickened her movements, making his breath start escaping in pants.

"Amy, I can't…I'm going to cum if you don't stop."

"Yes, please do," she whispered, excitement lacing her tone.

"It's messy," he ground out, not wanting to horrify her.

Her only reply was to move down his body, and then he felt the pad of her tongue licking across the head of his straining erection. That was it – her tentative movements sent him over the edge, and he yelled out, as he felt the explosion start surging forward.

"Amy," he warned as her lips closed around the top of his arousal while her hand continued moving up and down.

Her reply was again non-verbal as she sucked him hard, the tip of her tongue sliding across his head.

His body tensed as his release washed through him, feeling like it started at the tip of his toes, and traveled all through his body, before exploding through his shaft.

As he felt the first wave of his pleasure leave him, Amy never let go, her mouth continuing to suck him even harder, if that were possible.

He looked down as his body continued releasing into her warm mouth. Her eyes were closed, pleasure consuming her face as she sucked on him. After several moments, his body fell back to the bed, completely sated.

Amy's lips relaxed, releasing his head as her fingers continued to trail up and down. She gently licked along the still sensitive flesh for a few more moments, touching him as he began to soften.

"So amazing…," she again muttered before she finally crawled up the bed. "Thank you."

He looked at her incredulously as she thanked him. What blew him away was that she was completely serious.

"No, really, the thanks are all on me," he said with a huge grin as he quickly reached out and grabbed her, flipping her onto her back and half covering her body with his, before he reached down and kissed her, hard.

When he lifted his head, they were both slightly breathless, but she had a glow in her cheeks that hadn't been there the day before.

"You're on bed rest, woman. Quit looking at me like that, or I'm going to forget," he warned, though a smile played on his lips.

She smiled at him before her eyes grew sleepy. With much more gentle movements, he flipped over on his back, and pulled her in tightly against him. She didn't hesitate as she snuggled against his chest, then fell asleep within a minute.

Lucas wasn't far behind her.

Chapter Seventeen

"Thank you for calling the doctor. I…uh…don't know what happened yesterday. I think maybe I haven't been eating enough or something. The baby seems to zap a lot of my energy," Amy said with a small smile while rubbing her belly.

She was nervous and didn't know how to deal with it, or what to say. She'd never woken up with a guy before. She knew they hadn't had sex again, but sleeping all night with him seemed so much more intimate of an act, and they'd done it two nights in a row. She was already falling in love with Lucas and needed to back up and figure out what she was doing. If she wasn't careful, she'd be devastated when everything came to an end, and she had no doubt it would eventually end – whatever it was they had going on.

One minute the guy was being an arrogant jerk, and then the next, he was fretting over her and making sure she was well. She couldn't figure him out. It was all so confusing, and she was more scared than she'd ever been before. That said a lot, considering the way she'd grown up.

Lucas had spent an entire day and a half with her at her apartment. She napped off and on and started feeling much better. By the second afternoon, she was well enough for a trip to the doctor's office.

They didn't speak on the way there, both of them lost in their own thoughts. Amy was anxious to make sure nothing was wrong with her pregnancy. Once she knew everything was okay and she could actually see the baby moving inside her, she'd feel better.

She and Lucas walked straight back to the doctor's office, where he then gave her privacy as she changed. As they waited for Dr. Scott to come in, Amy laid upon the table with Lucas sitting next to the bed. She would've much rather Lucas waited in the front office, but she could tell there was no way he was going to miss the ultrasound.

The door finally opened. "Well, you look much better this afternoon, Amy. Let's see how your little one is doing, shall we?" the doctor said, as he headed directly over to the ultrasound monitor. He rubbed some sort of goo on her belly, causing her to jump from the coldness.

There was nothing for a few moments and then, there on the monitor, she saw a perfect little face. "This is our new three-dimensional ultrasound monitor. We get a much clearer image of the fetuses. It's still a little early to determine the sex, but it looks like all is healthy and well," Dr. Scott reassured them.

He took down some measurements before speaking again. "It looks like your due date is December seventeenth. You're just over three months along. Your child is fully formed and about the size of a peanut in its shell, but the heartbeat is strong and developing nicely. Would you like to hear it?"

Amy and Lucas both nodded. Suddenly the only sound in the room was a gentle thumping. No one said a word as the monitor picked up the heartbeat of their child. Tears of utter joy welled up in Amy's eyes and freely spilled over, running down her warm cheeks. She couldn't help but look at Lucas, to silently share the amazing moment with someone. His eyes were wide with wonder and when their eyes met, there was a new light in them. A light of hope for this new little being that would soon be in their arms.

It became so much more real to Amy as she looked at the screen and saw her infant nestled safe inside her body as the room filled with the strong rhythm of her heartbeat.

She could do this – she had to. No matter what it took, she'd make a good mother, even though she didn't think she was ready, she'd better get there quick, because she'd never let her child grow up thinking she wasn't safe or loved.

Family.

I finally have a family, Amy thought, emotions overflowing. She hadn't wanted to get pregnant so soon in her life, but as she listened to the beautiful sound of her daughter, or son's, heartbeat, she was grateful it had happened.

◊◊◊◊◊◊

Lucas looked from the monitor to Amy's face and saw tears streaming down her cheeks. The moment was so moving, he became a bit choked up and had to turn away. His child was strong and safe. Amy was beautiful, and he was glad she was the one carrying his baby. He could see the love and excitement shining through her.

They may have started things the wrong way, but he knew it would work out. They had no choice but to make it work. He hadn't been looking to get married, heck, he hadn't even wanted a girlfriend, but life had a way of happening.

Dr. Scott printed them some pictures from the ultrasound and left the room so Amy could get dressed.

"I can meet you in the lobby," Amy said as she lay on the table.

"I'll wait," he challenged.

It was a test of wills as she glared at him, and he sat back comfortably, not even giving her the courtesy of turning around.

They were getting married soon, so why shouldn't he look at his fiancé? Besides the fact that he really shouldn't torture himself any more than he already had, it was a standoff and he wasn't willing to back down.

"Fine," Amy snapped as she sat up and got off the table on the opposite side from where he was sitting.

He couldn't take his eyes from her as she grabbed her clothes and turned her back to him. Without taking the robe off, she slipped her slacks on, giving him only a slight peak at the green panties she was wearing.

She quickly discarded the gown, and slipped her shirt over her head, ending his view of her sexy back. He'd never really thought of the back as sexy before, but the more he was around Amy, the more body parts he found erotic. His mind ran away with him as he pictured himself running his tongue down the delicate indent of her spine, all the way to the rounded top of her backside...

No, not the time, nor the place, he scolded himself as he stood and adjusted his pants, which were becoming uncomfortably tight.

"I'm ready," Amy said as she grabbed her purse and opened the door, not waiting for him, before she flew from the room and made a beeline out of the office.

Neither of them spoke once he caught up to her, both of them lost in their own thoughts.

Lucas helped Amy into the car and then started driving out of the city to his parent's house on the island. When they started crossing the bridge, Amy turned toward him with a perplexed look on her face.

"Why are we going to your parents?" she asked nervously.

"We have some wedding plans to discuss with them."

"Lucas, I'm not getting married – I already told you that. I won't be forced into a marriage for any reason. Just because a baby's involved doesn't mean we need to take a walk down the aisle. We can work something out so you can spend ample time with our child," she said with a bit of panic in her voice.

"Amy, I'm old-fashioned, and I believe a kid needs both parents. You won't raise my child alone and I won't argue about it anymore. I'm trying not to be a jerk, here, so don't make me push it, but there will be a wedding, that is, unless you just don't want to be a mother," he said, his voice remaining calm, though his heart was pounding.

"You're being ridiculous, Lucas. We barely even know each other. One night of lust doesn't make us qualified to raise a child together. I don't know hardly anything about you, and you know nothing about me," she said, her arms crossed.

"You're pregnant. I don't need to know anything else right now," he said, his voice final. He pulled the car up to his parent's mansion and shut off the motor, then turned to face her.

The only thing he had going for him was she really didn't know how ruthless he'd be. In reality, he knew he wouldn't actually take his baby from its mother, but she didn't know that. It was his only ace in the hole.

"I…" she started to protest.

"You can either marry me, or…" he left the sentence hanging, acting as if he were bored.

◊◊◊◊◊◊

The tone in his voice terrified her. There was a deathly calm to him – no anger, no pleading. She knew he wasn't going to back down. Amy bowed her head and dealt with the acceptance. She was going to have to marry Lucas for her child's sake, not because he loved her. He was giving her no other choice in the matter. She was frustrated she'd made the poor mistake of sleeping with him. She wouldn't regret her child. She just wished she'd made her with someone who would've walked away and never looked back, or who would've loved her unconditionally.

She wasn't willing, nor prepared, to share her baby with another person. Sure, it would be great to have a happy, loving family, but she couldn't think of many couples who actually stayed together. The divorce rate rose each year, and she'd never wanted to be added to that list of statistics.

When her protests stopped, Lucas opened his car door and slipped outside. She undid her buckle and jumped out before he came around. He grabbed her hand and led her up the large staircase to the front door, her heart pounding so hard, she heard the blood rushing in her ears.

They walked into the house without saying anything further. He'd made his point, she'd made hers – and he'd won. She knew he'd always win. She'd just hoped he wouldn't want to play in the game of fatherhood.

"Lucas, Amy, I'm so glad to see you. We have much to discuss. All the arrangements have been made. Amy, you run along with Katherine and get your gown picked out so we can get the alterations done," Joseph said, talking fast as he approached the two of them before they'd gotten past the foyer.

Amy was whisked through the house and shown flower choices and cake and then she was fitted into a dress that was far more beautiful than anything she'd ever thought of wearing.

Amy had pictured her wedding day when she was young – as most little girls did – and what Joseph had planned on such short notice was a dream wedding. It would've been perfect if the groom was in love with her. It would've been even more perfect if she believed marriage could last forever.

She had to reluctantly admit that she was being given more than most women. She would have a safe home where she'd get to raise her child. She wouldn't have to deal with trembling in the middle of the night, worried the neighbor was going to get high and knock on her door. She wouldn't have to panic over not having enough money for milk. She'd at least be safe.

She could deal with everything else as long as she had her child. She knew it was a marriage of convenience, but didn't people get married for convenience all the time, for what the other person could give to them. What made her any different? Sure, it would get lonely, but how lonely could she really be, having her child with her?

"You look stunning in this gown," Katherine said as she knelt before her with pins and thread.

"You've really gone to too much trouble," Amy said, guilt consuming her as she spent time with Katherine.

Amy wanted to talk to her, tell Lucas's mother her fears, but how could she?

"I know you're scared, dear, but it will all work out. Just give yourself some time. You probably feel a bit like you're in a shotgun wedding, don't you?" Katherine asked as she looked into Amy's face. Amy felt her eyes immediately tear up at the understanding tone in Katherine's voice.

"I…this is all just happening so fast," Amy admitted.

"I know. I don't think the Anderson men know how to move at normal speeds. Someday, I'll have to tell you a little of my own story. I almost didn't get my happy ending because of stubborn pride and foolish assumptions. Now, I'm a very happy woman, with a husband who adores me, and I him, and three beautiful sons. It eventually works itself out," Katherine assured her.

"I don't see how," Amy said, feeling defeated in that moment.

"Oh, sweetie, I'm so sorry you're hurting," Katherine said as she quickly stood. "Come here."

Before Amy knew what she was doing, Katherine embraced her. The hug was Amy's undoing, and she instantly broke down and started sobbing in the woman's arms, horrified, but unable to stop herself.

"There, there, dear. It really will be okay," Katherine soothed her.

"I know it will. I just…these hormones…always crying," Amy stuttered as she sobbed on Katherine's shoulder.

"I remember that well, even though it was many years ago that I was pregnant," Katherine said with a gentle laugh.

Katherine pulled back and Amy wanted to fall forward again into her comforting embrace. It was times like these, in her life, that she missed having a mother the most.

"I know it doesn't feel like it, but soon the hoopla will be over with, and then all you have to worry about is settling down with your husband, and preparing for your baby. I'm always going to be just a phone call away if you need me, okay? I'm not just spouting words, either. I truly mean that. If you need anything, you give me a call," Katherine said, forcing Amy to look in her eyes.

"Okay," Amy answered with a watery smile. She was starting to really fall in love with Katherine, looking up to her like the mother she wanted so badly. She already loved Joseph, and thought the one great thing about her marriage to Lucas, was getting parents, even if they weren't truly hers.

She and Katherine finished her fitting, and then headed back downstairs, where they found Joseph and Lucas in the family room.

They stayed at the house most of the day and had dinner with Joseph and Katherine. As Joseph dominated the conversation, Amy focused on Katherine, who sat by silently, for the most part, as her husband spoke. She had a quiet dignity about her, letting everyone know that – even though Joseph had the loudest bark – she was truly the one in charge. She was the kind of mother Amy had dreamed about having during her miserable years growing up.

By the time Lucas took Amy back to the apartment building, she was almost asleep on her feet. She'd been through an exhausting day but, for the most part, it had been a good one. She always enjoyed visiting with Joseph and Katherine, and nothing had been greater than seeing the ultrasound of her unborn child.

She must've looked at the picture a hundred times throughout the day. She'd choked up when Lucas had handed the photo to his father, and she'd seen the sheen of tears in his eyes. She knew beyond any doubt her child would be loved beyond compare. She'd have a much better childhood than most children.

"Well, son, this is the greatest gift you could've ever given your mother and I," was all Joseph had said before he engulfed both of them in a bear-sized hug.

On their way home, Lucas placed his warm hand on her knee and kept it there the duration of the drive. At first, she'd tried to shake him off, but then gave up after he squeezed her flesh, letting her know he wasn't moving. Each time he touched her, she felt it through her entire body. She didn't think they'd have to worry about chemistry, at least not for a long while.

The two of them stepped off the elevator, onto their floor, and Amy headed for her door. "Not tonight, Amy. We'll use my apartment, instead."

"I want to go home alone, Lucas. It's been a really long day, and I need time to myself," she said with a hint of annoyance.

Lucas sighed as he steered her past her door and down the hallway.

"Amy, you'll be my wife in a few days. I'm not only taking you as a wife on paper. We'll live together, sleep together and be together in every way a husband and wife are meant to be. I'll only marry once. You'll be provided for extremely well and, in turn, I expect to be taken care of. You *will* share my bed," he again spoke in that voice that brooked no room for argument.

Her fatigue forgotten as her temper spiked and she became seething mad. She was getting sick and tired of him throwing his weight around and just expecting her to follow along with everything he demanded.

"Okay, Lucas. I've accepted we're to be married, and I plan on doing my *wifely duties*, but for the next few days, I'm not your wife, and I'd like to enjoy my apartment before my jail sentence begins," she snapped, wanting to strike out and hurt him.

◊◊◊◊◊◊

Amy had the opposite effect of angering him. Lucas had to keep from smiling. If she saw that, she'd think he was laughing at her, which, in a way, he was. He was actually looking forward to his upcoming nuptials. He would've never been happy with a woman who catered to his every whim. He had enough people willing to do that. He liked how his future wife had a strong personality and felt a desire to fight him. He knew he wouldn't get bored with her – ever.

He could push the issue and force her to stay with him, but he also knew to win the war was far more important than to win each and every battle. He'd already put her through the wringer that day, and her health was more important than anything else. He'd let her have this one.

"Fine. We'll do it your way. It will just make the honeymoon that much better," he said as he led her back to her door. He *really* couldn't wait for the honeymoon.

Just as she was about to go through the open doorway, he wrapped his arms around her and kissed her, long and hard. *Let her think about what she'll be missing out on tonight*, he thought as he watched her swoon.

He walked away feeling pretty good about himself; that was, until he got into his apartment – alone and in need of release. He sighed as he turned his shower faucet to cold and prepared himself for a hell of a long week.

Chapter Eighteen

"Breathe, Amy. Just breathe." She felt like she was about to hyperventilate as she stood in the dressing room in the huge mansion. She'd spent the morning being pampered for her wedding day.

Her hair was up in a bun, with curls cascading down her neck and face. Her makeup had been expertly applied to erase the dark circles, and highlight her eyes and mouth. Her nails were extended and painted. She didn't even feel like herself. They'd just placed her magnificent dress on her, and she was staring in the mirror at a stranger.

Who was the girl gazing back? They'd given her a few blessed minutes to calm herself, for which she was grateful.

"It's time, Amy," she heard Joseph softly call through the door before he opened it and stepped inside. His muted entrance was enough to make her turn her head. She'd never heard him speak so quietly before. He looked incredibly handsome in his tux. She definitely could see where the boys got their great looks. He was so alike, and yet so different, from Lucas.

Joseph had aged well. The biggest difference between Joseph and Lucas was their eyes. Lucas's eyes were always so focused and determined, where Joseph's were surrounded by laugh lines and always had a sparkle to them. He was far more relaxed than his son. She wondered if he'd been that way his entire life or if there'd been a time he'd held that same focused look.

As he approached, he kissed her sweetly on the cheek. "I'm so glad to finally have a daughter in the family. You're beautiful inside and out."

He wrapped his large arms around her in a gentle hug, his words meaning so much more to her than he could ever imagine. He had no clue how much she needed to be included in a loving family. She'd give up any amount of money to be loved the way Joseph loved his children. She was getting just a small piece of that now, and she didn't ever want to let it go.

"With your own father not here, I wanted you to know I'd be more than honored if you'd allow me to walk you down the aisle."

Amy's eyes were burning as she replied to his kind offer. "It would be my honor to have you escort me. You're the kind of father I always dreamed of having."

She couldn't say anything further because she got entirely too choked up as she looked into his kind eyes. He pulled her close for another hug, and she clung to him, hoping he'd never let go. She'd been so careful all her life to not get too attached to people, and yet, in a few short months, she was falling in love with an entire family.

"Now, now, you don't want to get all teary-eyed and ruin your makeup. I don't think my son could handle any delays. He's already pacing up and down the hallway. The preacher just led him to his spot at the altar," Joseph chuckled. Amy had her doubts about that, but didn't argue with him.

She took one final look in the mirror and then a fortifying breath, "I'm ready." She took hold of Joseph's arm and let him lead her from the waiting room. Music filled the air as they stepped through the doorway.

She gasped, and the only thing that kept her from running back the direction they'd come was Joseph gripping her arm. "I thought only a few people would be here," she whispered.

"Now, Amy, don't be frightened. My oldest son's finally getting married, and we couldn't hurt anyone's feelings by not including them in the affair," he said, making her feel guilty about her minor outburst.

Amy took a calming breath, ready to panic as they took the first few steps down the beautifully decorated aisle. She looked straight ahead, because she feared if she faced the strangers, she'd turn around and run.

She spotted Lucas standing on a stage, just a short distance from her. He took her breath away with how beautiful of a man he was. Their eyes met and held.

He gave her a smile that seemed to tell her everything would be okay.

Amy felt like the wind had been knocked out of her and she had to stop to catch her breath. Joseph looked at her quizzically, but she didn't notice. She didn't notice anything but the way her body quivered.

She was in love with him.

She didn't know how or when it happened, but somehow in the mist of their time together, he'd become an unstoppable force in her life. He was arrogant and bossy, demanding and pigheaded. He was also kind and gentle, giving and loving. He was the kind of man she didn't think existed.

He was also about to be her husband, but he didn't love her.

With the knowledge of living a life with the man she loved, knowing he'd never love her back, she didn't know how she was going to get through the wedding. How could she be with him every day, making love and raising a child, all the while knowing he didn't love her? She'd slowly wither to nothing.

Joseph prompted her, and she finally began to walk forward. She had to fight to keep the tears away.

Maybe he'll eventually fall in love with me, she tried to comfort herself. If he thought she'd somehow trapped him into the marriage, how would he ever trust her, much less love her? He knew she hadn't planned the pregnancy, but he was honorable in doing what was right for his child and, therefore, he'd always feel like he was trapped.

There was nothing she could do at the moment, so she'd continue down the aisle and get the wedding over with. She was a strong person. She'd just have to store away her love and try to survive as best she could.

◊◊◊◊◊◊

Lucas felt a moment of panic as Amy stopped halfway down the aisle. Was she going to turn and run? He wouldn't let her get far. He knew how badly she wanted her baby and, as much as it hurt him to trap her, he couldn't let them go. In the months he'd known her, she'd invaded his every sense, and he couldn't picture his future without her in it.

He breathed a sigh of relief as they began walking toward him again. When his father placed her hand in his and she stepped up to stand beside him, a quiet calm washed over him. He had her in his arms, and he wasn't letting go.

He barely heard the preacher speaking. He focused just enough to repeat the words he needed to say; otherwise, his mind was consumed by his beautiful bride.

She was a vision. He'd dated models and heiresses. He'd been with far more women than he should've, but none of them had been able to cause the tightening in his gut that Amy did. She had a natural beauty that outshone the brightest stars of Hollywood.

He'd move heaven and earth to have her as his wife forever. He was slowly falling in love with her. If she knew of his feelings, she'd know she had the power to drop him to his knees and beg her for mercy. That had happened to him once, and only once, several years ago, and he wouldn't let it happen again.

His mother and father were the only examples of true love he knew of. Every other couple he knew was together for what the other could bring them. It was just easier that way. If he gave Amy power over him, she'd slowly whittle him to nothing. He wouldn't let that happen.

He wouldn't let her destroy him. He'd be a good husband, and she'd be taken care of – never wanting for anything again. *Please, let her love me and not what I can give her*, he secretly added to his vows of love, honor and obey.

They finished the ceremony, and the preacher told him to kiss his new bride. Lucas gave a full-fledged smile.

"Gladly."

He bent her slightly backward and consumed her mouth, quickly forgetting they were standing in a room full of people.

He lost track of time and had no idea how long the kiss lasted. It had been too long since he'd last held her and tasted the sweet nectar of her lips.

"Ah, son, you have plenty of time for that during the honeymoon," Joseph interrupted the pair while slapping Lucas on the back. Amy turned scarlet as their guests laughed.

To all those witnessing the wedding, the marriage looked like a union of love that was going to last forever. The way each of them looked at one another could only be described as besotted.

"Everyone please follow the staff to the backyard, where the reception is taking place," Joseph announced as Lucas led Amy back down the aisle.

He looked at the large diamond shining on her finger, feeling a sense of satisfaction in knowing she was now his. He couldn't wait to get to the honeymoon.

In true Anderson fashion, they'd set up a spectacular wedding in only a week. Lucas watched his bride's facial expression as they passed through the crowd. She was in awe.

The yard had glamorous tents set up, filled with linen-covered tables. There was soft lighting, a dance floor, and an entire band playing music. Caterers carried trays of champagne and food, attending to the guests. On each table sat crystal, china and the most fragrant and colorful floral arrangements.

Lucas had wanted all the silly little traditional things. He didn't even know why. God knew it wasn't a traditional wedding. Amy probably thought it more appropriate to have guards with guns ushering her from station to station since he'd strong-armed her into the entire event.

He was surprised to see she seemed to be enjoying herself. Either his bride was full of surprises, or she was one phenomenal actress.

◊◊◊◊◊◊

"Can I have this dance?"

"Tom!" Amy exclaimed, immediately letting go of Lucas's arms and rushing over to her best friend.

With all the prepping she'd been put through during the week, she hadn't been to the office, and hadn't had a moment alone with him.

Seeing him looking so handsome in his tux made her eyes sting for the millionth time that day.

"You know, you're absolutely stunning."

"You have to say that. And, yes, I'd love to have this dance," she said with a watery smile.

He pulled her into his arms and began swinging her around the dance floor, making her feel like she was floating on water.

"You've been holding out on me. Where did you learn to dance like this?" she asked with surprise.

"I have an incredible mother who insisted her boys knew how to properly treat a lady. Unfortunately, our father never found the time to take her dancing, or even bring her flowers, for that matter. He ended up running off with his twenty-year younger secretary, and my mom's never been happier. Now, she goes dancing all the time," Tom said as he spun Amy in a circle.

"That's both tragic and wonderful."

"Well, the best part is, a year after dearest daddy ran off with the bimbo, she left him, running away with some surfer in Southern California who had a bigger…wallet," he said with a pause and a laugh.

"You're absolutely terrible," Amy said, the stress of her day lifting as time was suspended for a few brief moments.

"I really try. Your husband is currently glaring at the two of us. I just thought you should know," he said as he sent a wink over her shoulder.

Amy turned and saw Lucas's eyes narrow. Obviously, Tom's wink had been for him, and he didn't appreciate it much.

"Would you quit goading him."

"I can't help it. Before he steals you away again, I want you to know that I'm always going to be here for you, no matter what. If everything goes south, then you call me, and I'll come get you. My place certainly isn't going to be up to par with any house Mr. Anderson gives you, but it will be full of love."

"Thank you, Tom. You don't know how much that means to me."

"Well, you better not forget about me now that you're married and fat," he said with a teasing smile. She could see the insecurity beneath the teasing, though.

"First of all, I am so not fat, you horrible person. Secondly, I haven't had any true friends my entire life. You're the first, and I promise, you'll always be who I call when I need a shoulder to cry on. That also goes both ways. You better not forget about me."

"Amy, it's time to cut the cake," Lucas interrupted them as he placed a possessive hand on her shoulder.

"Okay," she said with reluctance. "Make sure you catch the bouquet," she called out as Lucas led her away. She got the reaction she was looking for when Tom began laughing.

◊◊◊◊◊◊

Lucas and Amy cut the cake and fed each other. They toasted their union and shared dances with family members. Lucas was surprised by the intense jealousy he felt as each of his brothers pulled Amy too close, for a married woman, and whisked her around the dance floor.

When she was dancing with Alex, she let out a delighted laugh at something he said. Lucas walked away from his dance partner without a word and reclaimed his bride. His brother laughed harder and kissed Amy on the cheek before releasing her.

"What were the two of you laughing about?" he questioned with jealousy as he spun her around the floor.

"He told me, if I came to my senses, I could call him, and he'd whisk me away from his boring older brother," she said, still smiling in delight.

"You're mine, and only mine, and the only one who'll be whisking you anywhere will be me," he stated and pulled her even closer so she'd have room for only him in her mind.

He kissed her until he could hardly stand anymore, and then he decided they'd spent enough time with people.

"It's time to go. Let's say goodnight to my parents and get away from here," he spoke as he took her hand and led her in the direction of his mom and dad.

Chapter Nineteen

Amy became incredibly nervous as Lucas led her toward his parents. This was it. They were going to be alone very soon, and she was terrified. She didn't know how to act as a married woman.

She wasn't worried about sex. They definitely had that part down, but she was worried about the before and after sex. Did she kiss him if she felt like it? Did she take his hand in hers? Did she tell him when the baby was kicking, so they could share the moment? Were those things too intimate?

In a regular marriage, she wouldn't need to ask herself those kinds of questions, but this wasn't a regular marriage, and she didn't know what was expected of her. It was terrifying.

"Mom, Dad, thank you so much for the wedding. I know I didn't give you enough time, and you still made it beautiful. We're leaving now," Lucas said as he hugged them.

"Thank you both. You're truly amazing. I'm very glad to be a part of your family," Amy added shyly.

"My dear, we're the ones grateful to have you in our lives. Now we finally have the daughter we weren't blessed with years ago," Joseph said, grabbing her in a hug and then passing her over to his wife.

"You two will have a wonderful honeymoon, and we'll get together for lunch next week. Now that the wedding's over, it's time to prepare for our first grandchild," Katherine added while hugging her.

Amy was so overcome by her amazing in-laws, she didn't know what else to say. Their love certainly outweighed everything else about the unusual union.

"Give us a few minutes to run upstairs and get Amy changed for your departure," Katherine said, while taking her arm.

Lucas looked as if he wasn't going to let her go until Joseph laughed and pulled him aside. "She'll be right back, son."

Amy loved that laughter. She quickly walked up the stairs with Katherine. She was nervous as they entered the bedroom and she saw the beautiful outfit sitting on the bed.

"Amy, I know all of this has been a whirlwind for you, but I want you to know I'm so happy to have you as a daughter," Katherine told her, once again making her eyes sting.

"Thank you, Katherine, I really do appreciate everything you've done for me. My dress is stunning, this wedding was beautiful, and your home so welcoming. I know saying thank you isn't enough, but really…thank you."

"Thank you is just right. I know this is none of my business, but I know this happened fast because of the baby coming. I also know my son can be stubborn and hard-headed. He's been hurt before. When a family's been given as much as we have, people tend to take advantage of you. Lucas has been with some greedy women, who he thought actually loved him. He'd never admit that, but a mother can see things others can't. Just be patient with him, dear. He truly is a good man."

"I love him," Amy told her, needing to say the words out loud, and wanting to assure his mother.

"Oh, honey, that's wonderful, but I already knew that. It's obvious every time you look in his direction. You'll be a good wife to him, and he'll be a good husband to you. Just remember, you've nothing to worry about because Lucas's growl is far worse than his bite. I can already see he worships you, and it gives my heart great pleasure to see the way you look at him," Katherine said. Katherine pulled her in for another warm hug, bonding them a little bit more. Amy hoped to never lose her. She was too emotional to say anything else.

"Well, we'd better get you back to Lucas before he starts hunting for you."

Amy changed quickly, and then the two of them returned downstairs.

Lucas led Amy from the house amid shouts of goodwill and much birdseed. They made their way to the awaiting limo, decorated with "Just married" across the window.

Amy gazed at Lucas, wondering what she should do next. Her wedding had been so much more than she'd expected, with him being attentive the entire time, but now that they were alone, she was nervous.

"Lucas…" She never got to finish her sentence, because Lucas pulled her into his arms and ravished her mouth.

She wanted him so badly that she didn't have a single thought of pushing him away. Her breathing deepened as her fingers tangled in his thick, dark hair, pulling him closer. He pressed even more tightly against her aching body, and she still felt like it wasn't enough.

Lucas was obviously as hungry for her as she was for him. Within seconds he unbuttoned her blouse and stripped her bra off. Amy gasped as he covered her breasts with his hands and then lips. He was molding her aching body with a sultry lover's touch and her body's reaction was clearly insatiable.

Her nipples ached as she pushed them into his mouth. When he clamped his lips over one rosy tip, she threw her head back and moaned. He switched to her other breast, giving her the full attention she needed and wanted.

Pregnancy had made her skin a thousand times more sensitive, every swipe of his tongue nearly sending her over the edge of ecstasy, each brush of his fingers, heating her core. He'd turned her to molten lava the only other time they'd made love, but this time, she felt like she was going to sink right through the seat.

When he released her nipple and trailed his mouth down her stomach, she began to tremble. He stripped her skirt and panties off in one smooth motion, and then he was trailing his tongue over the sensitive skin on the inside of her thighs. Her body moved restlessly around on the seat as she tried pulling him back up her body, but he only glanced up with smoldering eyes as he gave a slight shake of his head.

He began caressing her legs again, while his hands ran up and down her stomach, reaching over her breasts and then back down again. She felt his warm breath whisper over her most sensitive area, seconds before the wetness of his tongue began stroking her pink swollen pearl. Her body jerked at the intimate contact. Then, she could do nothing but feel as the pressure started mounting.

In only seconds she was falling apart, quivering as her body exploded. Before she had time to blink, Lucas crawled up her body, and took her lips, kissing her deeply with the taste of sex on his tongue.

She didn't think she could feel anything else after the explosion she'd just had, but as his tongue caressed the inside of her mouth, her body started to stir again, then began burning, needing the feel of him sinking deep inside her.

His hands moved down her body, gripping her back, as his knees parted her legs, opening her up for him. Then, with one hard thrust, he was buried deep inside her. Their breathing mingled together as her body tightened around him.

She erupted a second time, the explosion even more powerful than the first. She sobbed out his name as she lay quivering in his arms. With a cry of completion, Lucas let go and followed her over the edge of the cliff, before collapsing against her, both of them panting. Neither of them spoke as their breathing slowly returned to normal.

She didn't want to let go. She knew, once they broke apart, the awkward silence would begin. For now it was just two lovers enjoying the aftermath of what they'd shared.

They were still pressed together when the driver buzzed them, letting them know they'd reach their destination in five minutes.

Amy flushed scarlet as she quickly scrambled to get her clothing back in place.

"Where's my bra?" she asked in a panic, mortified at the thought of not being fully covered by the time the driver opened their door.

◊◊◊◊◊◊

Lucas laughed aloud at the horror on Amy's face at the thought of getting caught naked in the back of a car with her husband.

He pulled the bra from behind him and handed it over. She finished dressing in record time and scooted away from him. He straightened himself up, but he knew the clothes would be coming back off in a few minutes. He found it very endearing how his wife was afraid to be caught necking in the back of the limo.

He'd just finished loving Amy, far too quickly, and now he wanted to take her again, much more thoroughly. He could already feel his body hardening in anticipation of sinking into her over and over again, all night long.

They pulled up to the airport, where his private jet was awaiting their arrival. Lucas led her inside while the luggage was loaded.

"We'll be taking off in about thirty minutes, Mr. and Mrs. Anderson. Is there anything I can get for you while we're waiting?"

"Yes, Lana, thank you. We'll each have dinner, and I'll take a glass of bourbon. What would you like to drink, dear?" he asked Amy.

"I'd love some milk, please."

Moments later, Lana returned, "Here's your drink, Mrs. Anderson. Your meal will be out shortly."

"How are you feeling?" Lucas asked.

"Really good, actually," Amy replied. "I forgot to eat today, though, so I'm starving. I think I could consume an entire cow right now. Would it be rude for me to ask for two of the dinners?" she asked, embarrassed, but not enough to go hungry for the long trip.

"We have a full meal prepared for us, Amy. I don't think you'll have to worry about being hungry. I'm pretty famished myself. I didn't get much of a chance to eat with so much going on," he replied with a chuckle. He enjoyed how the pregnancy was affecting her, giving her curves an appealing softness, and turning her skin into one giant sex organ. He thought it may be wise to just keep her pregnant for the next ten years straight.

"Here's your first course." Lana set down an appealing plate with several appetizers in the mix, sending up tempting aromas. When Amy's stomach growled loudly enough for both Lucas and Lana to hear, he chuckled again. It was becoming a habit.

"You better dig in before my son starts doing more than growling," Lucas warned her.

Suddenly, Amy leaned over and kissed him, taking his breath away. "Your son *or* daughter," she emphasized, though she did it with humor, "is just fine. It's mommy that could consume everything in sight."

Lucas watched her groan as she took a bite of food, his already aroused body, jumping at the sound. He couldn't seem to take his eyes from her as she lifted the fork to her mouth, her tongue darting out to lick her lips, before she grabbed another mouthful. Finally, he managed to look away and begin on his own food, though he'd almost lost his appetite – well, for food, that is.

"I'll serve your salads after we're in the air," Lana said, then left them to eat.

Amy emptied her plate, then looked at what was remaining on his, with longing in her eyes. With desire clenching his gut, he speared a bite and slowly lifted his fork to her lips, nearly exploding in his seat, as she opened for him. She closed her eyes in pleasure and moaned. He didn't know if he'd make it until after dinner. He wanted to take her back to his bed, now.

What she did to him was impressive. The amount of pleasure she took in the simplest things was a total aphrodisiac.

"Amy, can we start this honeymoon on the right foot? I'd like for us to forget about how we got here, and at least pretend this has been a normal wedding, and now we're on the honeymoon of a lifetime," he said. He could see he'd surprised her as she tried to fully process his words.

Finally, her eyes filled with tears, and she nodded.

"These dang pregnancy hormones make me cry at the drop of a hat, I'm warning you now," she said with a watery laugh. "I'm not usually so emotional."

"I like you this way," he whispered as he leaned over and gently kissed her. Surprisingly, he did like her this way, soft and warm – and loving.

"We've been cleared for takeoff, Mr. Anderson. Please fasten your seat belts, and we should have a smooth flight. The wind is going in our direction, so we should be touching down in Paris at nine," said the pilot's voice over the intercom.

"I've never flown on a jet before, but I've seen the movies, and I have to tell you that this is much nicer than sharing a row of seats with a big sweaty guy next to me and a screaming toddler behind," Amy said with excitement.

Lucas burst out laughing. She really was invigorating. "I'd have to agree with you on that."

◊◊◊◊◊◊

During takeoff, Amy's face was glued to the window. She was fascinated by the whole event. She loved how the jet suddenly burst with speed. The feeling as they lifted into the air was unlike anything she'd ever experienced.

She had no fear.

She felt alive, adrenaline pumping through her system. She definitely had to add flying to her list of favorite things to do. She'd have to see if her husband would fly her to other places later. Maybe he would for their anniversary next year.

Once they reached cruising altitude, Lana brought them their salads. They ate several courses, including succulent lobster, which definitely didn't come from the bargain market's frozen department. After the final course was served, she leaned back and rubbed her stomach.

"You were right, Lucas, I'm stuffed," she said as a yawn escaped.

"Let's go take a nap, then – you look exhausted," he said as he got up and helped her from her seat.

"Can I get anything else for you, Mr. Anderson?" Lana asked.

"No, thank you, Lana. We're going to retire for the rest of the evening."

Lucas led her past the front seats, then down a hall. She tried looking around, but he was moving too quickly. They passed a couple doors, and she wondered how there was so much space in the jet. It had looked large on the outside, but not that big. At the end of the short hallway was another door. This one, he opened, and inside was a large bed, two nightstands, a flat screen television, and another door. She assumed it was a private bath.

"Your honeymoon suite, my bride," he whispered as he pulled her into his arms.

She instantly melted against him as he ran his hands up her back and slowly lowered his head to take her lips.

"It's perfect," she said when he stopped kissing her long enough to pull her shirt over her head.

"You're perfect. Now, let me properly make love to you. I've got all night long to worship your body," he said, his eyes bright with desire, making her feel incredibly sexy.

He slowly undressed her, stopping each time he took a piece of clothing off her, so he could run his fingers over the exposed skin.

Lucas spent the next couple hours doing exactly what he'd promised, and worshiping every square inch of her. When she'd reached the brink of ecstasy, and then some, he finally allowed them both to rest, pulling her into his arms, with her head lying against his chest. She was asleep within seconds, feeling hopeful about her future.

Chapter Twenty

"Amy, it's time to get up." Amy struggled to wake from the delicious dream she was having, her body sore and her eyes hazy, as she slowly managed to open her lids.

She didn't know how much sleep she'd actually gotten on the flight home, because Lucas had woken her a few times with the touch of his hands roaming her body. He'd made up for waking her, by sending her into a complete state of bliss, though.

"Don't want to," she finally mumbled, then shut her lids and started to drift back to sleep.

"We have to get into our seats. We've begun our decent," he said with a chuckle, making Amy groan in frustration.

"No," she stubbornly replied.

"You just have a bit of jet lag. You'll feel better soon, I promise." He ran his finger slowing down her exposed back, the sensations awakening her from the inside out.

Though, she in no way believed him, she finally managed to drag herself into a sitting position, her gritty eyes having a hard time staying open.

With a bit of help from Lucas, she made her way to the front of the jet and sat down. Lana, the perfect flight attendant, who was much too pretty for Amy's comfort, immediately set coffee down for Lucas, and milk for Amy.

She sipped her drink and picked at the muffin while the jet descended.

Once they landed, Amy started feeling a bit of excitement, even though she was exhausted. How could she not be excited with her first trip outside the United States? She was in Paris, a place she'd thought to only see in picture books.

"Where are we going first?" she asked as the jet moved slowly through the busy airport.

"To our room."

"We aren't exploring?" Disappointment flooded through her.

"I know you're excited to be here, but tonight we'll go to our room and rest, then start exploring the city tomorrow. I plan on taking you to every tourist spot there is, and then some less famous areas, that in my opinion, are the most beautiful parts of Paris."

"I suppose…" she trailed off. She was in the city of love, with her husband, and she didn't want to waste a minute of it on sleeping.

Lucas led her from the jet and straight to customs. Once they were done there, he took her to a waiting limo. As they climbed into the large back seat, her legs clenched together as pressure built up.

"As much as I'd love a repeat performance of our first ride in a limo, I know you have to be sore. I'll give you a day to rest," Lucas whispered in her ear, making her shiver.

She didn't feel all that sore.

The car pulled up in front of a huge building, not especially tall, compared to the places in Seattle, but incredibly long, with an L shape to it.

"Is this our hotel?" she asked.

Lucas began laughing as he looked at her, though she had no idea why. Had she already done something wrong?

"Are they not called hotel's here? Is it an apartment complex?"

He laughed more, and she started to feel self-conscious. She really had no idea what he found so amusing.

"I'm sorry, Amy. It's just that I'm not used to being with someone as innocent and unworldly as you," he said. She took immediate offense.

"Just because I wasn't born with a silver spoon, doesn't mean I'm ignorant. I just asked a simple question," she snapped and his laughter immediately died.

He gripped her hand and turned her head toward him.

"I'm sorry, Amy. I didn't mean that in a negative way. You're so refreshing to me, that's all. I've never brought a woman here before, though this city is the

Holy Grail to the many I've dated in the past. We're at the Hotel Ritz."

"Okay," she said with a shrug, not seeing what the fuss was all about. It was nice, beautiful, in fact, but wasn't a hotel, *just* a hotel – nothing more, nothing less.

He didn't say anything further as he led her from the car.

"Good evening, Mr. Anderson. It's so nice to have you here again," an impeccably dressed man said as he opened an ornate door for them to step through.

Amy's breath was taken away as she stepped inside the lobby. From the outside, the building was beautiful, but gave nothing away as to the interior. She looked around, her eyes wide as she took in the crystal chandeliers, sparkling in the light, exquisite antique furniture, and priceless decorations. People moved about the grand entrance, all of them looking like movie stars.

She was so far out of her comfort zone, she wasn't even on the same planet, anymore. She finally figured out why he'd been laughing.

"This is a hotel?" she squeaked.

"No. This is *the* hotel," he corrected with a gentle smile. "Only the best for our honeymoon."

She followed him as he went to the counter and the staff efficiently checked them in.

"Right this way, Mr. Anderson," a man said, and she was speechless as she was led down a stunning hallway to their room.

When the man opened the doors and she followed Lucas inside, she actually stumbled. She'd never imagined staying in such a place – not ever.

Lucas thanked the man, then led him out the door as she stood rooted to the spot, almost afraid to touch anything.

"This is the Imperial Suite. My father brought me here when I was a child, and even growing up in our mansion, I was impressed. There are two bedrooms, a grand salon, and our own private dining room. They say the bed is identical to the one in Marie Antoinette's bedroom in the Palace of Versailles. The style of furniture is of Louis XVI, and the artwork is French. Of course, we have all the luxuries of the twenty-first century, but being here feels like stepping back in time, to the day when Kings ruled the world," Lucas said, his tone quiet.

Amy looked at him, surprised by the delight in his own face. She didn't think anything could awe Lucas; after all he was a billionaire. A place like this was second nature to him.

"I now see why you were laughing."

"I wasn't laughing at you, Amy, truly I wasn't. I was laughing with delight because I love that you didn't know the most famous hotel in the world. I love that over the next two weeks, I get to see the awe in your eyes as I take you around this romantic and historic place. Whether a person is rich or poor, Paris is somewhere everyone should experience, at least once in a lifetime."

"Thank you, Lucas," she whispered, too emotional to add anything else. She wrapped her arms around his neck in an embrace, hoping her actions could show him, more than her words, how much she appreciated this experience.

"I'm going to draw you a bath, then we'll get some rest. It's late here, so we can get an early start tomorrow," he said as he tightened his arms around her.

Amy followed, feeling as if she couldn't be any more blown away with what she'd seen than she already was, but seeing the gold bathroom, filled with luxurious items, did it.

As she sank into the tub and drifted to sleep amid the scented bubbles, a smile played on her face. No matter what happened in the near future, she'd always have this. She'd make sure the memories lasted her a lifetime.

She didn't stir when Lucas lifted her from the tub and gently dried her off before placing her in the large bed.

The trip ended up being so much more than she could've ever imagined. They didn't bring up any of the problems that had been ever present in their relationship from the start. They simply got to know one another.

Each night was spent in the hotel, making love and holding on to one another, neither of them willing to let the other go. Amy thought, if their relationship kept progressing in such a positive way, they might have a real future together.

Lucas took her all across Paris. She was like a child at Disneyland. She loved the history and ancient beauty of it all.

They visited the Eiffel Tower, Notre Dame, the Champs-Elysees, the many gardens, art museums, and the places many visitors never had a chance to see.

He took her to romantic café's, where the food was exquisite, and the atmosphere divine. Then, before they made it back to their room, he took her dancing, seducing her each night on the dance floor.

It was a dream honeymoon, and she never wanted it to end, though she figured it had to be boring for Lucas as he'd seen it all before.

She was wrong on that aspect, though, as Lucas was visiting Paris for the first time through her eyes. He told her daily how much he was enjoying their trip.

Their last night in Paris was bittersweet. She was afraid to return to the real world, to end her time away. She didn't know what would happen when the magic of Paris wasn't surrounding them.

As he led her to the airport, she found herself fighting back tears, almost afraid of boarding his luxurious jet. Exhaustion overtook them as they reached cruising altitude and climbed in the soft bed. They both slept most of the red eye flight home. When they arrived back in Seattle, early in the morning, she fought jet lag and a heavy sense of melancholy at her honeymoon being officially over.

Chapter Twenty-One

Amy was truly happy in her marriage, even though it hadn't been what she wanted. After spending two weeks, receiving Lucas's undivided attention, she couldn't get enough of her husband. She also couldn't seem to get enough of his hands taking her to places she never knew existed. She became tense with anticipation at just the thought of his magical fingers stroking her skin.

"I've had a wonderful time with you, Amy, but it's nice to be home, now," Lucas said as he led her to the waiting car.

The sky was overcast, and a fine mist began seeping into her hair. Amy found herself fighting the urge to cry, though she really had no reason to be upset. She blamed it on the hormones again. She had five more months she could get away with that.

"I think I could've stayed there for a month straight," she admitted with a smile.

"Yes, Paris is addictive. I promise to take you back. Maybe, we'll take a family trip. My parents love Paris in the summer. I think Alex and Mark wouldn't mind joining us, too."

"Oh, that would be so much fun. Katherine and I could explore the museums for hours. I know that wasn't your favorite thing to do."

"Was I that obvious?" he said with a guilty grin. "It's not that I don't enjoy art, it's just that I've seen the places a hundred times," he admitted with a shrug.

"Thank you for taking me, anyway. I can't believe I got to see the desk where Victor Hugo wrote his books. It amazes me that he did them all while standing. What a treasured piece of history, and I got to be right there," Amy exclaimed, excitement brewing up again, just thinking about it.

They arrived at a small family diner, whose specialty was a fluffy omelet. Lucas led her inside. They ordered and then continued to visit until their meal arrived. All talking stopped as she consumed her meal as if she hadn't eaten in weeks. She was seriously worried she was going to gain a hundred pounds if she wasn't careful.

"I can't believe how much food I'm eating. You'd better stop me before I'm as big as a whale," she worriedly said to Lucas. Her morning sickness had ended, and hunger had come in with a vengeance.

"Remember, Amy, you're eating for two, and I can tell you now, if you're carrying my child, he'll be very demanding, even from the womb," Lucas said with laughter.

Oh well, she figured, he wasn't with her for her body, anyway. He'd married her because she carried his child. That thought put a little bit of unease back into her good mood. Amy decided to brush it off and not think about it. She was enjoying her time with Lucas way too much to let negative thoughts in.

"I have a wedding gift for you. I hope you like it because it would be difficult to return," Lucas said. She had no idea what else he could possibly give her. She didn't want any more material things from him. She wanted his heart.

She didn't care about his money or power. She didn't care about the trips to Paris or the massive diamond resting on her finger. She just wanted him to love her as much as she loved him.

"I didn't know we were supposed to get gifts for each other. I have nothing for you."

"Let me show you what it is," he told her as he helped her back into the car. They drove toward his parents' house, and she figured his present to her was hidden at their place, although she didn't understand why he needed to do that when they had two apartments in the city with plenty of space to keep a gift.

He turned and drove down a long driveway, and she was even more confused. Where were they going? They continued down the endless pavement that had beautiful trees shading their way. He stopped the car in front of a colonial style house.

He stepped out of the car and came around her side, opening the door. She stepped out, looking at him quizzically. They walked up the steps, and he opened the door, suddenly lifting her into his arms and carrying her across the threshold.

"Welcome home," he told her, before placing his lips on hers. Amy was speechless. He'd bought them a new home. Had he had it all along and just stayed at the apartments to be closer to work? She really hoped he'd never lived there with another woman. She didn't share well.

She had so many questions, but she was too afraid of the answers to ask them out loud. "This is really our house?" she questioned and he nodded. We have a real house!" she exclaimed as excitement consumed her.

She'd always dreamed of having a real home, with a real family in it, but had never thought it would happen for her. She knew she'd have a child, someday, but to have a husband and a beautiful house, too, seemed so unreal. She could barely breathe and was afraid to blink, in fear that it might all disappear.

Her arms wrapped around his neck and she pulled his head closer, not wanting their kiss to end. Her eyes closed as she enjoyed the feel of being in his arms. Maybe if they just didn't come up for air, the honeymoon would never end.

Lucas finally pulled back, his eyes glazed as he looked down at her. She smiled, suddenly filled with so much joy, she felt like she was going to burst.

"Our first stop can be the master bedroom," he said with a hopeful grin. Amy was tempted, really tempted, but her curiosity was getting the best of her, and she really wanted to see the place that was going to be her home.

"I think that's a much better stopping place on our tour," she told him as she pressed her full breasts into him, making a groan rumble out of his chest.

"I think you're a tad bit sadistic, Mrs. Anderson," he said before setting her back on her feet. She held on a moment, until she was sure her knees wouldn't buckle.

"Only with you," she said before smacking him on the butt and then taking off. She heard his intake of breath, knowing she'd shocked him.

It didn't take long for her to hear his urgent steps as he began chasing her. Amy laughed in delight as they ran through the house, her darting in and out of rooms, him right on her heels. There were so many doors, and passages, hallways, and hiding places, they could play the game all night long.

Excitement continued building as she did her best to keep the game alive. She slipped into a room, her breath taken away at finding a stunning den, one wall of it, nothing but a giant book shelf, reaching from the floor to the twenty foot high ceilings. It was currently empty, but she knew she'd have no problem filling it up. She was an expert at finding used books for a great price.

The home was sparsely furnished, which she liked. She had plenty of time to find items, and found it a real joy to bargain shop. It was a treasure hunt. On the rare days she'd had a few extra hours, she used to look through the many second-hand stores in the Seattle area, one day dreaming of decorating her own home with antique furniture.

People often didn't realize what they were throwing away, and she'd found priceless pieces of furniture too many times to count. If she'd had the money, or the space, she'd gladly have snapped them up.

She exited the den as she heard Lucas's steps drawing closer. After a few turns, she found herself in a state of the art kitchen, which had every appliance known to man. She couldn't wait to get in there and start baking. There was so much she'd missed out on in life, and now she'd get to catch up a little. She had an overflowing book with recipe after recipe in it from the hundreds of magazines she'd copied from. Since she'd aced all her chemistry classes, she figured she could do a decent job cooking – it wasn't much different than mixing chemicals.

She managed to tear herself from the kitchen, then found herself back in the entryway. The house had grown quiet, and she tensed, wondering where Lucas was. She'd been playing, but what if he was getting frustrated? She began to chew the inside of her cheek in worry as she climbed one side of the double circular staircase. Her fingers caressed the railing, making her feel as if she were royalty. It was the kind of stairs she'd seen in a few of her favorite romantic movies.

At the balcony, she had a choice to turn right or left, so she picked a direction and wandered a bit more, until she looked in one room and froze. Standing against the back wall was a beautiful crib with lace bedding and an intricate canopy protecting it. It was obviously old, but very well taken care of.

Her fingers stroked the hand carved posts as tears stung her eyes.

It was exactly the crib she would've chosen had she been searching. She could picture her newborn sleeping under the delicate quilt, protected beneath the white canopy.

Suddenly, Lucas was behind her, wrapping his arms around her waist. "This was the same crib I slept in as a baby. I know most mothers want to design their own nursery, but it would mean a lot to me, and my parents, if we used this crib for our child," he whispered in her ear.

"My mother made this quilt herself. She spent months on it while she was pregnant with me. She made one for each of her children and then saved them for her future grandchildren."

Amy was speechless. She was so touched by this piece of his family history, she knew she wouldn't be able to get any words out. She picked up the tiny blanket and brought it to her chest, bringing it to her nose next, to inhale the scent – envisioning Lucas as an infant, and the love of a mother's endless hours with each stitch made. It was the most beautiful thing she could witness and though her heart felt a sting of her own loss as a child, it was quickly warmed by the thought of her baby being loved, and never knowing the pains of loneliness like what she'd endured. Amy turned in his arms and with all the emotion she felt inside, showed him how much she liked the crib.

The chase through the house, the magnificence of it all, and finally this intimate moment, had all added up to a swelling desire inside her. She needed to touch the man she loved.

Lucas gently picked her up and carried her to their room. The rest of the tour would finish much, much later.

As they lay in the bed together, she cuddled under his chin while he rubbed her back and they continued to talk. “You must have noticed the lack of furniture. Some of the pieces here came from my parents, and the others I’ve picked up over the years. The rest of the place is for you to decorate. You can do what you want with it. If you want some help, my mother asked me to tell you she’d enjoy working with you to make this our home. In other words, she’s begging you to let her take you all over the city in a shopping frenzy. My mother really likes to shop, especially when it’s for someone else. You’ll be begging for mercy, but honestly, if you want to do it on your own, I’ll make an excuse up.”

Amy could tell he meant what he said. She could refuse, but she loved his parents, and she didn’t think she’d be able to deny them anything they asked of her. She enjoyed being with his mother and learning from her. Katherine would know everything about what babies needed. Amy knew nothing.

“I’d be very pleased to go with your mom, but I don’t know when I’ll have the time,” she said. Lucas took a deep breath as if he was trying to gain courage. That surprised her, as he seemed to never fear anything.

“What is it?” she asked.

“Amy, honestly I’m not trying to control you, but I think it would be best if you were to focus on you and the baby. You’ve already had health issues and will be very busy getting things ready for our new home and the baby. At your last visit, the doctor was concerned about your high blood pressure and is already threatening bed-rest. You may want to take an indefinite leave from the offices," he finally got to the point.

Amy had many mixed feelings. She was surprised that the strongest emotion she felt was relief. She was doing well at her job, but she didn't love it. There was so much stress involved, and all she could think about was her unborn child, anyway, which made work all that much more difficult. She could focus on her career after she safely delivered her child and was feeling better.

She didn't want to be completely dependent on Lucas, though. She did have a decent amount of savings already, due to the fact that she had very few expenses. That was her security blanket. It wasn't enough to last long if they were no longer together, but it would be enough to get her settled into a new place while she found a job.

"I'd need to train a new person. I'm okay with not working for now, though; especially since Dr. Scott said I need to stay off my feet as much as possible. I'll want to work again after the baby is a few months old, though, but it might be better if I didn't work for my husband."

Lucas looked relieved. "You don't have to worry about training someone. My dad has already taken care of all that while we were on our honeymoon. He brought in someone to fill your place until you were able to come back, and she's working great."

"Who's this new person?" she asked suspiciously. She didn't want some skinny, hot young thing working with her husband for countless hours each week. She knew there were many women out there who wouldn't have any problem sleeping with a married man, and that connecting door between their offices was far too easy to slink through.

The thought of another woman placing her hands on Lucas was enough to quicken her heartbeat, and she was ready to scratch the eyes out of this non-existent person. This was her family, and she'd do anything in her power to hold onto it.

Lucas laughed. It was obvious that he knew exactly what she was thinking. "Don't worry. She's a happily married grandmother of six, who is more than qualified. She actually worked for another division in the company, and my father feels it's high time she receives a promotion," he reassured her.

"Esther's been working with her the past week, and she's picked up on the job quickly. I think she'll do well for us in the corporate offices. Of course, it will no longer be such a pleasure for me going into work each day, knowing you're not there. I've gotten used to your scent invading every aspect of my workspace. I'll desperately miss it," he said while nuzzling her neck.

"I guess everything has been taken care of, then," she answered, feeling a little out of sorts, since she'd been replaced so easily. "I'll focus on getting our home ready for the baby."

Amy was scared, as she'd always worked hard, and now there wasn't much expected from her except to get the home ready and wait for their little one to be born. She didn't know what she'd do with the extra time on her hands.

It was going to be difficult turning their house into the perfect home, because if they didn't make it, which there was a good chance, considering why they'd gotten married, she wouldn't take anything from her husband. She'd come into the relationship with nothing, and she wouldn't feel right turning into one of those women who were out to get all they could.

Many people used Lucas and his family for their own selfish needs. Couldn't all those people see the Andersons were wonderful, with or without the money and power? Well, she planned on showing him how much she loved him for himself – and nothing else – for the rest of her life.

Chapter Twenty-Two

Amy spent the next few months getting her home decorated and ready for her newborn. She'd frequently stop whatever she was doing and rub her belly, astonished how it protruded further from her body each new day she woke up. She was elated at the thought of being a mother soon.

Her relationship with Lucas was going well, but there was also something missing. They made love insatiably, and when they were in the bed together, she felt cherished, like the most beautiful woman in the world.

When she was in his arms, everything was perfect. He still hadn't said the magic words she desperately wanted to hear, but she did feel loved by him. Maybe he just wouldn't be able to tell her he was in love with her.

She had to fight herself daily to not shout the words out to him. Each time they made love, she'd say them in her head over and over again. "*I love you, Lucas. I love you.*" How she wished she had the confidence to tell him how she felt. She was afraid he'd think her too clingy if she told him, and then he'd pull away from her.

She didn't know if she could survive if he didn't want her anymore. She'd begun to imagine the "happily ever after life" she'd read about in so many romance novels. She'd always thought it was only possible in fiction, but there she was, living it in her own ongoing novel.

Amy was lost in her thoughts as she attempted to read a book out by the pool. Her stomach was getting so much larger, as she was in the thick of her third trimester. She kept waiting for Lucas to become repulsed with her body, but he seemed to think the changes were sexy, if his body's reaction was any indication.

Even on the rare nights they didn't make love, she could feel the evidence he wanted her pressed into the softness of her backside.

"Hello, sexy," Lucas said as he sat down and nuzzled her neck. "How are you feeling, today?" He continued up her neck with an open-mouthed kiss that had her pulse skyrocketing.

"I'm great," she purred. "Want me to take you upstairs and show you?" she pleaded, as his kisses were already turning her body into a puddle of need.

He chuckled and pulled her into his lap, where he sealed their mouths together in a deep kiss. By the time they pulled apart for much needed air, she could feel the evidence of his arousal, and she was ready for him.

He slid her skirt up and took her right there on the lounge with her sitting atop him. She came fast and hard and then collapsed in his arms. "Now that was a great hello," he whispered as he continued to stroke her back.

"Dinner's ready," they heard a voice call from inside the house.

◊◊◊◊◊◊

Lucas quickly covered Amy, having forgotten their maid could've walked out at any moment. He forgot the rest of the world existed when she was wrapped in his arms.

He didn't like to lose control that way, and he sat uncomfortably while his body tried to return to normal.

"I'm sorry," he said a bit sheepishly. "I was just coming out to say hello, but you make me go a little crazy."

She laid her hand on his face while looking into his eyes. "Don't be sorry. I wanted you just as badly, and no one caught us," she said, sounding a bit defensive. "I want to make love to you as much as possible, before our child takes up all the room, and you won't be able to reach me anymore," she finished self-consciously.

He looked deep into her eyes and spoke honestly, "You're beautiful, Amy, and your body changing with our child growing inside of you only enhances that beauty. I want you all the time, and that won't ever change." He continued caressing her as he spoke.

They sat together for a while longer until hunger finally had them getting up and going into the kitchen, where they shared a pleasantly quiet dinner. They retired early to bed and made love again. As she reached her peak, she quietly whispered, "I love you," not being able to hold it back any longer.

She felt him stiffen at her words and feared she'd somehow broken the rules of their marriage. He said nothing, but he didn't push her away. She lay in his arms, feeling desolate, and wanting him to repeat the words to her.

She felt like he loved her, but maybe she was wrong. Silent tears fell down her cheeks until she finally fell asleep from pure exhaustion.

◊◊◊◊◊◊

Lucas remained motionless while holding Amy as he waited for her breathing to even out, assuring him she was finally asleep. *She loves me*, he thought in awe. He'd seen the signs of her attachment and felt she was falling in love, but he was so afraid to open himself.

There'd been too many women who'd spoken those same words – not because they loved him, but because they loved his money, his power, and all he could give them.

He knew, deep down, that Amy wasn't one of those women, but she already had him wrapped around her fingers. To give her his love seemed like he'd be giving up the last piece of himself. He wasn't ready to do that yet. He had to have something left, he tried to reason.

He knew his father would be disappointed in the way he was behaving, but he'd been scorched in the past. When he was younger, he'd fallen in love, only to find the girl with his college roommate.

Wherever there was someone who wanted to use him, there was also another person who despised him for being born with the proverbial silver spoon. What frustrated him the most was that these people didn't even try to know him. They just saw dollar signs, not the man beneath. It tended to harden a person.

He fell asleep, for the first time having a restless night with his wife. Guilt ate at him, but he pushed it back in the recesses of his mind until it no longer affected him.

Lucas eventually gave up on sleep when he woke for the fifth time, and got out of bed. He stood beside Amy for a while, gazing down at the innocence on her face. There was no way a person could act that well. Each day he spent with her, he started to trust a little bit more. His walls were slowly starting to crumble.

◊◊◊◊◊◊

After she told Lucas she loved him, he started coming home later each night. She was seeing him much less. She could feel him slipping away from her, before she'd ever really had him. She figured she was going to either give this her all, or let go. She couldn't live in the marriage halfway anymore.

In the beginning she'd told herself she could do it. She thought she could do anything for the sake of her child, but what kind of mother would she be if she was so depressed, she couldn't even function?

It was killing her a little bit more each day as she watched him pull further away. She didn't say she loved him again, afraid that if she did, he'd ask her to sleep in a separate room.

They were making love less often, too, partially because he was gone so much more, but a lot had to do with her being so far along in her pregnancy, and she was perpetually exhausted. She'd had a few months in the middle where she'd felt great, but the beginning had been hard, and the end was even worse.

The doctor was keeping an eye on her, as she was swelling too much, and he was worried her blood pressure was too high. He'd put her on bed rest for ninety percent of each day, and she was getting tired of it.

When her blood pressure was finally under control, the doctor told her she could move around a bit more, and that some fresh air might do her good. She decided to get out of the house for a while.

She was going into the office to surprise Lucas with a romantic lunch, lovemaking, and a confession. She was going to tell him how much she loved him and how much she wanted the marriage to be real.

If he didn't return her feelings, then she'd let him go and get on with her life. She knew he'd want to be a part of her child's life and that would have to work out, but she couldn't live like roommates any longer.

She knew he still had the power to take her child away, but as she'd gotten to know him, she didn't think he could ever remove a child from her mother. Besides, there was no way Joseph and Katherine would ever support it. They had too much love and respect for family.

Amy was feeling nervous on her drive to the office. She hadn't been there in a while, and she was scared he wouldn't be happy with the interruption. She planned her visit when she knew he'd be alone and she could just slip in. She didn't want to run into Tom. She hadn't told him about what was going on, feeling as if it was a betrayal to Lucas to say anything negative about their marriage.

She was hoping he could love her. *Please*, she prayed, *let him love me as much as he loves our unborn baby.*

She walked into her old office, which was empty, and pulled her coat a little tighter. It was long and covered her well, but she knew that all she had on underneath was skimpy black lingerie. It had been hard to find something sexy when her stomach was protruding out about a foot from the rest of her body but, unbelievably, she'd hit the jackpot and felt somewhat sexy for the first time in a very long while.

She wasn't really self-conscious about her body, as Lucas had always raved of her beauty and complimented often on her body changes. His excitement to meet their child was one of the reasons she loved him so dearly. Some things unplanned turned out pretty great.

She cracked the connecting door quietly and then stopped where she stood, her heart shattering. Lucas wasn't alone. There was a skinny redheaded woman wrapped around him, and they were locked in a passionate embrace.

Her hair was a mess, as if they'd already been making love for hours. Her shirt was hanging open, and her skirt was hiked up, showing her garter. She was stunning in a way Amy could never hope to be, she thought in agony.

This was the reason he wasn't coming home to her much anymore. He was having an affair. She'd doubted he could love her, but there had been growth in their relationship, or so she'd thought. No matter what else, though, she didn't figure he was the type of man to cheat.

Up until the last month, they'd made love all the time. She thought he was satisfied – more than satisfied, even, as their love-making always seemed so frenzied, as if they couldn't get enough of each other. He was always ready to sink deep inside her, and that was something a man couldn't fake.

She was horrified to think that maybe he was picturing his mistress as he made love to her. Maybe that was how he was always so ready. Amy knew she could never compete with someone like the stunning redhead.

She only stood there for a couple of seconds, but it seemed like an eternity. Her whole world began to crumble, and she didn't know how she was still standing.

She closed the door and ran back to the elevator. She could feel hot tears streaming down her face as she quickly escaped to her car and sped home. She had her answer. She'd never stay with a man who cheated. She couldn't do it.

Chapter Twenty-Three

"What do you think you're doing, Laura?" Lucas spat to the redhead, whom he'd dated months before he and Amy had become involved.

She'd walked into his office moments earlier, with her famous pouting expression, stating that they needed to have a talk. He'd told her there was nothing to talk about, but she'd come around his desk and sat in front of him, spreading her legs open, so he had no choice but to notice she was wearing nothing underneath her short skirt.

He couldn't believe at one time he'd desired her. She was as fake as Amy was real, and he wanted her out of his office immediately.

"You need to get out. There's nothing left between us," he said between clenched teeth as he backed his chair away from her. "You also know I'm a married man and am no longer on the market."

She just smiled at him with what she thought was a seductive stare and ripped open her shirt to show her ample breasts spilling from her bra.

He stood up to physically escort her from the room when she wrapped herself around him and locked her lips to his. He was so stunned, he stood motionless for a few seconds before his hands came up to her waist and pushed her from him.

"Baby, you know you want me," she said, sounding falsely hurt.

He was done with her games. He marched over to his desk and pushed a single button. "Security, I need you in my office immediately."

Within a minute, two large men came into the room to see the still half-naked woman trying to wrap herself around their boss. "Please escort this woman to the outside of the building and never let her in again," Lucas said tightly, barely able to control his rage.

"Yes, Mr. Anderson. Right away," they replied professionally, while each of them took one of her arms and led her away.

Lucas sat back in his chair and rested his hands on his head. All he could think about was Amy. She was real, where the women before her had been as fake as Laura.

When Amy smiled, it was with warmth and light. When she laughed, it was like music, the sound so infectious, you couldn't help but join her.

He loved how she was with his family, how warm and giving. She'd had such a miserable childhood, filled with despair and fear, hunger and insecurity. He didn't understand how she'd managed to turn out so well.

He loved her pride, the way her eyes lit with fire when she felt he was being an ass – which lately, was all the time. He'd seen some of the light fading from her eyes as she sent him longing looks, but she never complained, just continued being there for him whenever he needed her.

"Hey, Lucas, you busy?"

Lucas looked up, irritated at being interrupted. He quickly pushed it down as he stood to greet his brother.

"What are you doing home, Alex? Aren't you supposed to be in Spain this whole month?"

"Yeah, but we got done early."

"Usually when you get done early, you spend the rest of your time locked up in some beach hut with one of the local girls," Lucas teased him. Out of all the brothers, Alex was certainly the playboy of the family. There were more pictures of him, with different women, across all the gossip magazines than Lucas, Mark and their cousins, combined.

"I was thinking about it, but then dad called and asked me to come home. He said something's going on that he didn't want to talk about on the phone, and that I should get back as early as possible."

"I haven't heard anything. When did you talk to him?"

"He called three days ago. I was hoping you could fill me in. You live right around the corner. I figured he'd tell you about it," Alex said, starting to look a bit worried.

"You know dad. I'm sure it's nothing," Lucas said, though he wasn't convinced. Joseph didn't normally disturb the boys unless it was important.

"Let's get Mark down here, and see if he knows anything," Alex said as he pulled out his phone and dialed. Luck was on their side when Mark was already in town, and agreed to meet them in a half hour.

Lucas and Alex continued chatting until he arrived.

"Whoa, Lucas, you look like crap," Mark said as he stepped in the room.

"Thanks, right back at you," Lucas snapped.

"Hell, brother, I always look good. Don't you know that the ladies really dig the whole jeans and boots look?"

"I'll stick with my suits," Lucas replied.

"Suit yourself. Ha, get it?" Mark said, laughing at his own joke.

"Mark may be acting like a pain in the ass, but he's right, you don't look your best. What's going on with the stressed out face? I thought married life was supposed to be all lovey, kissy, and crap," Alex said.

"It's none of your business – and that goes for you, too, Mark."

"Hey, if you can't perform for your wife, I can always lend a hand," Alex said with a wicked grin. "She's hotter than the fourth of July," he added with a whistle.

Before Lucas knew what he was doing, he flew out of his chair and pinned Alex to the wall.

The brothers were all about the same size, and had wrestled all throughout their lives. He never would've been able to pin Alex so easily if he hadn't stunned him with his unusual attack.

"That's my wife you're talking about," Lucas growled. Then as he realized what he'd done, he released Alex and began pacing the room.

"Holy crap, you're going crazy. I thought this whole marriage was a thing of convenience. You know, one-night-stand, pregnancy, and all that," Mark said, as he moved closer to Alex just in case Lucas decided to go nuts again and the two of them needed to pin him down.

"It was…or is…or…I don't know," Lucas thundered.

"You're in love," Alex said, wonder filling his voice. "I didn't think that was possible. I mean, if that happened to any of us, I just assumed it would be, Mark."

"Hey," Mark snapped. "Focus on Lucas."

"I'm not in love…" Lucas paused as he thought about Amy. He couldn't imagine not having her with him every night. Even with pulling away from her, he still knew she was in the house. He still climbed in bed with her every night. He still… He loved her.

He loved his wife.

So why was he chatting with his brothers instead of running to her? Because he was an idiot.

Suddenly, all he wanted to do was go home and wrap her in his arms and tell her repeatedly how much she meant to him. He was done pushing her away from him. Without realizing it, his mouth turned up in a huge smile as he thought about his future.

He'd stop for roses on the way home. He realized he hadn't purchased any for her, yet. He'd make up for that and so much more.

"I've got to go. We'll discuss dad later. Thank you, both." He tossed the words behind him as he took off running out the door. He missed the looks of confusion his brothers shot each other.

◊◊◊◊◊◊

Amy couldn't keep the tears from falling as she drove from the office to her beautiful home. She sat in the car, gazing at the place with deep anguish, knowing she'd never sleep there again in the arms of her husband. How could he have cheated on her? She'd given him her body freely, and her love, as well.

She pulled herself together enough to walk inside. She slowly climbed the stairs leading to their bedroom and, once again, a few tears slipped from her eyes and she bit her lips to muffle her sobs. It wouldn't take her long to pack, as she wouldn't take anything she didn't consider exclusively hers.

She packed some clothes and baby items and then took the case back to her room. She looked around with one last glance and then took off her wedding ring. She sat at the vanity and wrote her husband a note.

She set her ring on top of the letter, grabbed her suitcases, and walked out the door without allowing herself to look back again.

She had no idea where she was heading or what she was going to do when she got there. She just knew she had to get away. She was afraid if he came through those doors and wrapped his arms around her, she'd melt and beg him to love her and not run into the arms of another woman. She'd already given him her heart. She had nothing left to offer. She had nothing he wanted.

Amy drove onto the freeway and headed south. After several hours, she passed through Salem, and it didn't feel far enough. She was starting to feel a little sore, though, and pulled over at a rest stop to stretch.

It was after five, so she crossed her fingers that Tom had left work, then dialed his number. She needed a friend to talk to.

"Hey, Amy, what's going on?"

The sound of his familiar voice made her lose her composure and tears started pouring again, her sobs coming on so strong, she couldn't get the words past her throat.

"Amy? What's going on? Where are you? You have to speak to me. Okay, I'm getting really scared. Just tell me where you are, and I'll come get you," Tom said, his voice filled with panic.

"I…I left," she managed to get out.

"You left to where, honey? Tell me where you are. I'll get there as quick as I can," he said. She heard the sound of his car starting as he waited.

"One sec," she choked out, and then took several deep breaths in, trying to get her emotions settled down.

"Take your time, calm down, and let me help," he said, his voice soothing, helping to calm her.

"I'm not in Seattle. I left," she finally managed to say with only one hiccup.

"What do you mean, you *left* Seattle? Where are you? I'm coming right now," he demanded.

"Lucas, he had a woman at the office," she said, her tears falling freely down her cheeks.

"I'm going to kill the bastard. I swear, I'll rip him apart, piece by piece," Tom said, his indignation managing to bring a weak smile to her face.

"No, I don't want you doing that. I just…I had to leave."

"I understand. I really do, but I told you if you ever needed to go anywhere, then to come to me. Tell me where you are and I'll come get you," he tried again.

"I just need a day or two alone. I'll call you back tomorrow, okay?"

"No, that's not okay. You're huge pregnant, in the middle of I can't even imagine where. You tell me where you are. I'm coming to get you!"

"I'll call, I promise," Amy said as she hung up. Her phone immediately rang again, but she ignored it. After the third time, she turned it off, saying a silent apology to Tom. She knew she owed him big time, but she just needed to be alone a few days to get everything sorted out.

It took another hour, but she finally managed to get her tears to stop so she could leave the rest stop. She didn't want to be there when it got dark.

She merged onto the freeway again and continued driving south. After a couple more hours, she was in Springfield, next to Eugene. She'd always wanted to visit, so she took the next exit that would take her downtown.

She pulled off the freeway, into the business district, and started to look around for a cheap hotel. She passed the Hilton and shook her head. That was beyond her price range at the moment. Finally, she found a little dive of a place and pulled in.

She walked inside, so tired she could barely hold her head up. The man behind the counter was leering at her in a way that really frightened her, especially with the smell of alcohol seeping from him.

"I'd like a room for the night, please," she asked quietly.

"Do you have a credit card?" he hacked at her.

"No. I have cash," she responded, not wanting to use her credit card, and not trusting the man to have her information.

"Well, we normally require a credit card, in case you steal anything..." He leered again.

"Oh, then I guess I'll have to find another place," she stated calmly, even though she felt as if she was going to fall over at any moment.

"I guess we can do it on cash this time," he said, a bit desperately. She wasn't going to stay in the place if there wasn't a double lock on the door. She didn't trust the guy.

"Thank you," Amy responded and filled out the small card he handed her. Then she received her key. She grabbed her car and drove to the parking spot in front of her door.

She wearily got out of the rig, grabbed her suitcase and opened the motel room door. She gasped at the horrid smell of cigarettes and stale beer, feeling her stomach turn. Flashbacks of her childhood instantly came to mind from the smells of the room unleashing all feelings of insecurity, fear and abandonment. She was too scared to even open a window, as the neighborhood she was in didn't seem the safest. She wasn't going to be Mrs. Anderson anymore and would have to get used to life like it had been before her marriage.

She didn't really care about the room; she was just so empty from the betrayal of her husband cheating. She'd been in his arms the night before, and then he was in the arms of another just a few short hours later. Thank goodness for her exhaustion, because she fell into a restless sleep, almost immediately.

Chapter Twenty-Four

"Then where the hell did she go?" Lucas shouted to his cook, Rosa. He knew it wasn't her fault Amy was gone, but he had no one else to take his fear and anger out on.

He'd come home, anticipating holding his wife and telling her how he felt. The roses were clutched to his chest. He'd opened the door and called out to her. When there was no answer, he hadn't felt panic; he'd just headed up the stairs, where he figured she was taking a nap.

She'd been more tired lately, and he'd been worried about her health, as well as that of his son or daughter.

He quietly stepped into their bedroom and looked around. He frowned slightly when she wasn't there, but he figured she was in the bathroom. He walked over to the door. She wasn't there, either.

As he turned to walk back out to grill Rosa with more questions, his eye caught a glimmer of light from the table and he stopped to notice it was her ring sitting on the table, atop a piece of paper. Instantly, he was furious. She'd left him. He felt it. She'd told him she loved him, and yet, still she'd walked out on him. He'd drag her back, no matter where she'd gone.

She wasn't going to make him into a fool and leave him alone and vulnerable. She'd lied to him. He was sure she had taken all she could get her greedy hands on in the process of leaving. This whole time, she'd just played him.

He slowly picked up the paper and looked blankly down at it, not wanting to know what she'd written, but unable to stop himself from reading.

> Lucas,
> I love you so much more than words could ever say. I know that wasn't part of our arrangement, but I couldn't help it. I thought I could do this still, even knowing you can't ever love me, but I can't. I can't stand by while you act so cold, and I can no longer live here, while you're leaving me to be in the arms of another woman. I know you love our child, and I won't try to keep her from you, but I have to get away for the sake of my own health. I'll

contact you after the baby is born, and we can arrange something then. I'll return the car just as soon as I can get things worked out. I hope you find whatever it is that you're looking for.
Amy

He read the note about ten times, not understanding what was going on. He wasn't cheating on her. Why would she think he was? He went from anger to confusion in the space of a heartbeat.

He calmed down and re-read the note. He needed to find out what was going on and not just jump to conclusions.

He slowly walked down the stairs, almost as if he was in a trance. He walked into the kitchen where Rosa was cooking. "Hello, Mr. Anderson. You're home early," she said, as if nothing was wrong. This attitude made his temper come to the forefront again.

"Have you seen my wife?" he asked with a bite to his voice. She turned toward him, with her brows puckered. "She left a while ago," she said, perplexed, as if he should know this.

That was when he'd shouted at her, demanding to know where Amy was. He'd immediately felt bad and calmed himself down.

"I apologize, Rosa. It's just that Amy's gone, and all I have is this note," he said as he thrust the note in front of her.

She scanned the piece of paper, and then her breath hitched as she re-read it. She looked at Lucas with suspicion on her face. He knew Amy had become friends with Rosa and the two of them spent a lot of time together.

"I didn't cheat on my wife," he began defending himself. He didn't need to explain anything to her, but he didn't like the censure he saw in her eyes. She immediately looked down, as if she knew she'd been glaring at her boss.

"It's not my business," she stated.

"Can you tell me where Amy has been today?" he asked.

"Didn't you see her, Mr. Anderson? I packed her a lunch, and she was bringing it into your office. She said she wanted to surprise you with a romantic lunch because you've had to work so late every night. She was very excited when she left. She came home much sooner than I expected she would, but I assumed she'd just forgotten something, because she was only here for about fifteen minutes, and then she rushed back out the door without saying another word."

Lucas suddenly sank down into the chair next to him. His legs wouldn't support him any longer. "No," he cried out with such devastation in his voice that Rosa put her hand on his shoulder.

He knew Amy must've come by the office when Laura was in there. If she'd been there at the wrong moment, it might have looked like he was having an affair. He slowly got to his feet. "I have to make some phone calls," he said as he walked out of the room.

An hour later, he again cupped his head in his hands. He'd spoken with his security guards and found out that, yes, she'd been there at noon and had left within five minutes. She'd been there only minutes before they'd escorted his unwanted visitor out.

So, she thought he was having an affair. It seemed to him that her not trusting him was a little convenient. Why had she not marched in and asked what he was doing? He assumed she was thinking she'd found him in the arms of another woman so she could get past the prenuptial agreement and take him for all he had.

She thought wrong.

He called up the banks to find out how much she'd taken. After another half hour, he hung up the phone and once again felt shame. She'd taken nothing. He'd put a trace on all the credit cards to find out where they'd been used and found she'd not used any of them.

Not only had she not used any of them today, but she hadn't used them once since his mother and she had furnished the house. There were zero purchases. Why had he not paid attention to any of that? He never noticed she hadn't been out shopping – or gone anywhere, for that matter.

He wandered into their bedroom, feeling an aching need for her to be there. He liked going baby shopping with her. She was so excited about each new purchase. He thought back over those trips and how they'd pass through the malls, and she never even looked at the jewelry stores or the many fashion boutiques.

He looked into the small jewelry box his mother had given to Amy and noticed the few pieces he'd picked up for her were still in there. She'd taken nothing but a few clothes and the car, which she said she'd return.

The car!

He was suddenly jumping to his feet and running back into the office. He'd been feeling hopeless about how to possibly find her, since she wasn't using the credit cards, when he realized there was tracking on the vehicle. He always added it on, in case of theft or an accident.

Within moments, he had the vehicle located. He glanced at his watch. It was eight in the evening. He called his pilot and told him to get the jet ready. They'd be heading to Eugene within the hour.

Lucas jumped in his car and dialed his father as he drove toward the Seattle Airport. Joseph listened as Lucas explained everything that had happened.

"Get her back, son. She's the best thing that's ever happened to you," his father said when finished.

"I've been so stubborn and stupid, Dad. I love her, but was afraid if I gave her my heart, she'd have everything. I finally realize it doesn't even matter, because without her in my life, I have nothing anyway," he finished on a strangled note.

His dad gave him a moment to compose himself and then let him know he and his mother would be there for him if he needed anything.

"Thanks for everything, Dad. I'll be home soon," Lucas promised before hanging up.

He felt a little better after talking with his father. He knew how much his parents loved Amy. He couldn't have a single conversation with them without hearing them praising her for one thing or another. Amy could often be found at their house during the day, working on something for the baby.

Amy and his mother had finished the nursery together. They'd made beautiful stencil designs on the walls and sewn curtains. He'd asked one day why she didn't just go buy the items, and she'd looked at him like he was a child. *"It means so much more when they come from the heart. When our child grows up, she'll know that her grandma and mom loved her so much they wanted to make her first room the best place ever,"* she'd simply stated.

Lucas reached the airport and was in the air within thirty minutes of his arrival. "The flight will only take about forty minutes, Mr. Anderson," came the pilot's voice over the intercom. His attendant brought him a much needed drink once they were airborne.

He arranged transportation to his wife's location to be waiting for him the minute he landed. He stepped off the jet and into an awaiting town car. He gave the driver the address and was horrified when he reached the hotel where she was staying.

He knew she was there, because her car was sitting out front, looking completely out of place.

"Would you like for me to wait?" the driver asked.

Lucas handed him several bills. "No thanks. I have other transportation," he said as he walked to the front doors.

The clerk behind the filthy counter looked Lucas up and down in awe. "You looking for a room?" he asked, looking past him. Lucas figured the man was looking for the cheap hooker he figured Lucas had with him. Lucas wasn't full of himself, but he also knew the guy didn't get clients like him there – ever.

"My wife checked in here earlier today. I need to know which room she's in. She'll be checking out," Lucas said with authority.

"I can't give out information about my customers," the man's voice shook, as he didn't quite meet Lucas's eyes.

Lucas was ready to grab the weasel of a man by the shirt and throw him against a wall, but he knew, if he remained calm he'd get his way more easily.

Lucas placed a hundred-dollar-bill on the counter, and he saw the little man practically drool. "Amy Anderson's room, please," was all he said as he kept his fingers on the bill.

"She's in room twelve," the man said without any further argument. He handed Lucas the key and snatched the bill off the counter before the rich man could change his mind. Without another word, Lucas walked out and didn't stop until he reached door twelve.

He stood listening and didn't hear any sound, so he inserted the key, and the knob turned easily. He started to push the door open when a chain halted him. He peeked through the crack and saw her lying on the bed, shivering in her sleep, curled into herself with her hand protectively over her stomach.

Lucas pulled the door back toward him a few inches. Then he gave it a quick jerk inward, and the chain snapped without much effort. He was aghast at the lack of security in the building. Amy didn't even wake as he stepped into the room.

The smell of the place was enough to turn his stomach. He needed to get her out of there fast – before there was any lasting damage to her and his child.

He sat on the side of the bed and gently shook her. With a gasp of alarm, Amy jerked awake and sat up, her eyes round with terror.

"Oh, thank goodness it's only you, Lucas," she said as her breathing slowed back down. Considering the area of town she was in, as well as the sleazy man at the front desk, he understood her uneasiness.

Once her initial fright was over, she realized where she was, and that he was there with her. She looked at him with worry in her eyes.

"How did you get in here? How did you know where I was?" she questioned.

"There's tracking on your car, Amy, and before you start shouting about me spying on you, there's tracking on all our vehicles. It's a safety precaution in case any of them are stolen." He held up his hand as he tried to delay the fight. "I know you have a lot to say about what you think has happened, but I'm really uncomfortable with having you and my child in this unhealthy environment. I've reserved a suite at the Valley River Inn, which is only a few miles from here. Let's head over there, get some food, and have our talk," he said with his usual calm, commanding voice.

He didn't wait for Amy to say anything. He just gathered her things, which were pretty minimal, considering nothing was unpacked. He walked her bag out the still open door and placed it in her car.

When Amy still hadn't said anything or budged, he walked into the room, scooped her up in his arms as if she weighed nothing, and gently deposited her in the front passenger seat of the car. He placed a couple more hundred-dollar bills on the nightstand with a note that said "For the lock," and then he quickly pulled out of the slum motel's parking lot.

Lucas programmed the hotel address into his GPS and was at the Valley River Inn within ten minutes. There was hardly any traffic that night, making it quick and easy. Amy said nothing on the drive over. She sat in the passenger seat with her head turned away and her arms crossed.

Chapter Twenty-Five

Amy had such a myriad of emotions running through her at once that she didn't know which to focus on first. The emotion at the forefront was love. Her love for Lucas burned deep within her chest. Her life without him seemed endless and empty.

She loved him too much to be able to sit back while he had affairs with different women. She knew the redhead wouldn't be the last. He was vibrant, handsome, and every woman's dream-come-true. Look how quickly she'd fallen for him.

Upon their arrival to the hotel, she obediently followed him in. She was too exhausted – emotionally and physically – to fight him anymore that night. She'd just have to rationally explain she wasn't the type of woman who would sit back while her husband slept around.

They entered the beautiful suite, and her nerves were stretched to the breaking point. He hadn't spoken to her since he'd whisked her out of that disgusting motel. She wasn't sorry to see that place go.

Maybe, after they talked, he'd let her stay in her old apartment until the baby was born. He knew she was on strict orders to not be working right then, as it could cause harm to the baby. She'd never do anything to hurt her child. Her hand caressed her stomach as she sat on the couch and waited to see what he had to say.

Lucas stepped over to the phone and placed an order for food. Then he sat down next to her.

"Amy, I've never been as terrified as when I realized you'd left me. How could you not realize what you mean to me?" he began speaking. She opened her mouth to respond, but he gently shook his head and pulled her into his lap.

She knew she should struggle, but even though he was the reason she was in so much pain, she longed for the comfort he was offering. He began rubbing her back in slow circles, and she had to fight the tears wanting to spill again. She didn't see how there was a single tear left in her body.

"Look at me, please," he tenderly pleaded with her. She finally turned to look in his eyes. They seemed so filled with love and sincerity.

"I love you."

Tears - they fell freely down her cheeks, and her body shook gently with sobs at finally hearing the words she'd yearned to hear for so long.

"I love you, and only you," he said again as he gently wiped away her tears. "What you saw today was not me clinging to another woman. She's an ex-girlfriend who was trying to get me back. If you would've stayed a moment longer, you would've seen me push her away as soon as she made her move. I had security remove her from the premises. Talk about being in the wrong place at the wrong time..." he finished with a sheepish grin on his face.

She stared at him, a ray of hope starting to bloom within her broken heart. He was saying he loved her, and maybe she really had jumped to conclusions. "Why would you think I'd cheat on you? Do you think so little of me? Making love to you is the best sexual experience I've had in my life, but it's so much more than just sex. I can never get enough of you. Why in the world would I need to go to another woman when I have you to myself every night?" he asked with confusion.

"It's logical that you'd want a woman like her. I'm not sophisticated or gorgeous. You got trapped into being with me because of the baby. It just makes more sense, than you actually being able to love me," she broke off with a sob, and could say nothing further.

Lucas lifted her chin and placed his lips on hers. She immediately responded, as she always did, to even his lightest touch. He pulled back quickly, but gently.

"Amy, I admit we didn't start out the best way, but none of that matters, anymore. All that matters now is how we feel about each other and how we feel about our child," he said while running his hand over her stomach.

"I love you so much. I'm sorry I've been a fool. I was afraid to give you my heart because you already own me in every other way. I'd walk through fire for you. I'd hunt you down to the edges of the universe. I can't, and won't, live without you. You and our child are my reason for survival. Without you both, there is no joy or passion in my life. There is no meaning," he said.

She believed him.

He loved her!

She'd never, in her life, felt such tremendous joy delight as at that moment, sitting on her husband's lap, with his arms wrapped tightly around her. She could see the love in his eyes and feel it exuding from his body. Peace filled her at the realization that everything would be okay.

"I love you so much, Lucas. I think I've loved you from the very first time we met. I tried to fight it, but there's no fighting a man like you. You're who I want to be with the rest of my life."

Amy threw her arms around Lucas's neck and kissed him with a hunger that would keep them up for a very long time that night.

◊◊◊◊◊◊

They got up early the next day and started the drive home with Amy feeling much better about her return trip. Lucas drove with one hand, while his other rested on her leg, or at least the part of her leg that her stomach wasn't covering.

"I honestly don't see how you desire me when I'm as big as a cow."

"You're stunning, Amy. Pregnancy has given your skin a beautiful glow. I can't complain about the added curves, either," he said with a wiggle of his brows as he looked pointedly down at her larger breasts.

"You're terrible, Lucas," she admonished, though she secretly loved how much he worshiped her body.

They chatted the entire five-hour trip, taking more time to know all the things about each other that neither of them had spoken about before.

"Why did you go into business?" he asked when he found out she didn't really like the world of high finance.

"I needed security, and the business world pays well."

"What do you really want to do? You know, you can be a stay at home mother if you want. I want you to do whatever makes you happiest." The sincerity in his voice made her brave enough to tell him about her dream.

"I've always loved antiques. They fascinate me. When I'm holding an old Wagner cast iron pan in my hand that I know was made over a hundred years ago, I get a thrill. I know it doesn't make much money, unless you're really good at what you do, but I've always thought it would be kind of great to buy and sell antiques. Though, I'd probably have a hard time parting with most of them, so it could just end up with me hoarding a lot of stuff you'd consider junk. I took a couple electives in school, though, and found out that I have a real knack for spotting genuine items, and I'm also really good at restoring them, without causing damage," she said, hoping he wouldn't think she was being ridiculous.

"That's great, Amy. You should do what you love. Besides that, my mother would love to spend hours on end shopping with you, doing what she'd consider, treasure hunting," he said, his voice filled with excitement.

"Do you really mean that?"

"Definitely. I think it's a great idea. I'll have a shop built next to the house with plenty of room for you to store your items and also work on them. We can hire a nanny to help with the baby, even if it's just so she can sit down in the shop with you and hold onto her if your hands are too dirty."

Amy smiled when she realized he'd called their child, a *her,* for the first time. She'd been calling her a girl, and he'd been calling the baby a boy, since they first found out about the pregnancy, though they'd chosen not to know what the sex of the baby was.

"Thank you, Lucas. You don't know what that means to me," she said as she leaned over and placed her head against his arm.

"I want you to be happy, Amy – really happy. I'd do anything to make that happen. This is the easiest thing in the world to give you.

"I really like the idea of spending more time with your mother," she said, meaning it.

"She'll love that, too. So will dad. That will give him more time to do whatever it is he does, that he always tries to keep from mom. She always finds out, though," Lucas said while laughing.

"Your father is nothing but a gentle teddy-bear, who adores his wife."

"You are most certainly correct on that."

Upon their arrival in Seattle, they headed straight to the mansion, as Joseph had called a family meeting. They walked in the door, hand in hand, and Joseph and Katherine were right there to greet them.

"Oh, honey, we're so glad you're home safe. The next time my son is acting out of turn, you just call me up, okay? You're always welcome here – more than welcome, in fact. You're wanted. We both love you so much, Amy," Katherine said as she wrapped Amy in a warm embrace, making her cry again.

"I love you, too" Amy said, not even attempting to hide her emotions.

"I think it's long past time you started calling me mom. Of course, that's only if you're comfortable with it," Katherine said as she pulled back, her own eyes filled with tears.

"It would mean more to me than anything else in the world. My mother wasn't deserving of the title. She wasn't evil – just very, very sick. I used to dream about having a mom like you in my life. Now, not only do I have this striking man, who actually loves me, but I get you, too."

The two women cried together as Joseph and Lucas looked at each other with suspiciously bright eyes, themselves.

"Well, what about me, darling? Do you have room in your heart for a father, too?" Joseph asked with a smile. He was attempting a joke, but she saw the vulnerability in him, amazed that he'd ever be worried about her answer.

"I can't believe you'd even need to ask. I owe everything to you, Dad – everything. You were the one who had faith in me from the beginning, when so few others did. You gave me a chance, and brought me into your home with open arms. I love you more than words could ever describe. I promise to never run off again, no matter what. I was foolish to do so in the first place. I knew better than to think Lucas would ever cheat. But even if he did, I knew I could come here, to you, and that you'd still love us both. Thank you for giving me the security I've always searched for."

Amy couldn't say anything more, because Joseph pulled her in tight, squeezing her shoulders, but being careful of her stomach. She cried on his shoulder for a minute before he let go.

"Alex and Mark are waiting in the den. Let's get your face cleaned up, then go have a family meeting," Joseph said a little gruffly.

Amy walked with Katherine to one of the guest bathrooms and washed her face before they joined the rest of the family.

Lucas collected her at the door and she followed him to the sofa, where he pulled her onto his lap and they waited for Joseph to speak.

"Your Uncle George called me a couple weeks ago to let me know Amelia was sick. He didn't want me to say anything until the test results came in, because he didn't want anyone to worry," Joseph said, his voice choking up.

"Dad?" Mark questioned, but Joseph just held up his hand, his face a mask of pain.

"It's not good. She has stage four ovarian cancer, and it's already spread to other organs. She seemed perfectly healthy on the outside, everything normal, so they didn't know until it was too late. The doctors said she won't last long," he finished.

"We need to go there," Alex said.

"I'll call the jet," Mark offered.

"No. I flew out there last week and George begged me to wait. He knows you all want to say goodbye to your aunt, but he's devastated right now, and he just wants his last days with her as normal as they can make them. She's turned down all treatments, because the doctors told her there was nothing they could do, but possibly give her a few more weeks, and she'd be real sick during them. George fought her on it, but she wants to be lucid for her last days with her husband and children."

"How are Trenton and the others handling it?" Lucas asked.

"Not well. They're holding in there right now, but it's just so unexpected. I know they feel like they've been cheated. They have been. They're losing their mother, not getting enough time to deal with it, let alone say goodbye."

"Can we do anything?" Lucas asked. He was the one who had the hardest time accepting that something couldn't be done.

"Unfortunately, we can't. All the money in the world still can't prevent such an ugly disease," Joseph said, his anger evident.

"We just needed to let you know. Your cousins will need you," Katherine spoke up.

"Of course, Mom," Mark answered.

"That was all I needed to tell you. Hopefully, she proves just how stubborn the Anderson's truly are, even if the Anderson name comes by marriage," Joseph said as he looked over at Amy. She gave him a watery smile.

She hadn't met his twin brother, George, but she'd often heard about him. She hurt for the man, not able to even imagine what it must be like for him to watch the love of his life slip away, right before his eyes, and not be able to do a thing about it.

"Even an extra month would be a real blessing," Alex said, knowing his father didn't think Amelia would beat the disease, but was just hoping for more time.

"Yes, in cases like these, a month can be all the difference in the family having time to accept the plans of a higher power."

They finished up for the night, Lucas walking out to the car with Amy and helping her inside.

It had been a long and emotional few days, and she was exhausted. She wanted to do nothing more than lie in bed with Lucas and have him hold her, reassuring her that everything would be okay.

That's exactly what he did.

Epilogue

"Push, baby, push. You're doing so great. I see her head," Lucas mumbled in a terrified whisper.

"Arrrgggggg...," Amy grunted as she used her last remaining strength and gave a final push. She collapsed back against the bed as she heard the sweetest sound imaginable.

The first cry of her beautiful baby girl.

Then, before she knew it, the doctor was placing their newborn on top of her chest, and Amy looked into the scrunched up face of her daughter throwing her very first temper tantrum.

"She definitely has her daddy's temperament," Lucas laughed as he rubbed their daughter from head to toe, making sure she was okay. "I think she's hungry and letting us all know about it," he chuckled.

Even exhausted, Amy looked from her husband to her baby girl and felt pride and happiness as her family grew. She could see the affection and wonder shining in Lucas's eyes, and it was the most beautiful sight in the world.

"Jasmine would like to have her father hold her now," Amy said. He gently picked her up and held her closely against his chest. The tiniest movement of her breathing was the most amazing feeling in the world. The night before, he'd been feeling her kick from inside the safety of Amy's womb. Now, he was holding her in his arms.

The doctors quickly cleaned Amy and Jasmine, and then the three of them transferred rooms. They were there no more than a few minutes when a knock sounded on the door.

"Can we come in?" said the subdued voice of her normally booming father-in-law.

"Come in, come in, Dad. Meet your very first granddaughter, Jasmine Katherine Anderson," Lucas said proudly.

◊◊◊◊◊◊

Joseph gently took his granddaughter from his son, and a tear spilled freely down his cheek. Things hadn't turned out badly at all, he thought to himself. He was in a hospital, holding his brand new granddaughter, and his son was happily married.

His son should be thanking him, but Joseph knew better than to ask for any praise for all he'd done to get those kids together. His beautiful granddaughter was all the thanks he needed.

"You two have done really well," Joseph said as he smiled at Amy and Lucas. "She's the most beautiful girl I've ever seen in my life."

He reluctantly handed the baby to his Katherine and watched a glow come over her face as she sat in the rocker and held the precious gift against her chest, while humming a lullaby. "We almost got a Christmas baby," Joseph laughed. It was December twenty-third. They all agreed Jasmine was the perfect gift for the entire family.

"Guess we'll have to work on giving Jasmine a little brother born on Christmas next year," Lucas said as he looked at his wife hungrily. She was still the most beautiful thing in his universe, even after the hard labor she'd endured.

"Now, son, I sure want a ton of grandbabies running around that empty old mansion, but you may not want to scare your wife off. It never is a good idea to talk about child number two when she's still feeling the pain from the first one." He winked at Amy.

"The pain's already forgotten, Dad. I already love her more than I could ever imagine being possible, and I want to give her many siblings. I love Lucas so much, and that love needs to be shared with the wonderful children I know we'll make."

Joseph's heart enlarged a bit more at how much affection he felt for his new daughter. He truly loved her like she was one of his own kids. Since she was married to his son, she was his family now. He bent down and kissed her cheek.

There was another knock on the door, and then Amy's face broke out into a huge smile as Tom stepped through the doorway, carrying a huge teddy bear, balloons, and a large bag of chocolate.

"Tom, I'm so glad you finally got here," Amy said to her best friend.

"There was an accident on the freeway, or I would've been here an hour ago," Tom replied as he bent down and kissed her on the cheek.

"Come and meet your goddaughter, Jasmine," Amy said. Tom's eyes instantly filled with tears as he took the precious bundle in his arms.

"She's perfect, Amy. Just like her mom," he told her, while trying to hide the tears filling his eyes.

They all visited for over an hour, as Joseph watched the interactions of those he felt such devotion to. He was pleased Amy had such a good friend by her side, and elated his son had such a wonderful wife.

"You did so well, Amy. You're such a strong woman, most certainly an equal match for my son. We'll leave you kids alone so you can rest, now," Joseph said as he helped his wife to her feet.

Katherine walked over to the bed and passed her granddaughter to her mother, where she immediately started to root for food. That gave them all a laugh.

"I love you, Mom. I'm so glad you were here," Amy's voice caught.

Katherine brushed a kiss across her cheeks, "It's a priceless moment in my life. Thank you," she replied and then walked hand in hand from the room with Joseph.

The two of them turned a corner, and Joseph's eyes twinkled. "Well, Katherine…One son down, two to go. I like being a grandpa, and I'm getting greedy now. I want new babies every year for the next ten years or so," he stated, as if he would indeed get his wish.

"Now, Joseph. I admit this turned out well, but you won't be doing any more meddling in our sons' lives. They can find their own mates and find their own way," she said sternly, even though she knew it was a futile battle.

Joseph just wrapped his arm around his wife and whistled a tune as they headed for their car. He already had the perfect bride picked out for his middle child, Alex…

◊◊◊◊◊◊

Unfortunately, a few weeks later, George's wife, Amelia, passed away, causing heartbreak among the family, who'd so recently celebrated the birth of a new life.

The entire family flew to Chicago to be with George and his children, Trenton, Max, Brianne, and Austin. No one said much as Amelia was lowered into the ground, forever laid to rest.

Joseph tried speaking to George afterward, but he closed up, too hurt and angry with the world to try and be comforted. It was a day of devastation for everyone, but especially George.

Joseph watched in agony, as his family fell apart before his very eyes. When the service was over, it seemed each of them went a separate way. Instead of leaning on one another, they were scurrying around, trying to lick their own wounds.

Joseph hoped in a short amount of time, they'd come back together. He knew the only way they'd truly heal was if they did it as a family.

With broken hearts, he and Katherine, Lucas, Amy and Jasmine, Alex and Mark all returned home, not able to do anything more for George or the kids, though they would've if they possibly could.

"Time, it will just take some time," Joseph said aloud on the return flight.

"Yes, it will all work out..." Lucas agreed.

ABOUT THE AUTHOR

Melody Anne is the author of the popular series, Billionaire Bachelors, and Baby for the Billionaire. She also has a Young Adult Series in high demand; Midnight Fire and Midnight Moon - Rise of the Dark Angel with a third book in the works called Midnight Storm.

As an aspiring author, she's written for years, then became published in 2011. Holding a Bachelors Degree in business, she loves to write about strong, powerful, businessmen and the corporate world.

When Melody isn't writing, she cultivates strong bonds with her family and relatives and enjoys time spent with them as well as her friends, and beloved pets. A country girl at heart, she loves the small town and strong community she lives in and is involved in many community projects.

www.melodyanne.com. She makes it a point to respond to all her fans.

You can also join her on facebook at:

www.facebook.com/authormelodyanne,

@authmelodyanne.

She looks forward to hearing from you and thanks you for your continued interest in her stories.